BITE RISK

S.J. WILLS

Simon & Schuster Books for Young Readers
NEW YORK   LONDON   TORONTO   SYDNEY   NEW DELHI

SIMON & SCHUSTER BOOKS FOR YOUNG READERS
An imprint of Simon & Schuster Children's Publishing Division
1230 Avenue of the Americas, New York, New York 10020
This book is a work of fiction. Any references to historical events, real people, or real places are used fictitiously. Other names, characters, places, and events are products of the author's imagination, and any resemblance to actual events or places or persons, living or dead, is entirely coincidental.
Text © 2023 by S. J. Wills
Originally published in Great Britain in 2023 by Simon & Schuster UK Ltd.
Cover illustration © 2023 by Jose Manuel Real Lopez
Cover design by Sean Williams © 2023 by Simon & Schuster, Inc.
All rights reserved, including the right of reproduction in whole or in part in any form.
SIMON & SCHUSTER BOOKS FOR YOUNG READERS
and related marks are trademarks of Simon & Schuster, Inc. For information about special discounts for bulk purchases, please contact Simon & Schuster Special Sales at 1-866-506-1949 or business@simonandschuster.com. The Simon & Schuster Speakers Bureau can bring authors to your live event. For more information or to book an event, contact the Simon & Schuster Speakers Bureau at 1-866-248-3049 or visit our website at www.simonspeakers.com.
Also available in a Simon & Schuster Books for Young Readers hardcover edition
The text for this book was set in Archer.
Manufactured in the United States of America
0723 OFF
First Simon & Schuster Books for Young Readers paperback edition August 2023
2 4 6 8 10 9 7 5 3 1
Library of Congress Cataloging-in-Publication Data
Names: Wills, S. J. (Children's author), author. Title: Bite risk / by S.J. Wills.
Description: New York : Simon & Schuster, 2023. | Series: Bite risk ; 1 Identifiers: LCCN 2023022823 | ISBN 9781665938006 (hardcover) | ISBN 9781665938013 (paperback)
ISBN 9781398520967 (ebook) Subjects: CYAC: Werewolves--Fiction. | Horror stories.
LCGFT: Werewolf fiction. Horror fiction. | Novels.
Classification: LCC PZ7.1.W5743 Bi 2023 | DDC [Fic]—dc23 LC record available at https://lccn.loc.gov/2023022823

For Rob, Fraser, and Cameron

CHAPTER ONE

I'm so busy repairing the tripwire across the front porch that I almost forget to take Mom her dinner. It's only when I hear her clanging about downstairs that I realize it's nearly eight o'clock. The streetlights cast a feeble yellowish haze as far as the house, but I don't need them— the moon is more than enough. It hangs heavy and ripe over Tremorglade, watching everything we do.

At least the explosive charges are finally set round the outer perimeter of the house, and the graphene nets are checked. Satisfied, I sit back on my heels and watch the neon warning bunting flapping in the breeze. All safe for tonight, even if I did leave it a little late. Dangerously late, Mom would say, if she knew. She always complains that I never change, and I point out that I definitely will, just not this month, but it never makes her crack a smile. She doesn't think we should laugh about that stuff.

My eyelids feel like sandpaper and my fingers are sore from twisting the wires, but I shuffle to the fridge and haul out tonight's meal, wrinkling my nose as ever at the smell. In my haste, I pull the shelf out too far and it tips forward, its contents thudding wetly into my chest. Great.

The clanging downstairs is louder now. Mom's getting antsy, like she always does around this time. I should've left dinner with her ages ago, but I got distracted.

The basement stairs are steep and the light stays off when I flick the switch. It happens from time to time. We don't always keep up with the bills and occasionally the electricity company notices. Mom will call them first thing tomorrow and plead for mercy until she gets paid at the end of the week.

I hold the tray against my chest with one hand and feel my way down the wall with the other, treading super carefully on the stone steps. I don't want to fall and injure myself right now. Especially not before Mom's eaten.

There's a soft moan as I approach the bottom of the stairs and I feel guilty for my lateness.

"Sorry, Mom, it was just really fiddly tonight." Plus I reached level twenty on Happy Trappers, but she doesn't need to know that.

Silence. I get the feeling she's not in the mood to hear excuses.

I can't see a thing in the darkness now, so I take my phone out of my back pocket and fumble to turn on the flashlight. I accidentally shine it right in her eyes, and she rears back. A flash of white teeth.

"Sorry, sorry." I place the tray and the phone on the basement floor so the beam of light points up at the ceiling and pick up the slab of raw beef. It's as big as my head, and I realize I've forgotten to cut it up. The bone is still in it. It might not even fit through the bars of the cage.

Too late now, though—she can smell it. At once, she looms out of the darkness, fast and hard. There's a sharp metallic clang as she throws herself against the door, making the whole cage rattle, then she retreats a little.

Better get on with it.

I throw the meat on the floor and stamp on it to flatten it, trying not to splatter the neatly folded clothes she's left to the side, then pick it up and step forward, holding it next to the cage at arm's length.

She doesn't move from the shadows.

She's waiting for something.

If she thinks I'm going to open the door she's got another think coming, although I doubt what's going through her mind right now could really be described as thoughts.

Sensations, maybe. Hunger. Rage.

Blood from the meat is oozing over my wrist, dribbling down the statutory notice welded to the middle of the cage door: CAUTION—BITE RISK.

"Come on, will you, it's heavy."

My arm's getting weak, I'm dead tired. Even though it's Confinement, I was seriously considering staying in tonight and just chilling out in front of the TV. But now I can't, plus she's messing with me. A wave of irritation overtakes me, and I shove the meat in farther, the bone resisting against the bars, then finally pinging through.

It's all she needs.

A millisecond later her teeth are bared and snapping, claws ripping at my sleeve as I struggle to withdraw my arm through the bars.

Adrenaline surges through my veins as I yank back in panic, eventually remembering I need to let go of the meat. But my knuckles are in the way, bashing against the iron cage. At last my hand slithers through and I crash-land on the floor into the puddle of bloody meat juice.

I sit there for a moment letting my heartbeat return to normal. It's okay. She's tearing into the beef, crouching, watching me with her yellow eyes.

My arm still seems to be attached to me, though there's a thin red line down the back of my hand where the tip of one fang has caught it and drawn a neat incision. It's just a scratch. Could have been a lot worse. Stings so much, though.

I rub my back and tut. "Mo-om."

Chunks fall from her jaws, and a pink-tinged string of saliva drops to the floor as she makes short work of her dinner. In my annoyance, I'm tempted to take a photo right now and put it on the internet, but she'd kill me.

It's ten past eight, according to my watch. There's a dull throbbing at the back of my head and around my shoulders—the usual Confinement headache—but I'm wide awake now, thanks to that little shot of adrenaline.

Too fidgety for a movie now, and with no electricity anyway, I decide to hang out with Elena after all. Unlike me, she'll have had her dad and brother sorted out hours ago.

I leave Mom to it and head gingerly up the stairs, out the door, and through the garden, skipping neatly over the tripwire and heading to Elena's house across the road, where there's a faint light seeping between her bedroom curtains. Earlier, when I was setting the tripwires, I could hear her singing. She has a pretty good voice.

It's a warm spring evening; the scent of the first cut grass is in the air. The bunting and luminous DANGER signs mark the hazards at every house, like twisted birthday-party decorations. Up and down the road loads of kids are out, the younger ones playing, older ones standing and scrolling on their phones or talking in groups, tranquilizer guns slung over their shoulders. Even little Mika, who started Caretaking only a couple of months ago, is already settled on her front porch in the wheelchair she's using while she recovers from her operation, cleaning the barrel of her X50 like a veteran.

Rudy and Asim are in the middle of a ten-pin bowling game in the street. A few toddlers have been plonked in the handy fenced-off area around the hazel tree, where they're happily chucking handfuls of grass at one another and eating bugs. They've all been ready for ages.

I should be more organized, I know. *Set up, lock in, watch out.* The protocol we all need to follow.

Here in Tremorglade, because we're so isolated, we don't have to put up with many of the horrors that the rest of the world does—deadly weather, plagues, violent crime, and marauding pirates.

We just have to live with one another's mistakes.

CHAPTER TWO

Music drifts down from one of the upper windows of Elena's house—that's her brother Pedro's bedroom. He always wants something upbeat and poppy blasting into his cage for Confinement. Elena usually starts off by singing to him, and then puts the player on for the rest of the night. She wears headphones in bed as her room is right opposite his, but she keeps her alert bracelet on so she'd know if there were ever a problem, which there never is. Well, there hasn't been for ages, anyway.

Pedro swears music helps, so he's been playing various tunes to himself during Confinements and recording his reactions. So far the results have been . . . marginal. In that maybe, *maybe*, a bit of electropop turns his rage level down a notch. Half a notch. Maybe.

I've just mounted the first step up to the front door when it crashes open and Elena appears, her grin wide and mischievous. Her long bangs are stuck to the light brown skin of her forehead and she's out of breath. Been dancing, probably.

Then she does a double take. "Whoa. Did you just kill someone?"

I look down at myself. In the moonlight, and standing right under the streetlamp, it's quite a bit worse than I thought. My T-shirt has a large, uneven circle of blood with spatter marks all around it, and my trousers are unpleasantly wet on my thighs. My milk-white arms have red streaks up them. There's a sickly butcher-shop smell coming from somewhere, and I think it might be me.

"Oh, no, I just . . . kind of fumbled Mom's dinner. Should I go change?"

"Nah. Don't worry about it. The blood spatter is actually an improvement on those trousers. It hides the pattern nicely."

"Thanks."

She punches me amiably on the arm. "You are such a doofus, Sel."

There's no denying it. Being a doofus is pretty much my thing. If you can drop it, fall over it, break it, tread on it, or choke on it, you can bet I'll have done it.

At school in target practice everyone stands back a good few extra feet on either side, ever since I hit our teacher. It was a practice dart, obviously, not one of the proper ones—that would've killed her outside of a

Confinement night. But even the practice ones hurt when they pierce your flesh. It was an accident, but if I'm honest I can see how she might think it wasn't—she was standing behind me at the time. I'd slung the tranquilizer over my shoulder at the end of a session but forgotten to put the safety back on. She gave me detention every night for a month: just me, a bunch of targets, and a lot of rounds of darts. Even that hasn't noticeably improved my aim.

"Shady Oaks?" I suggest.

Shady Oaks Retirement Community is where our friend Harold lives. We play cards together, and he's the only adult in Tremorglade who won't tear us to shreds if we get too close tonight.

We take our bikes and ride to the other side of town. The whispering of the river accompanies us all the way, a dark ribbon glimpsed in the gaps between houses and shops, meandering gently downward along the western edge of Tremorglade, growing wider until it meets the forest, where it falls away in a hundred-foot-high waterfall. Behind us and to either side are the mountains that hold Tremorglade in a horseshoe-shaped embrace. It's like nature knew the world was going to end up a warring, crime-ridden, disease-blizzard-and-drought-afflicted mess, and set aside a little nook to keep a lucky few of us safe.

Around the halfway point we pass the Wellness Center. There's no one there tonight, of course. All of us kids are first-aid trained, though. If any of us were to get seriously injured, we'd just have to try not to bleed out until one of the medics opens up in the morning. A car-sized delivery drone lifts off from its drop zone in the grounds and buzzes off, propellers a blur, sweeping up and over the trees, back in the direction of Hastaville. It will have picked up this month's expired tranq darts, dropped fresh ones, and brought medical supplies or equipment for us. Its red light blinks into the distance before disappearing.

We get everything by drone—some as big as that one, others small enough to fit into the palm of your hand. A lot of places use them these days, since they're much harder to hijack than vehicles. That's not a problem here— we're just too small and too remote to be worth the trip. We can order off the internet and have stuff dropped to our doors, although we do try to buy from local shops when we can because Mom says it's important to support the community. I don't think I've ever met a visitor from out of town.

As we ride, I'm conscious of the usual low-grade anxiety and nausea dragging at me. We call it the doldrums. Us kids get a ping on our alert bracelets at the onset of dusk once a month, but none of us needs it. Our bodies know, and they don't like it. Everything gets heavier. The air feels oppressive, as though the adults suck the energy out of the atmosphere as they Turn.

Mom doesn't remember the doldrums being a thing when she was young, even after the Disruption, but old people always think things were better in the past. The dizziness, headaches, and nagging sense of doom are always gone by morning, but most of us kids sleep badly on these nights. The guidance says we should go to bed at a sensible time on Confinement, once we've done our duty, although we're supposed to be ready to spring out of bed if there's an alarm, tranq at the ready. Who's to say what's a "sensible time," anyway? These nights belong to us.

I've wondered what it would be like if I could ride my bike fast enough to keep up with the daylight around the Earth, a hair's breadth in front of that sundown moment through time zones, and never get caught. Behind me, the tidal wave of adults convulsing, their bodies bulging and bursting, the full moon remolding them until they're all Turned, while I fly on, light and free as a swift.

Turning. That's the official term. A very prim and proper word when you consider the gory flesh-erupting process it's referring to. More commonly known around here as "getting long in the tooth," "buying a real fur coat," "coughing up a hairball," "on the way to the vet," and so on. My personal favorite is "digging in the litter box." And what you have, when all the eye-popping and hair-sprouting is done, are the beasts themselves: the Turned.

We generally use their nickname, which is Rippers. For obvious reasons. We don't keep them in cages for fun.

Other languages have their own names for them, of course, but no matter what you call them, they're the same across the world, and have been since the Disruption twenty-five years ago. Since then, every full moon, from dusk till dawn, everyone over the age of about fourteen, sometimes fifteen, Turns. *Almost* everyone, that is.

I won't bore you with the technical details, how they work out the exact night it's going to happen—but it's due to the "synodic month," which is an average of 29.5 days. It has something to do with the precise moment the moon is fullest, and which dawn or dusk it's closest to. Suffice to say, the nerds do the math and it gets automatically added to your Seekle calendar. Your local council also makes sure no one can miss it. Rumor is that things get weird some places way up north. Like, they have months on end when the sun doesn't even rise, and with no dawn or dusk to trigger their bodies, Turning is unpredictable, glitchy. You might Turn for twenty-four hours, or it might be a whole week, before waking up dazed and drooling. How messed up is that?

"Oof, it feels worse tonight, don't you think?" I say.

Elena shrugs. She gets the doldrums a bit too, but always seems to be able to brush them off—tonight her knotted frown is gone and she holds herself straighter, swerving around potholes like a level-sixty Ripper on the

Extreme setting of Happy Trappers. She smiles to herself, her dimpled, round cheeks flushed a deep rose-bronze with the exhilaration of speed and the wind in her face. The doldrums definitely affect some people more than others. It probably helps that Confinement is the one night she doesn't have to worry about her dad.

Just before we get to Shady Oaks, the chain pings off my ancient bike, as it regularly does. Neither of us can get it back on, so we walk the short distance the rest of the way, before dumping the bikes on Shady Oaks' wide lawn, which is dotted with circular flowerbeds. The grounds run right down to the line of tall pines that mark the very edge of town and the start of the thick forest. The building itself is single-story, modern brick, with shrubs against the walls. You can just about hear the hum of the waterfall—the river hurling itself down that sheer drop before continuing through a deep gulch away into the forest.

When we knock on the open door of Harold's room, he looks up from shuffling a pack of cards and his eyes light up. "Ah! Finally! My willing victims!"

Harold's little terrier, Eddie, trots over to me and licks my leg. I tickle him behind the ears, and he closes his eyes in bliss for a moment before curling up at Harold's feet again.

Harold is Immutable, which, as you know, is pretty rare. He's the only adult in Tremorglade, in fact, that doesn't Turn, though there are others scattered around the world. Apparently, they tend to form little clubs, have Confinement pizza nights and stuff like that. When I say little, I do mean little—according to its website, the Hastaville Immutables Society has four members in a city of a hundred thousand.

But here in Tremorglade, Harold's only company is us. We got to know him properly a few years ago, when he fell over in the grocery store right in front of me, and I helped him get to the Wellness Center. We kind of hit it off—he's different from the other adults, and I don't just mean because he's Immutable. He doesn't hide his disdain for Mayor Warren, who as well as being a sort of ceremonial figure, is ultimately responsible for organizing Confinement night in Tremorglade—his council pairs adults with Caretakers and constantly nags us about following the guidelines.

Warren wants Harold to be more responsible, to make the most of his Immutability. So he tried to make Harold a community support officer, with the job of patrolling the streets on Confinement nights to check us kids were all behaving appropriately. Harold suggested that, instead, maybe Warren should check his own behavior for the rest of the month when he wasn't Turned, because frankly the town's administration left a lot to be desired, and maybe he should focus on all that and leave the kids the heck alone.

Now Harold raises an eyebrow at the state of me,

but merely declares that tonight's game is Go Fish. We watch as he deals, his trembling, liver-spotted hands sending the cards carefully in more or less the right direction, though Elena and I have to intercept one or two before they slide off the table. We go around a few times and, as ever, I'm out of luck. Then Harold asks Elena the question I was too scared to ask earlier.

"So, how's your dad's job search going?"

My stomach tightens. I keep my eyes on my cards but can't help holding my breath. Lucas has been job hunting online ever since his wife, Valeria, Elena and Pedro's mom, died three years ago. Which would be fine, except that he's been searching for jobs as far away as Colmea, where Valeria grew up, and loads of other countries too. Anywhere but Tremorglade, in fact. Elena says he thinks they need a new start. She has mixed feelings about it, because it would mean leaving her best friend—me—but on the other hand, she's never been anywhere else, and thinks it might be kind of exciting. *Exciting?* Dangerous, more like.

"No luck," she says, and I breathe again.

I don't get it. Elena and her family watch the news like the rest of us. They *know* what it's like out there. They see the crime levels rising, the Rotting Plague epidemics, the sudden weather anomalies that sweep away whole communities, leaving broken homes and broken people. In some towns, I've heard people are sloppy on

Confinement. In those places, it's the kids who have to take cover, while Rippers roam the streets mauling each other and killing livestock—and worse. In the morning, crows peck at the corpses. I saw it on a documentary, and the images are burned into my brain.

We live in literally the safest little nook on the planet right now. Why would anyone give that up?

"Got any threes, Elena?" Harold asks. "So how many jobs is that now?"

"Go fish. Twenty-two job applications in fifteen different towns." She sighs. "He keeps getting close, had a few video interviews, but then they give it to someone else at the last minute. It's really getting him down."

Harold catches my eye. That's an understatement, and we all know it. The nights Lucas is howling to feed on human flesh are his best ones these days. In between applying for jobs online, he mostly sits watching the TV. Sometimes he cries, even when it's cartoons. Other times he gets angry and breaks stuff. He refuses to apply for jobs in Tremorglade. Luckily Pedro has a decent-paying job fixing computers, even though he's only nineteen. Otherwise there'd be no money coming in to their family at all.

Not much gets past Harold. People talk to him, so he knows most things that go on around here, which is both good and bad. Good because he can see both sides of arguments and sometimes even fix problems for us, and bad because it's hard to hide anything from him.

I ask him if he's got any aces and he chucks two across. Still doesn't give me enough for a trick.

"Here. How's your mom doing, Sel? Getting enough work?"

Mom cleans for people all over town. None of them are exactly generous with the wages. The only reason I have a laptop and phone is because Pedro fixed up some rejects for me—they're practically from the dark ages, slow and buggy, but they mean I can play Happy Trappers along with everyone else, and access FIN— Friends International Network—too.

I shrug. "I mean, she works a *lot*. We're fine." I know where this is going—Mom's told me not to accept any more money from him, because we're not charity cases. But he's pretty determined.

He saved up a lot from his job before he retired—some financial thing, sounds boring, but it was obviously lucrative and means he can afford to live here. Shady Oaks is definitely top-end accommodation. It has large en suite rooms and a communal lounge with views over pretty grounds. Although it's a retirement community, I'm not sure it meets the definition of "community" right now. There are six rooms and at the moment only two of them are occupied—he has room one, and Dora has room four across the corridor. The rent is too expensive for most people to afford, but the company that owns Shady Oaks doesn't seem bothered that it's more than half empty.

Seems like Harold's money is burning a hole in his pocket. There's no one in town, adult or child, that he hasn't paid over the odds to do some chore for him, and often it happens to coincide with times they really could do with the money. He notices stuff like that.

Harold takes the hint and changes the subject, leaning back in his chair, perusing his cards like a restaurant menu.

"I've got another appointment at the Wellness Center tomorrow." He grimaces. "Getting poked and prodded. Those people, Sequest. They're relentless. Why're they so interested in what goes on in our bodies, eh? It's suspicious if you ask me. Taking liberties. Someone should look into it. I'm thinking of withdrawing my consent."

Elena and I swap eye rolls. This is a familiar complaint. Harold's really got it in for Sequest. It's the nonprofit company set up to find a cure for *corpus pilori*, the virus that causes Turning.

You can still find old reports online, about the first recorded cases. My mom told me that initially it was just one of those weird news stories from a long way away. She was around the age that I am now. Then it started to spread, far more quickly and easily than should have been possible. But then *corpus pilori* was no ordinary virus. It was smart. After it infected you, it usually hid in your body for a month or two, quietly infecting everyone around you, until it made its presence known in a way you couldn't miss. There was widespread panic.

Pretty soon the Rippers were everywhere, and lots of kids were killed before the whole caging protocol was organized. They called this time the Disruption. Government after government around the world collapsed, followed by different leaders who soon failed too, unable to deal with the fallout. But in the midst of this mess, a small number of independent scientists grouped together and pledged to make things better. They called themselves Sequest.

Sick of the incompetence, impotence, and corruption of the politicians, they began to coordinate a proper response. They set up an international network of the best scientific minds, and pooled all the research, so that any breakthroughs could be immediately shared. They built Wellness Centers in every town to act as both clinics and research labs, invented the alert bracelet and Caretaking systems, and recommended the Confinement night guidelines that most places adopted as rules. Their one defining purpose: to act in the best interests of humankind.

For a while the residents of Tremorglade thought they'd escaped Rippers, because of how remote we are.

Corpus pilori found a way.

The first person who Turned here was a middle-aged bank manager called Irene. She burst out of her cottage, killed a bunch of her neighbor's chickens, and went on a rampage. Tremorgladers had hoped not to have to use the cages and tranqs they'd stocked up on, but they were more or less ready for Irene. She got tranq'd pretty quickly, but not before she'd claimed a human victim—her neighbor. He came out to see what was happening to his chickens and received a personal and brutal demonstration. There's a memorial statue of him in the town square—in his pajamas, surrounded by chickens. I often wonder if that's really how he'd have wanted to be remembered. Afterward, there were rumors that Irene had secretly visited her sister in Hastaville weeks earlier, though she tearfully denied it.

No one had ever seen the like of *corpus pilori*. Infected adults passed it to their offspring, who were born with it already in their bodies, dormant.

But here's the thing. Those babies have grown and become . . . us. Children and young adults who are basically *over it*. It's all we've ever known. Life goes on, you know? And ninety-six-point-something percent of nights are fur-free. So, yeah, aspects of it are a pain, but Turning is nowhere near as bad as puberty, so Pedro says. I must admit, when my time finally comes, I'll miss the camaraderie of Confinement. But it's likely I won't Turn for a couple of years yet.

And there have been benefits: Sequest scientists have used the data they gather from their Wellness Centers across the world to research cures for all sorts of things—cancers, heart problems, foot funguses, you name it. Loads of new treatments have been discovered, which never would have happened if it hadn't been for *corpus pilori*. Their quick antibiotic treatment saved Mom's life when she had an infection a few years back, and I'll always be grateful for that. It's not their fault they haven't found the one cure they set out to find. And I seriously doubt they're trying to mind-control us, or whatever it is Harold thinks they're up to today.

Elena tuts. "Hold your cards closer to your chest, Harold, unless you want me to totally destroy you."

"Ooh, fighting talk!" he grins. "We'll just see about that, young lady." He twiddles his hearing aid, causing it to emit a tinny screech. "Got any twos, Sel?"

"Take 'em." I watch him lay down yet another trick. "What have you got against Sequest, anyway?"

"What have I got against them?" he gasps, wide-eyed. "They steal my blood! Every month! And no one does a thing about it!"

I shake my head, laughing.

Harold continues, "What does Dr. Travis want with my blood, eh? I'll tell you." He leans across the table, and whispers. "To drink it."

Elena lets out a snort and slaps another card on the table. "You could be right there."

We'd rather stay sick than visit Dr. Travis, with her

freezing cold hands and conviction that all children are faking illness, even if you have a temperature of forty degrees. She's had a particular disdain for me ever since that time I thought I had a deadly rash, but it turned out I'd left a red pen in my pocket. But we have to see her regularly anyway when she comes to do blood tests and other things at school. I think she really enjoys sticking that needle in my arm every month, although she complains about my "shy veins" that don't always cooperate. Can't she see? They're not shy, they're terrified. If she was nicer, I bet she'd get bucketfuls out of me.

Us kids get tested loads, adults much less often. It's our blood that reveals when we're about to Turn for the first time. Somewhere on your chart you get a big spike, and that's when you need to make sure your cage is ready and organize things with your assigned Caretaker. Harold's chart must be flat as a pancake.

"I get why they want ours," I tell him. "But I don't see why they want *your* blood. You're never going to Turn."

"Yeah," Elena says. "But maybe that makes it all the more important. A baseline to measure everyone else's against."

Harold raises one eyebrow. "Ooh. I'm a baseline, lucky me! Nope. It's experimentation and they're evil scientists, is what it is."

He wins at cards, as usual, but shares his winner's

sweets with us—fizzy laces today. They tingle on my tongue as Elena and I walk our bikes back toward home just after midnight. We're really supposed to stay close to home all night on Confinement, near to whomever we're Caretaking—in my case, my mom, and for Elena, her dad and brother—but most of us interpret that . . . flexibly. It's the only night that is truly ours, after all, and Harold thinks the responsibility laid on us is unfair, so he keeps quiet about our exact whereabouts. It's another reason we get along. He hates snitches as much as we do.

But not everyone around here can be trusted. Unfortunately, as we round the corner back into our road, we run into a reminder of that.

CHAPTER THREE

Ingrid Rossi is standing under the lamppost outside my house, staring up at three pigeons huddled together on top of it. They're cooing softly, like she's making them jittery. I know exactly how they feel.

She spots us. "Well, well, where have you two saddos been? Far from home, breaking the rules again."

The hypocrisy is strong with this one. Ingrid lives in Juniper House, the children's home. It's close to Shady Oaks, which is why she's Dora's Caretaker. Another one of those stupid decisions from up high that goes to show how little anyone in the mayor's office actually knows about the young people in their town. I never worry about running into Ingrid at Shady Oaks, though, because once dusk's fallen and she's done the absolute minimum of checking Dora's cage lock, she's well out of there—finding trouble wherever she can. Harold always ends up doing the explosives perimeter around Shady Oaks' grounds, despite his arthritis, and despite it not being his job.

Two more figures float out of the darkness farther up, like shark fins breaking the liquid surface of the night—Fee and Loretta. There's no one else around now—tiredness has claimed the younger children, and most of the older ones are inside, probably playing Happy Trappers. The other residents of Juniper steer clear of Ingrid, so she hangs out with these two: rich kids who get a kick out of proximity to violence. They like to get into enough trouble to look hard, but not enough for Mommy and Daddy to cut off their allowances.

Fee is wearing a pristine white dress that shows off her tan—the kind you have to pay for if you live in Tremorglade and it's only April. Everything about her is glossy and smooth. Loretta has perfect dark brown skin with a dewy glow. Her black hair runs tight along her scalp into a puff on top of her head, held by a jeweled clip that glitters in the moonlight. Next to them, Elena and I look like we've been run through the waste disposal.

Ingrid may not have that kind of sheen, but she doesn't need it. Her red hair is scraped back into a business-like ponytail that suggests preening is a waste of her precious time. She hates most people, but she's developed a special kind of loathing for me over the past few years, and for the life of me I don't know why. The only thing I can think of is the time she tripped over my bag outside class and broke a tooth. For a while after that, she'd spot me and just . . . go for me, out of nowhere. Shoving, punching, kicking. That got her suspended a couple of times. Amy and Bernice, who run Juniper House, have been warned that if it happens again, she'll be chucked out of school for good.

Since then, the physical attacks have stopped. But she makes up stories about me, rumors about bad stuff I've supposedly done—to her, and to other people. It's all lies. The worst was when Amy and Bernice's cat, Hinky, got killed, probably by a fox, and Ingrid claimed it was me. I mean, no one believes her. But it hurts. I'd never do anything like that. I've never done anything to *her*. It's like she just picked me as the villain in her story.

"Get lost." Elena's not intimidated, despite the fact that Ingrid is at least a head taller, Tremorglade's tae kwon do champion, and full of sharp angles whereas Elena is soft and rounded. "Go bother someone else." She flicks a dismissive hand at Fee and Loretta, who are approaching slowly but indirectly, staying close to Ingrid, like sulky moons in orbit around an inhospitable planet. Fee flicks her glossy blond hair, while Loretta examines her perfect, deep red nails then glances up with a smirk. My feet tingle, wanting to run, but I'm stuck.

Ingrid's gaze swings up and down my body. Her icy blue eyes absorb the state of me. I try to discreetly pull my damp trousers away from my bum crack where they insist on clinging, while holding my bike with the other hand.

"Wow. You really made a special effort tonight, hey, Sel? So glam! You two on a date or something?" Fee and Loretta giggle. Even their tinkly laughs sound like money.

In a smooth movement, Ingrid brings her tranq around and points it at me. Those hard, bright eyes narrow down the sight. Her left hand brushes an auburn curl away from her forehead, then moves to support the barrel. The X50 is heavy, even though it's the lightest of the tranqs. It takes a big dart to knock out a Ripper.

"The penalty for being away from home on Confinement is death."

Death? The penalty is definitely not death. We're not barbarians. Mom would ground me, though, and I'd probably get a talking-to from the mayor. Plus, all the grown-ups would give me that disappointed look, like they thought I was better than that. They rely on us.

Public shame, *that's* the penalty. The adults are under the impression that it works.

I go very still. You never point a tranq at another person, not even as a joke. Especially not when it's loaded for Rippers. The safety's on, but her thumb is right next to it. I stare down the barrel, imagining the glint of the needle inside.

"Put that down." Elena steps in front of me. I can't see her expression, but it seems to have the desired effect.

Ingrid lowers the tranq and slings it over her shoulder with a chuckle.

"Just kidding around. Why're you so uptight? I'm totally safe with tranqs, unlike your clumsy little friend here."

"He's not clumsy."

"People get hurt around him, a lot. But maybe you're right, he's not clumsy. That means he does it on purpose. Could it be that lovely Sel is not such a great guy? Not such a *good boy*. If only they knew what you're really like. Cat killer." She spits, and it lands on my shoe. "You know what, I think it's my civic duty to show them you're not the Goody Two-shoes you pretend to be. Someone should report you to the police."

The police force around here is basically just Sergeant Derek Hale, although he's got a couple of part-timers on his team to help out. Not that there's anything to help with, apart from giving out fines for people who don't pick up dog poo, and doing school assemblies about "Responsible Caretaking." He gets all his orders from HQ in Hastaville and can't make any decisions for himself—from what I can tell, if he sneezes, he has to get permission before he can wipe his nose. That doesn't stop him from acting like he's some top detective in a movie, though—he wears mirrored sunglasses almost all the time, way into the evenings, until he actually starts to bump into things. As one of the few people with a car here, he drives his police cruiser around with the window wound down so he can make gun shapes with his hand as he passes and chews gum with his mouth open. If he ever had to deal with an actual crime, he'd probably get so excited he'd choke on it.

Hale and his team are just as useless on Confinement nights, of course, but with a better excuse. And by common consent, none of us kids will tell on any other, no matter what. But our unwritten code means nothing to Ingrid. When she eventually Turns, it won't make much of a difference. She's already a full-time monster.

I shrug in what I hope is a careless way, feigning interest in the pigeons on the lamppost. There are now some on the rooftops near us, where they've gathered to watch the show. They're cooing and grunting weirdly, mirroring my rising panic. My throat feels like it's closing up. There's a buzzing at the edge of my hearing, like a mosquito has got into my head.

"I haven't done anything wrong." My voice is shakier than I would like. "And I never killed Hinky. I bet it was you."

I regret saying it immediately. Hinky spent most of his time curled up in Ingrid's room at Juniper. She used to buy little sprats to feed him as treats, out of her allowance.

"Oh, you are a *piece of work*," she says, her voice low and dangerous. She raises the tranq again and moves her thumb directly over the safety. One tiny slide and it'll be armed.

"Ingrid, no." Even Elena sounds panicky now.

Ingrid aims the tranq slowly between me and Elena as though choosing her prey. Fee and Loretta stand frozen, eyes wide. Even they're unnerved by her behavior tonight.

My throat is dry, my heart skittering in my chest. Next to me, Elena shifts her weight, like she's preparing to make a lunge for the tranq. I want to stop her, but my arms are jelly. I try to speak but all that comes out is a strangled squeak. An instinctive cry for help. The buzzing in my head is now deafening.

People say there are no such things as miracles, but sometimes there's no other explanation.

Right then, something incredible happens.

Pigeons start crashing into Ingrid's face.

CHAPTER FOUR

She doesn't see the first one coming. It slams into her temple out of nowhere, sideways like it's been shot from a cannon. She's almost thrown off her feet. Her head snaps round and the feathered body drops to the ground. Slowly, her hand rises to touch the place it hit. Blinking, she regards the dead bird at her feet.

"What the—"

Then the rest of them come. Birds drop from the sky like hailstones, smashing into the ground, bouncing off her head and then her arms when she raises them to protect herself. There's a sickening, slopping drumbeat of soft, fragile bodies hitting concrete at speed. Fee and Loretta are a few meters away, and it takes them a moment to react to what they're seeing. Then a pigeon smacks into the ground right in front of Fee, sending a splatter of gore up her tanned legs and white dress, and that finally releases them from their stupor. They scream, grabbing at each other, trying to run in different directions before finally fleeing, crouched over, around the corner.

I can't move. A sick bubble rises in my throat. My hands reach out instinctively to try to catch some of the birds, but it's ridiculous, hopeless.

There's a powerful tug on my shirt—Elena—and I'm dragged under my next-door neighbor's porch.

The pigeon hail is mainly concentrated where Ingrid is standing, though a few stray birds are swooping wildly up and down the street. The feathery tornado seems to be expanding—there's a rush of air on my cheek, a lump whizzes past, and the window behind us shatters as the bird hits it. A droplet of blood lands by the corner of my eye. We duck, making our bodies as small as possible, using a hedge as cover.

I can barely see Ingrid now for the flying bodies, the torrent is so thick. She's in a defensive crouch under the lamppost and they're piling up around her.

It feels endless, but it can only be seconds, maybe half a minute since it started. All at once, it's over.

The sky is empty again. Silence. Then, a thin, reedy noise escapes Ingrid, like air from a leaky balloon. I launch myself forward involuntarily, and Elena tightens her grip on my arm. When I glance back, her eyes are glassy with horror.

"Where are you going?" she asks.

I shake Elena off and walk unsteadily to Ingrid, stepping around the mess, while trying not to see it. Some of the birds are moving, most aren't. Ingrid's whole body is shaking. Her head jerks up when I gently touch her back, and the whining sound she's making cuts off. Her face is covered in blood and gunk and feathers, unspeakable juices dripping from her hair. "Are ... are you okay?" I ask.

For a moment she regards me with confusion, as if she doesn't know who I am. Then her mouth twists into a grimace. "Get. Away. From. Me."

"Let's get you home—"

Both her fists shove forcefully into my stomach, and I stagger backward, stumbling over the small bodies. "*I hate you*," she whispers, repeating it over and over hysterically while I walk numbly backward. Finally, she seems to run out of breath and her anger subsides back into whining.

"Leave her," Elena says quietly, arriving at my side. "She'll go home eventually. Wanna come over to my place?" I can tell she wants to pick over what just happened, but I can't face it right now. I need my bed.

"Let's talk tomorrow."

I watch as my friend reluctantly goes inside her house. Ingrid's still in the middle of the street. The sound of her wailing is oddly quiet as I open my own door. And when I shut it behind me, I don't hear it at all.

» » »

I barely register the dawn alert buzzing on my wrist a few hours later and enjoy a blissful extra ten minutes dozing until my phone pings with a text. My fingers fumble across the bedside table, push the phone over the edge, and finally retrieve it from the threadbare carpet. The text is from Elena.

*YOU OK? WHAT **WAS** THAT?*

Last night's apocalyptic weirdness returns to my brain and jolts me awake.

When I open the curtains and lean out of the window, there they are. I didn't dream it. Bird bodies lie strewn in my garden and in the street. A ginger cat is sitting serenely in the middle of it all, washing itself like it's just had breakfast. It probably has. My stomach turns over. I'm not going out there until the street cleaners have finished.

I struggle to make sense of my thoughts—gears won't click into place. Did I do it, somehow? I wished for rescue, sure. I thought Ingrid was going to kill me. Did I *make* the pigeons attack? Do I have some kind of . . . power?

The idea doesn't feel like wish fulfillment, it feels like a nightmare. Those poor creatures.

And Ingrid. A surge of sympathy for her is immediately quelled by remembering her absolute hatred of me. I knew it before, but last night I truly felt the strength of it—a furious dark loathing.

We'll never be president of each other's fan clubs, that's for sure.

As I go to close the window, I notice something metallic hanging off the tree branch just outside. At first, I think it's a Frisbee—a disc, only about the size of my hand when I spread my fingers—but then I see it's caught on the branch by wires sticking out of it.

Seems like pigeons weren't the only things falling from the sky last night.

I reach it easily, unhooking it to bring it inside. It's a drone—the propellers have mostly broken off, but there's still half of one, bent, coming from the top. They don't normally crash—they have sensors to avoid it.

Another memory from last night: that buzzing. I thought it was in my head but actually, I wonder if it was this.

This one is different from the other drones. There's nowhere to hold cargo, and on the bottom of it is black mesh that reminds me of the speaker on a music player. I look it over for a while, baffled, and then Harold rings.

"Forgot to give your mom's cake tin back last night. Does she need it in the next few days? I can drop it off."

"Nah, it's fine. She's got loads." I'm still considering the drone in my hands.

"What's wrong?"

I laugh. He can always tell. I fill him in on last night, and then describe what I've just found. "I guess I should report it, right?"

"Sounds intriguing. No hurry to do that, I reckon. Isn't this Pedro's area of expertise?"

It's not a bad idea. I tell him I need to go and let Mom out, then hang up, before chucking the drone on my bed. I'll take it to Pedro later.

Mom looks even more tired than usual when I let her out of her cage this morning. Dark circles under her eyes. Bloodstains at the corners of her mouth, which she missed with her hanky. She's got a long cleaning shift to do later too.

Most people get their Caretakers to leave a key within arm's reach just outside the bars, so they can let themselves out at dawn, but Mom won't hear of it. She insisted we save up to splurge on one of those heavy-duty cages with an electronic keypad on the outside of the door, because she saw a load of online ads about how much stronger and safer they are. We had to get a backup battery for it too, so it won't fail when our power goes out. It doesn't even have a remote I can leave for her. I've got to punch in the number on the door, old-school style.

So when I come down, she's already been awake for a while, sitting on her blanket fully dressed, hands in her lap and reading a book like she's in the dentist's waiting room. She always leaves her clothes and something to read within reach, just outside the bars in a neat pile, so she doesn't trample on them or rip them during the night.

As I jab the buttons, I try to persuade her again to buy a remote for the door. It would be so much more convenient. For her, I mean. It's not just because I want to stay in bed longer.

Okay, it is a bit that.

"It's not like you could accidentally key in the passcode. Massive furry mitts, no opposable thumbs." I hold mine up and do a little thumb dance to demonstrate. "Everyone else lets themselves out."

But she's not having it. "Do you think I care what everyone else does?" she asks, lips pursed as she steps through the door. "No such thing as too careful, Ansel." She's the only person who calls me by my full first name. Literally everyone else calls me Sel, including at school. When she's angry it's "Ansel Archer."

Mom can't bear the thought she might hurt someone as a Ripper—waking up to find her claws and teeth have taken someone's life.

I circle my finger around my lips to indicate she's got a few stains left on hers. "Missed a bit. You look rough, Mom."

She dabs around the corners of her mouth and gives me a sour glance, eyeing my wild hair. "What's your excuse? Those opposable thumbs can't hold a comb?"

Despite her exhaustion, her tone is light and teasing, full of relief that nothing happened. She can't remember anything about the nights she Turns—no one does—and it's only when she wakes safe in her cage that she can be sure everything's okay. She once told me it's like a huge, heavy blanket falls on her and presses her to the ground. Next thing she knows, she wakes up to the smell of blood, a sticky mouth, bad breath, and aching fingers.

We don't discuss the lunging and growling, or the howling. On the stroke of midnight they all howl. Up and down the street, across the whole town. No matter how many times you hear it, it's eerie. I recorded Mom doing it once because I thought she'd be curious, but she dismissed it as "caterwauling" and made me delete it.

"What's that?" Her sharp eyes have caught the scratch on my hand. Her voice is suddenly tight. I cross my arms, tucking the offending mark out of sight.

"Nothing, the knife slipped when I was cutting up the beef."

Her anxious gaze searches my face. "Really?"

I snort and roll my eyes. "What else is it gonna be? If you'd got a bite out of me, don't you think it'd be a lot worse than that? Have you *seen* your fangs? Oh, right, course not. Well, I'll take a photo next time to show you."

"You will *not*."

That puts an end to the questions.

Upstairs, we sit at the kitchen table to eat our freshly baked cinnamon rolls. Mom prepared them yesterday so

I could pop them in the oven first thing today. She loves messing around with dough and pastry, even the fiddly stuff like croissants and doughnuts. She says it's an art. Mom's at her happiest when she's icing a sponge cake or drizzling a sugary glaze over buns.

Crisp flakes of pastry fall from my lips as we listen to the radio news. I learn, mostly to my relief but also somewhat to my disappointment, that I am not, in fact, a pigeon-whisperer.

The dozens of birds that suddenly started acting weird didn't come in response to my call, after all.

The radio says there was an unusual weather event last night affecting Tremorglade, Hastaville, and Yojay—the valley towns. Some kind of storm high up, a weird atmospheric pressure thing that messed with the birds' internal navigation instincts. We don't normally get that stuff. It's a northern thing. I hope it doesn't mean we'll get more of their nightmarish weather.

"Well, how about that!" Mom exclaims. "Did you notice anything like that last night?"

"Yeah, a bit," I say noncommittally. I don't want to get into exactly what happened because then she'll want to check Ingrid's okay, and Ingrid will tell her I was at Shady Oaks last night. Mom likes Harold and helps me keep an eye on him, although she's not wild about the fact that he keeps trying to give us money. I haven't mentioned how much he hates Sequest either—she's always fundraising for them, since they took such good care of her. And if she knew Elena and I spent Confinements at Shady Oaks, she'd decide he's a bad influence. She wants me close to home those nights, following protocol, in case she needs shooting.

It's overkill if you ask me. The system works without us having to babysit the whole time. Escapes just don't happen anymore. The last one was years ago when Mrs. Harris's rusty cage lock broke. She cleared out the tropical fish tank with a couple of gulps, ate the family dog, and gouged three slits right through the living room door before her daughter tranq'd her through the window. Now they have a titanium Impregnacage with a timer lock and CCTV.

No one in Tremorglade has ever got farther than that, not since the Disruption.

Okay, so I got a little sloppy last night reaching through the bars. But the important stuff—the locking in . . . I would *never* take chances with that. Our cage is totally secure. Then there's the tripwire across the porch, which can spring the graphene net down instantly. And if that misses her, there's the explosives perimeter. A special little mix we call stun pops, just enough to stop her in her tracks and give her a nasty headache, but nowhere near enough to kill her in full Ripper mode. It's a tried and tested formula around the world. Everything's marked in neon, so humans can't miss it. Luckily Rippers don't pay attention to signs.

Even if she *did* make it beyond the perimeter, there are always dozens of kids up and down the road with a fully loaded tranq and an itchy trigger finger who'd be happy to deal with an escaped parent, no matter whose it is.

There's no point trying to persuade Mom to stop worrying, though. I'll just enjoy my tiny bit of freedom.

What she doesn't know can't hurt her, I think to myself.

Like my pigeon-whispering powers, it's another of my assumptions that turns out to be wrong.

CHAPTER FIVE

Next Confinement, Elena says she's busy, so I ride to Harold's on my own, feeling miffed. It's not like she hangs out with anyone else much—only Pedro, and he's not an option tonight, being of the fang-and-claw persuasion. She won't tell me what she's up to. What if she's bored of me and just wants to spend the evening playing Happy Trappers, or on FIN, chatting with her online pen pal Trix in Rheitzland? I don't begrudge her friendship with Trix—I chat with my FIN friend Chad all the time online and miss him when we haven't messaged for a while. But Confinements are special. She can talk to Trix anytime.

I don't understand her lately. She's got ants in her pants. Even if her dad doesn't manage to get a job outside Tremorglade, she wants "a change of scenery." She's been trying to persuade me to go hiking with her over to Hastaville. Hiking! Like she's not aware of the big red warning signs at the edge of the forest specifically telling you not to do it. Like she's entirely forgotten what happened to Remi Colletto and his family three years ago.

Remi was sixteen. Good at sports, an outdoorsy type. His whole family was adventurous. Anyway, they got it into their heads to go camping, never mind the warnings. What could go wrong? Obviously, from here, there's only one direction to go, so they set off down the road through the forest, a nice safe waxing moon due over their heads all week, of course. Six of them, from Grandpa Colletto all the way down to little Wren, still in Babygros.

None of them ever made it home. They were killed and eaten by a starving bear that had been roaming the outskirts of Yojay, where they'd apparently set up for the night. Locals found their bloody clothes, little pieces of them the bear missed still inside. Tragic, the newsreaders called it.

Harold reckons it was Sequest, of course.

Me, I'm not so sure it was a bear that ate them either, but I have a different theory. The folks in Yojay have a reputation, if you know what I mean. They get hungry.

The thing is, the forest is safe—close to Tremorglade. Sure, there are wild creatures, foxes, deer, and even wolves, but they're timid, they don't like coming close to town. They leave us be, and we do the same. That's less true the farther away you go.

Elena's got to be joking about the hiking. She'd better be.

I fret about it all evening while playing cards with Harold, and fare even worse than usual.

"I'm not even sure you're trying," Harold scolds me.

"Sorry. Bit distracted today."

"That'll be Sequest experimenting on your brainwaves," he says. That at least raises a bubble of laughter from my chest.

"Yeah, probably."

But he's not laughing. "They're up to something," he insists. "Did Pedro take a look at that drone?" For the first time, I feel a twist of doubt about my friend. His Sequest rants are funny, but I hope he's not turning into some kind of actual conspiracy nut.

He winces.

"You all right?" I ask.

He twiddles his hearing aid. "Headache." For a moment I worry he's about to attribute that to Sequest as well, but then he smiles wearily. "Just the doldrums. And I've been out all over town running errands—think I've overdone it."

"It's worse lately, isn't it? The doldrums." Elena reckons I'm imagining it, but it definitely is. The nausea, the headaches, the general out-of-sorts-ness. "Do you want a painkiller?"

"No, it's all right, don't make a fuss."

"How about one of your juice drinks?" I lift one of the little glass bottles from the newly delivered box on the floor. He mixes his own recipe nonalcoholic punch for the monthly Howler parties held in the town square before Confinement nights. He orders all sorts of interesting juice and soda concoctions off the internet. Most of them taste like cough syrup, although they're very popular. It's frowned upon to drink alcohol in the twenty-four hours before Confinement— drunk is dangerous when you're supposed to go into your cage nice and quietly.

He waves it away. "Not now, thank you. Come on." He nods at the cards in my hand. "Your go."

I select a three of spades and drop it on the table before realizing it was a stupid choice. I've just thrown away a trump. But Harold doesn't seem to notice—he's staring into the distance, frowning.

"Ingrid was in such a rush before dusk." He shakes his head. "Do you mind if we check on Dora quickly? I want to make sure she's locked in properly. I'd never forgive myself if anything happened to her."

Harold is very protective of Dora, despite the fact she's horribly rude to him, and incredibly nosy. He regularly finds her poking about in his room. He just takes it, though. She's pretty much as unpleasant as Ingrid except seventy years older so she's had more practice. In that way Ingrid is the perfect Caretaker for her. They deserve each other.

If you so much as pass Dora's room when the door's open and glance in, she'll jump down your throat in a way her Ripper self would be proud of. She guards her room as though she's got diamonds in there instead of a load of flowery cushions and lacy doilies and a whole series of books with wartime nurses on the covers. She just about puts up with Ingrid locking her in, because she has no choice, I suppose. But she shouts at her a lot, according to Harold. I can understand why Ingrid doesn't hang around.

We open the door to Dora's room quietly, as though we're afraid of waking her up, even though Rippers don't sleep. She's standing in the center of her cage, all bony and stiff, very still, a low growl simmering in her throat, having heard us coming. Her fur stands out in untidy graying tufts, the knees on her back legs bowed toward each other awkwardly. There are low voices, and it takes me a moment to trace them to the speaker on a shelf—she's put an audiobook on. I listen for a few seconds while Harold bends to check the padlock. Two characters are discussing what they'll do when a baby is born and worrying what will become of them. I struggle to imagine Dora caring enough about anyone to follow this kind of story. I guess there's always more to people than you think.

I quickly lose interest and absentmindedly take hold of one of the cage bars to give it a test rattle. Dora immediately goes for my hand, causing me to jump back, banging into the small bedside table.

"Watch out for her teeth!" Harold gasps.

"It's okay. She didn't get me," I reassure him.

"No, her *teeth*." Harold gestures behind me, where I've jolted the bedside table, sloshing a full tumbler that I now see is home to a set of dentures, grinning pinkly in their watery lair. I grab a few tissues from the box and quickly clean up the spill. For some reason the sight of Dora's false teeth makes me sad: all neat and orderly in the cleaning fluid where she put them before dusk made her a monster.

Elderly Rippers are weaker than younger ones, but it's all relative. You still wouldn't set one free, not unless you want it on your death certificate that you had your intestines torn out by a retiree. Under the molting, patchy fur, there's a sinuous flex of muscle, and Ripper skin is so tough that even mosquitoes can't puncture it. That's why the X50 darts are so strong.

Harold straightens up, reassuring the irritated Ripper now pacing up and down, hissing and yowling. "All secure. There we go, Dora, sorry to disturb you." He sighs, his gaze roving around the room for a moment, sweeping the shelves with a slight frown, as though he's got the feeling something's out of place. Then he gives himself a little shake, and we head back to his room to restart our game.

We've barely played another hand when—

Ping

My alert bracelet vibrates on my wrist, and I stare at it in surprise. Eddie leaps to his feet and starts yapping until Harold puts a calming hand on his back. "That sounded like an alert."

It is. An escape. I'd forgotten what they sound like, we haven't had one for so long. Anyone can send an alert, but the system grades them according to how many it's received for the same incident, in the unlikely event that someone has just sat on their bracelet and managed to select an address randomly. This one is flashing red, which means there have been multiple reports. It's real.

To my shame, my first thought is that I hope it isn't near here because then I'll have to do something about it.

Then I read the alert and my stomach lurches, like I've just stumbled off a cliff.

It *is* nowhere near. It's all the way across town:

15 Albermore Terrace

My address.

Harold sees my expression, the way I grip the arms of the chair as I stand up unsteadily. "Sel?"

"Mom," I croak. "It's Mom."

CHAPTER SIX

I make it across town in record time, my sneakers punishing the pedals on my bike so viciously, I'm scared they're going to fly off. My mind is filled by a single question: *How did this happen?* I distinctly remember clicking the lock shut, seeing the red light come on, wishing Mom a good night, then tugging at the door to check.

Doesn't matter. Just get there.

I push myself so hard that when I finally reach my road, there are sparks floating at the edge of my vision and my breath is coming in harsh rasps. By some miracle my bike chain has stayed on.

There are a few kids spaced out, their backs to me, tranqs pointed down the side alley of my house, where we keep the bins. The closest two—Asim and Rudy—turn around briefly when they hear the spin of my wheels, then shift their focus ahead again. I toss my bike to one side as Asim nods toward the alley.

"There. She went for Rudy but ran straight into the stun pops, got flamed, and backed off behind there."

I glance at Rudy, heart in my mouth. He's standing just outside my front garden, legs planted apart like we've been taught. His heaving chest is the only sign of what just happened.

I need to shut her down before she makes another move. Those three stun pops have left a gap plenty big enough for her to get through if she tries again at the same point.

Our front door is hanging off one hinge. I don't see the graphene net, so it must have triggered, but for some reason it didn't stop her.

A clattering from the side of the house reminds me this is not a question for right now. I raise my own tranq. This is my mess. I need to clean it up.

"Safety off," someone says from behind me.

Right. I flick it.

The gap down the side of our house is a dead end— Mika's house next door has an extension that goes right up to our wall at the back. The alley is covered in shadows as I approach. If Mom's down there, she's quiet and still, which is not a normal state for a Ripper. She might be hurt. If the stun pops got her, she might—

Some instinct gives me a millisecond's warning

before a huge body launches at me from the darkness and I lose my footing in panic, slipping and letting off an uncontrolled volley of darts into the night sky. The big bin goes flying and lands on top of me just before the Ripper does, knocking the breath from my lungs. The hinged lid smacks open onto my face, forming a barrier between us, Mom's jaws snapping behind the other side of the flimsy plastic. I have about half a second to live.

There's a *snick* sound, and a yelp, and almost immediately the movement stops, and Mom goes slack. The pressure on my chest subsides as she slides off the bin, collapsing onto the garbage now strewn on the ground from torn black bags. I struggle up and kneel at her side.

"Mom..."

I run my hands through her fur, surprised at how soft it is, and realize it's the first time I've ever really touched her as a Ripper. My fingers press against the warm skin underneath—her side moving up and down under my hand. She's alive, just knocked out.

"You hurt?"

Mika rolls forward up the garden path toward me, flicking her bangs out of her eyes. She lowers her tranq to her lap.

I manage to shake my head.

"Sorry I couldn't get her before she went through the stun pops. That's gonna hurt tomorrow."

I look where she's pointing, at Mom's hind leg. There's a large, charred section of fur with blood seeping out at the edges.

I can barely speak due to my bursting lungs, and to shame. It chokes me. What have I done?

"Mika, thank you. I . . . "

"Sure." She shrugs like she's only done the washing-up for me. If it wasn't for the tremble in her voice and the haunted look on her face, I'd think she was fine with it. She's not fine with it. Tonight is going to feature in her nightmares.

What have I done? Not just to Mom, but to my friends. My neighbors. Now it's all over, there's a small crowd of them standing around.

"You better get her inside."

Rudy and Asim pass us, hoisting a tarp between them, all business.

A couple of people head down the side of the house to find the darts I let off—hopefully they'll just be embedded in the fence, not lying on the ground waiting to jab someone in the foot. A clean-up team will be dispatched tomorrow, but it's better if those darts are found sooner rather than later. I shudder as I realize I could easily have killed someone with my panicky trigger finger.

It takes eight of us to roll Mom on the tarp and slowly manhandle her back through the front door, her head bumping sickeningly and tongue lolling as we descend the stone steps to the cellar.

Once she's finally inside the cage and we close the door, we stand to get our breath back, and I see the others surreptitiously taking her in.

She's beautiful. A silver-gray top layer of fur, each hair tipped with black, a delicate coppery tinge over the shoulders and down her spine. Her eyelids are slightly open, irises glinting gold through the slit. No one gets to check out a Ripper like this, normally. They're in constant movement, have inhumanly quick reflexes, and are perpetually full of violence. Now, the sheer size of her, the muscular legs and neck, the razor teeth . . . everyone drinks it in, fascinated. Them seeing Mom this way, utterly helpless, feels indecent. I almost snap at them to stop staring, but I owe them more than I can ever repay. They did their jobs when I failed to do mine.

I really hope the wound will have disappeared by tomorrow. Sometimes they do, but Rippers usually only have little grazes from throwing themselves against the cage all night. This one's almost certainly going to persist through her Return and need treatment.

The other kids gradually peel off back home, except for Elena, whose arrival I hadn't even noticed. She goes outside and brings in the graphene net, which she found in a flowerbed. It's got a huge hole in it.

. I sit on the floor of the cellar, unwilling to leave Mom alone yet. Elena comes to sit right next to me, arm round my shoulders, and then the sobs break free. My whole body shudders with the enormity of what's happened.

I've been so stupid. Complacent. I put everyone in danger.

None of them have told me off, none of them judged me or asked how the cage door got open—the lock worked fine when they shut it just now. None of them wanted to know where I'd been or did so much as tut. That will come tomorrow, for sure, when the adults wake.

For now, though, the horror and the disgust are all mine.

CHAPTER SEVEN

MAY—29 DAYS
TO NEXT CONFINEMENT

I get a visit from Sergeant Hale the following day. It's a Saturday, so I wouldn't be at school anyway, thank goodness. I'm not ready to face that just yet.

Hale comes down to the basement to see our setup to figure out what went wrong. Mom stays upstairs on the sofa—her leg is really hurting. It's got a big dressing on it that she'll have to get changed twice a week at the Wellness Center so that it doesn't get infected. She insists she'll be able to work on Monday.

I think she might be in shock. Or maybe it's the after-effects of the tranq. She hasn't been angry. She doesn't even blame me. It's much worse than that—she blames herself.

Back upstairs, Sergeant Hale sighs and gets his notebook out. We wait, subdued, while he writes in it, ignoring the hammering and clattering at the front of the house as Mika's mom attaches a new door for us.

He sucks his teeth. "Seems like you just didn't lock it properly, Sel."

"But . . . I did. I definitely did." I swear I clicked it into place. I remember doing it, just as I've done it hundreds of times before. "The little red light came on, like always."

"Maybe it's faulty," Mom offers. "It's my mistake, I bought it. I fell for those ads that said it was super secure. I'll get an old-fashioned padlock immediately." She sounds so apologetic. I can't bear it.

Hale shrugs. "Sure, as an additional measure it would be wise. But ultimately, this is on your Caretaker." He fixes me with a significant look.

"What if someone let her out on purpose?" I speak the thought the moment it occurs to me. Ingrid's hateful face swims into my mind.

Hale stiffens. "That's a serious accusation. Who else knows the lock passcode, apart from you and your mother?"

No one does, except for Elena, but I'm not telling him that.

He takes my silence as an answer.

"So where were you, Sel?"

"Just hanging out with friends. You know. Riding my bike. I wasn't . . . far away." It's the same thing I told Mom. I don't want to get Harold in trouble. It's not his fault— he's never pressured me to visit on Confinements; it's my choice.

"What friends? Elena, right?" Hale flips over a page in his notebook.

"No." It comes out louder than I intend. He glances up in surprise.

"No? You two are pretty close, right? Always hanging out, from what I hear."

"No, I mean, yeah, but no, we weren't . . . on this particular occasion. She had other stuff to do." I lick my lips. For some reason I feel like I'm lying, even though I'm not. What does he mean, *from what I hear*? Who's he been talking to? Why are Elena and I even a topic of conversation?

"So she was busy? Out as well? Doing what?"

I shrug dramatically. "No idea. Why don't you ask her?" As soon as I've said it, I want to take it back. *Great job keeping her out of it, Sel.* But Hale presses on.

"So who were you with?"

"It was just . . . you know, random kids from school. I can't remember. I don't really know most of them."

He lets the silence grow for a moment, giving the lie some space so we can all appreciate what a whopper it is. Even the hammering noise from fitting the doorframe stops for a few seconds. Everyone at school is intimately acquainted with the details of one another's lives, whether they want to be or not. We know extended family histories, daily routines, favorite foods, birthmarks, test scores, toilet habits.

Hale's pencil scratches on his notebook. What can he possibly be writing that takes this long? He's probably just doodling to make me uncomfortable.

It's working.

"Ingrid," I add, sweating. "I was with Ingrid Rossi." Mom's eyebrows draw together skeptically, but she says nothing.

The pencil pauses, then scratches again. Ingrid's name. My stomach twists with a nauseous mix of spite and shame.

"Derek," Mom says, "this doesn't have to go any further, does it?"

"I'll have to make a report, I'm afraid, Mrs. Archer." Mom flinches at his formality. "It'll go to Police HQ in Hastaville, but I doubt there'll be consequences as it's his first offence, and no one else got hurt. And frankly, they've got bigger problems in Hastaville, as you know. Murderers and robbers round every corner." He waits for me to look at him, and I notice that his eyes are puffy underneath like he doesn't get a lot of sleep. "You're a good kid. I get it. We have it easy here, you forget how important it is to be careful. I hope last night reminded you that Caretaking is life and death. We leave you kids alone for *one night* a month, that's all. Just … from now on, do what you're supposed to do. Got it? Maybe get yourself on the next New Caretakers' course for a refresher."

There's a lump in my throat that stops me speaking.

Mom jumps in and apologizes again and says, "Yes, we will." *We* will.

"That wasn't true about Ingrid, was it?" Mom says, the moment Hale is gone.

"She was there!" I insist, slightly too loudly. "Making my life a misery, as always." It's barely a lie—it just wasn't precisely last night, that's all.

"You kids have got to stick together. You're so young. You shouldn't have to—" She breaks off, miserable, mortified. "I know there's some bad blood between you two. Be kind, Sel."

This is too much. Except for Ingrid, us kids *do* stick together. Last night proved that. "Bad blood? She bullies me, simple as that. You don't see it. You're never around, are you?"

Her face goes still and blank, and I'm immediately remorseful. She works so hard for the two of us, and I know she wishes she had more time with me. How have I turned this into an argument? Yet again, I've found a way to hurt her. Every time I open my mouth I make things worse.

"I . . . didn't mean that."

She nods, resting her head back on the sofa cushion. She needs to sleep, though I can't see how she'll manage it with all the hammering still going on. I leave her and head upstairs, rubbing my eyes. They feel sore and irritated from all the crying last night.

I lie on my bed for a while, nose pressed into the space between the mattress and the wall, where I can see the giant house spider who has made a home down there. It's oddly comforting, having her (I've decided she's female) just living there quietly the whole time, regardless of anything I do or don't do. I guess she comes out at night to hunt, or something. She doesn't need me at all—she only asks that I don't vacuum under my bed, and that works for both of us.

I plan to spend the day in my room, wallowing, but Elena texts in her usual polite fashion:

Get here now.

I obey.

We're in Pedro's room, staring at the pieces of drone laid out on the floor—the one I found in my tree last month. I'd forgotten about it, what with everything else. He's taken it apart—there are little screws, and chips, and colored wires, and pieces of plastic and metal that he's carefully separated.

I'm just relieved to have something to think about other than what a terrible person I am. "So it really was a speaker? How did it end up stuck outside my bedroom window?"

I look to Pedro for explanation. He's lying on Elena's bed playing Happy Trappers on his phone, wearing a brand-new T-shirt with a picture of a cartoon Ripper wearing headphones, captioned: *Music too loud? Bite me.* He doesn't take his eyes off the screen, and Elena answers for him, bubbling over with excitement.

"That's what we wanted to know. So I ran a few tests last night, using an app that Pedro has on his phone. And sure enough, there was some noise coming from above, the whole night."

"What, over my house?"

"Over the whole town, from what I could tell."

So *this* is what she was doing last night instead of coming with me to Harold's. I'm still miffed, albeit now for a different reason: that she didn't tell me what she was up to. But I'm too intrigued to sulk about it for long.

"I didn't hear anything. Must have been pretty quiet."

"That's the thing, actually. It was really loud, but *we* couldn't hear it." Her face is lit up; she's pretty pleased with herself.

"That . . . literally doesn't make sense." I cross my arms over my chest.

"It does!" Elena insists. "Tell him, Pedro."

Pedro finally speaks from the bed. "Infrasound."

I wait, but he doesn't immediately elaborate, instead continuing to smash his thumbs against the phone screen, trying to tranq a deadly digital Ripper.

Most of the time, I'm happy that I'm not an adult. But then I remember Pedro and I think it might be okay, as long as I can be like him.

I used to think it was his clothes. He knows what suits him and wears it well. He's got this fake-feather jacket, which gives him a kind of badass angel vibe. But when he let me try it on, I might as well have been wearing a bunch of dead pigeons. When he hangs out with his mates, they look like an album cover for an indie band. Most of them act like they haven't noticed we exist, but Pedro's never too cool to be nice to his little sister's friends.

For his last birthday, Elena got him another T-shirt, with a picture of Fen Zhao on it—his favorite actor, from *Plague Terror*. It's a still from the movie. They don't make many new movies these days, since the Disruption, so when they do, we *all* stream them, over and over. Pretty much everyone I know can recite most of the scenes by heart. Old movies are harder to relate to, since there was no such thing as Turning back then. There's a rumor that *Plague Terror 2* is coming out soon; I'm not sure Tremorglade's internet will be able to handle the massive surge in demand there'll be the moment it's available to stream.

Pedro is a little bit of a fanboy when it comes to Fen Zhao—he actually sent the shirt to Fen's agent, asking for her to sign it, but never got it back, even though he sent return postage. He says he doesn't blame Fen, it'll be her agent's fault. Although I'm not sure why Fen's agent would steal Pedro's T-shirt. She must be loaded, what with her client being in those blockbuster movies.

Finally Pedro gets to a break in the game, and glances at me. "Infrasound—sound waves that human beings can't hear, but they're there. Ultrasound waves are high frequency, and infrasound are low frequency. Elena measured eighteen hertz last night. Below what we can possibly hear. But it was seriously loud."

"Eighteen hurts?" I frown back at the drone pieces on the floor. My physics is hazy. I vaguely remember Ms. Boateng teaching us something about thunder and dog whistles but after the test I kind of cleared it out of my brain.

"It's a unit of measurement," Elena clarifies.

"If you say so." I clamber over the bed to sit next to Pedro and watch him play. I marvel at how he can multitask even on level fifty-eight.

"And the interesting thing was, it started right at dusk, and cut off at dawn, like someone threw a switch," Pedro says.

"But . . . why?"

"Now, that is the big question, my friend. And whichever way you look at it, the answer's not good."

"It's not?"

"But it helps explain why your pigeons were acting weird."

"How?" Then I do a double take. "Hang on, what do you mean, *my* pigeons?"

"They dive-bombed Ingrid at a crucial moment, right? Elena told me you thought you might be the pigeon-whisperer or something."

I glower at her, and she shrugs innocently.

"I did not think that."

"'Kay."

I tut. "Anyhow, they explained it already on the radio. It was the weather."

"Nope." He doesn't take his eyes off the phone as he answers. He's on a tricky bit, trying to time a net drop just as the Ripper passes underneath, but it's a fiendishly unpredictable one and keeps changing direction. "We did a little bit of research this morning. When flocks of birds act like they did that night, it's not because of weather. It's because they think they're being attacked by a predator."

"Like an eagle or something?"

"Or a drone, dropping suddenly and crashing into that tree next to your house."

I take it in. Those poor creatures. So terrified, they fled right into the ground. That would at least explain why nowhere else in Tremorglade had pigeon hail.

"And on top of that," Pedro continues, "they would probably have been extra spooked."

"Because of Ingrid?"

He laughs. "No, dork. She only has that effect on you,

buddy. I'm talking about the infrasound. It turns out pigeons can hear it, unlike us. They'd normally be asleep at that time, but something was bothering them. Then I guess they thought they were being attacked by this weird noisy thing and panicked."

"You sure it wasn't the weather? The radio said it happened in other places around the northern valleys too."

He grunts in annoyance as a survey flashes up on his phone, pausing the action.

What's your favorite song?

That's the only downside of Happy Trappers, it's chock-full of ads where you have to answer stupid questions to carry on with the game. He finally gives me his full attention.

"Does that sound like the way weather behaves to you? I mean, some types of weather can produce infrasound effects. But have you ever known a storm to start from nothing, on the dot of dusk, and stop just like that at dawn?" He clicks his finger and thumb.

"I suppose not. Hey, type in 'Your butt,'" I tell him, pointing at his screen. Elena rolls her eyes, but Pedro humors me and keys it in. The screen flashes and won't accept it.

"Sorry, dweeb. It's too smart for your juvenile humor."

He types in the name of a track by Federal Agenda—"Moonlight Disco"—before finally drop-kicking the Ripper into a box. "Anyhow, as to why the radio was saying that . . . I don't know. Could be completely unrelated, I guess. Your pigeons and those northern pigeons acting up for different reasons."

"Stop calling them *my* pigeons," I mutter.

Elena, who has been shifting impatiently this whole time, jumps in again.

"I saw them, Sel. The drones, just like this one. With Pedro's telescope. Once I started to look for them, they were all over the place. High up enough that you don't see them from the ground. No lights on them, not like the delivery ones."

The drone is black underneath, I notice, apart from the glint of its internal wires. Like it was designed to go unnoticed in the night sky.

"Aaaannnnd, that's not all," Pedro adds, checking his score then chucking the phone on the bed. "It's not just pigeons that are affected by that kind of noise. Humans, too, even though we can't hear it. Some more than others. It can cause headaches, nausea, even change your mood, make you feel scared for no reason. Ring any bells?"

My jaw drops. "The Confinement doldrums!"

"Maybe."

"Who would do that?" My mind is racing.

Pedro's face breaks into a grin. "Oh, now that's the easy part. Show him, Elena."

She crouches, turning over one of the pieces of plastic from the drone. I follow her pointing finger to a tiny logo.

Sequest, Inc.

"Maybe Harold's wild conspiracy theory isn't so wild after all."

CHAPTER EIGHT

On Monday, Hale comes and gives us a school assembly on Confinement Responsibilities. I don't know if it was already planned, or if Friday night's events prompted it. Either way, it's excruciating. It feels like he's addressing me directly, but it's hard to tell when he has his shades on.

"Some of you aren't taking this seriously," he intones. "May I remind you all that the protocol is 'set up, lock in, *watch* out.' Not 'chill out.'"

I can practically feel a vacuum form around me as the entire room looks anywhere but at me. Apart from Ingrid, two rows in front, who swivels around and catches my eye for a good few seconds before facing forward again. I guess she had a visit from Hale too, after what I said.

Well, she can't hate me more than *I* hate myself.

It gets worse.

Back in class, Ms. Boateng reminds us that today is

PSHE day and puts on a video. The entire class groans when we see what it is.

Your Changing Body. Cringe. Honestly, do they think we're six? Like we don't already know this stuff? I could give you the whole spiel in my sleep. But yet again, here we go.

The black screen brightens to white and the presenter comes into focus. He's sitting on a tall stool, with his back to us and then, as though he's just heard us come in, he glances over his shoulder at the camera, spins to face us, and his orange face breaks out into a delighted cheesy smile.

"Hey, you!" he says. "I'm so glad you're here!"

There's a collective swish of fabric on plastic as we all sigh, slump back in our seats, and wait for it to be over.

The presenter explains that we'll know when the change is coming. In a simpering voice he says our blood tests will tell us when our first Turn is approaching, but there are usually other signs too. A mild temperature. A prickling sensation over the whole body. An obsession with checking out the moon and an uncontrollable urge to sing to it. A hankering for raw flesh.

Elena swears she won't get that last one, being a vegan. She's determined she'll crave tortilla chips, dipped in her late mom's favorite tomato-and-onion sauce. Valeria showed her how to make some of the Colmeyan national dishes without meat, so Elena can cook up a spicy feast with pretty much any vegetable you can think of. I mean, I've never heard of a vegan Ripper, but if anyone can make it happen, it's Elena.

I'm thirteen, so I might have a couple of years to go, or it might be soon. I'll probably be a late developer, though—I'm really skinny and short, so I don't look my age at all. My arms are like pale twigs, with faint blue veins showing under the skin; it's hard to imagine super-strong muscles bulging there instead. My best attribute is my hair. It's thick, dark, and slightly wavy—Mom says it's movie-star hair, same as my dad's was. I kind of hope it'll be reflected in my Ripper self somehow, as human features sometimes are. Maybe I'll have a longer bit of fur on top of my head, or something. I'm curious to see. If I Turn before Elena, she's promised to come around that first night, and take a photo.

"Don't be afraid," the *Your Changing Body* presenter is saying, smiling like he's learned how to do it from a book. "It's perfectly normal. No harm will come to you. Just as you have done for your parents or guardians, your loved ones will follow a few simple precautions to keep you safe. They'll take good care of you and treat you with dignity and respect."

A couple of shifty half-smiles are shared around the class.

For some loved ones, it's a chance to have a little fun.

You can see it plenty on the internet if you search on

Seekle for a site called Righteous Rippers. Usually, it's older teenagers who've got their younger siblings to film them, or set up an automatic camera to do it themselves. Then they upload the videos to the site, for laughs and likes. There're prizes for the best ones: Angriest Ripper; Strongest Ripper; Funniest Ripper; Flashiest Ripper, and so on. Squirting an entire can of cream into a Ripper's mouth through the bars. Getting them to catch meatballs—there's a scoreboard for that. Seeing what random non-food item they will eat. I saw one where a guy was dressed as Red Riding Hood, cape and all, so that at dusk he busted out of it and ate a sheep carcass that was wearing a granny costume. It got about a million likes.

Mom thinks Turning should be a private thing. She doesn't even like to show when she's upset, so the idea of being watched when she's literally bouncing off the walls in slavering fury is a big no-no. It's a pretty old-fashioned view of something that's just a fact of life, but things were different when she was a kid. Mom would never want to be on Righteous Rippers; she'd feel so humiliated.

Except, I remember with a painful lurch, that I've already humiliated her.

I check Ingrid in hopes of seeing her squirming too, but she's looking stonily at a spot on the wall about a meter over the TV screen, where the school's motto is rendered in embroidery on a framed canvas: *Protect Your Future*, it says, around a picture of a padlock and a target. I reluctantly turn back to watch the final section of the video.

The presenter tells us that we mustn't worry about any of this, that Sequest is here to help us and take care of us. All I can think at this point is, *Yeah, but why do you hate pigeons?*

He introduces a short video of a man Turning in slow motion. The guy starts off huddled modestly under a blanket, but that soon falls off once his body puffs up like popcorn. They haven't even made it soft focus to smooth out the grossest bits, where the eyes bubble and bulge and stretch and burst. Slow-motion close-ups of thick hairs starting as black dots under the skin, expanding, becoming lumps, the epidermis resisting, then suddenly cracking open as the fur shaft razors through. Calf muscles trembling, then shivering uncontrollably, taken over by rolling waves of flesh, surging and collapsing like jelly in an earthquake. It doesn't happen all neat and logical. Sometimes random parts get the fur first, then it gets sucked back in for a few moments as the flesh expands, like it got ahead of itself: bits of bone, ligament, arteries and even organs thrusting outward in chaotic volcanoes of remolding body, until finally, everything ends up in the right place. The right place for a Ripper, that is.

Even Ms. Boateng looks a bit seasick by the time the credits roll.

CHAPTER NINE

MAY—21 DAYS
TO NEXT CONFINEMENT

"I knew it!" Harold exclaims as I sit with him drinking tea and eating lemon cake in Shady Oaks' community lounge.

Pedro, Elena, and I have been back and forth about what to do with the drone, and with the information we now have. What we really want to find out is *why* Sequest is blasting infrasound at the town. It feels like the kind of thing it'd be polite to let people know, and they haven't. Which makes it a secret.

"I think we should ask the mayor," I tell Harold. "Warren might know what it's for, and if not, he'd want to find out, I'm sure."

Harold makes a disgusted face, like he does any time the mayor is mentioned. "No. You can't trust him."

When deciding to move to Shady Oaks, Harold made what he describes as a fatal error. He failed to account for the fact that his window looks out in the direction of the nearest neighbor: Warren. Which means that every morning he is treated to the sight of the town's most powerful resident coming out onto his porch, stretching and picking up his newspaper, wearing only his underpants. Harold's checked with Sergeant Hale and apparently it's not actually a crime. The two of them are friends, though, so he would say that. Not even Tremorglade is free from institutional corruption.

"Warren is an establishment man through and through," Harold says with distaste. "The sort that doesn't question things. And if he *does* know what's going on, he's in on the secret, isn't he? No. You need to do some investigating of your own. Quietly."

"How am I going to—"

There's a distant clang from down the corridor, like something's been dropped in the communal kitchen. Must be Dora.

"Shhh!" He slaps a hand on my arm to quiet me abruptly, like we're hiding from a special forces ambush, instead of a grumpy old lady getting herself a cup of tea.

We wait for a few minutes, expecting her to come into the lounge, but she doesn't. Then we hear her door closing. Harold relaxes again.

"This drone thing." He bites his lip. "Have you told your mom?"

I shift uncomfortably. "Not yet. You know how she

feels about Sequest. All the fundraising she does. I don't want to worry her without proof."

I expect him to tell me off, but he nods. "Probably sensible. You must be discreet. Keep it to just us: you, me, Elena, and Pedro."

"All right."

But Harold won't let up. "I mean it. In my experience, with these big organizations, when people start asking awkward questions . . . they don't like it. They can get nasty. We must protect those we care about." He nods in the direction of the kitchen, meaning Dora.

I try not to smile. He's really getting into this. "Okay, sure. But come on, what can they really do to us?"

He leans over and makes me look him in the eye. "Those people already take your blood, Sel. They have the power to do other things to you. And to your family. What about the lock on your poor mom's cage?"

I blink in confusion. "What about it?"

"Are we sure it was an accident?"

I swallow. We aren't sure. But my prime suspect isn't Sequest.

"Even if they weren't responsible, they might use it to make you look bad, so people won't believe anything you say. I saw something like that on an episode of *Deadly Business* once, this pharmaceutical company got a corrupt policeman to plant evidence on someone who'd witnessed their crimes. These kinds of people play dirty."

As so often with Harold, he's taking this too far.

"*Deadly Business* isn't a documentary, Harold, it's a drama. And Mom's escape happened before we started looking into any of this. Don't get paranoid on me. I know you don't like Sequest, but I doubt they're breaking the law, or giving us the doldrums on purpose."

Harold's not really listening. "Don't you think it's convenient, hmm? That the only people who might complain about it are the ones with the least influence: children."

"Harold, there's no reason they'd *want* to make us sick. It's literally the opposite of why they exist."

He sits back with a sigh. "If you say so. How about some more cake?"

In the empty kitchen, I cut another slice of the lemon cake I brought for him. I made it myself, following Mom's special recipe. Harold insisted we leave it in here in case Dora wanted any, and I can see one more big slice has gone.

There's a hard tap on my shoulder, and I nearly knock the whole cake to the floor.

"Why were you talking about infrasound?"

I take a deep breath. "Good morning, Dora! Did you enjoy the cake?"

"Shut up about the cake. Are you poking your nose into things you should be leaving alone?"

Someone's been listening outside the lounge, it seems. I eye her warily. It strikes me that I don't actually know anything about Dora's previous life. Maybe she was a physics professor or something.

"Do you know something about infrasound, Dora?"

"No," she snaps. "And neither should you. It's not your concern."

I can't help it—I laugh. Her eyes narrow in anger. "Dora, look, it's fine. Harold was . . . helping me with some physics homework. I can just Seekle it."

Dora's black pupils glitter at me. "I wouldn't do that if I were you." Her tone is cold and steely. "Stay off Seekle and mind your own business, if you know what's good for you."

At that moment, Harold pops his head round the door of the kitchen. "Ah! I came to find out if you were going to let me starve to death in there, Sel, but you two are having a lovely chinwag, I see. About searching for things on Seekle? I think it's admirable, the way these young people can take control of their own education now, don't you, Dora? The internet is a marvelous thing. So much information at the touch of a button. I wish I could get the hang of it."

I can't help but smile to myself. Harold struggles with his computer. Watching him try to use it is excruciating. I usually have to Seekle things for him and print them out.

Dora pushes past him to the counter with her plate, giving me the evil eye.

"Oops, I'm in your way, sorry!" Harold mutters, and I can tell he's embarrassed for her.

We watch as she shuffles back to her room, not before taking the slice of cake I've just cut for Harold.

Harold's smile fades. "Oh dear. She's quite unsteady. I do think perhaps we should get her one of these emergency necklaces, like mine." He fingers the plastic button on the string round his neck. He often doesn't carry his phone around, so Mom and I thought it would be a good idea to get the button for him. If he presses it, our phones both get a notification so we can go check he's okay. He jokes that I'm his Caretaker.

"She seems fine," I say.

"Hmm. In some ways. The other day I came back from a walk and found her in my room again. With a knife."

I gasp. "You're kidding me."

"Oh, I knew she didn't mean anything by it, but I'll admit I was rather taken aback. Said she was tidying up. I suggested putting it in the kitchen drawer, and off she went happily enough." He clocks my uneasy expression. "I'm perfectly safe, it's her I'm worried for."

"Just . . . be careful, okay? Maybe lock your door."

As we head back to the lounge with more cake, I can't help but wonder if he's paranoid about the wrong things.

CHAPTER TEN

After Harold wipes the floor with me at cards, I walk over to Elena and Pedro's, keen to offload my thoughts.

But the moment I round the corner into our road I get déjà vu. Ingrid is standing under the lamppost again, the one where she met me last time. She's leaning against it, staring not at pigeons this time, but at Elena and Pedro's house. Fee and Loretta are hanging around looking bored. I think about turning back and wandering the streets until they're gone, but then Fee spots me and says something to Ingrid, who moves off the lamppost and blocks my path.

I try to walk past, but Fee and Loretta move in front of me. Around us the street is quiet. Birds are behaving normally, the traitors, despite the presence of my nemesis.

"Learned how to use a lock yet, Sel?" Loretta sneers. "Or do you need a manual?"

My plan to remain calm collapses like a popped balloon. My hands ball into fists. "It was you, wasn't it? One of you let Mom out."

But Loretta's nose crinkles in a confused sneer. "What? Don't be stupid. We don't have a death wish." She might be acting, but my instinct tells me her reaction is genuine.

Ingrid elbows her aside. "I want to talk about the pigeons. What did you do to them?"

At that, I'm completely wrongfooted, my anger darting around, unsure where to go.

I notice Loretta rolling her eyes at Fee, who shakes her head. "Ing, let's go—who cares about the stupid birds?"

Ingrid doesn't reply, fixing me with her hostile stare.

I smile sweetly. "Don't you listen to the news? It was the weather."

There's a dramatic sigh from Fee, a not-so-subtle reminder that having to listen to me is ruining her day. Ingrid keeps her gaze on me but addresses them. "You two can get lost now, yeah?"

Their faces are a picture. Off-balance, like Ingrid's just pulled the rug from under them. Dismissed with zero attempt at politeness. They stand there in shock for a few seconds and then hesitantly walk away, casting hurt glances back. I think Ingrid might just have fatally offended her only friends, but she doesn't seem to care.

"Don't mess with me. I heard you and Elena discussing

it on the way home from school. Something about a drone. What did you do?"

I'm shaken. She's been spying on us?

Just as I open my mouth to express my outrage, there's a noise behind me. We move over to the pavement and watch as Hale's police cruiser swings by and parks, blue lights flashing. He gives the siren a quick *whoop whoop*, making Ingrid and me jump out of our skins.

He hops out of the car, jaw working on gum, and his mirrored shades swivel in our direction. For a glorious moment I think he's here to arrest Ingrid—maybe I'm a *police*-whisperer!—but then he does his cheery double finger-gun pose before trotting up Elena's front steps and rapping on her door.

Lucas answers in his pajama bottoms, mousy hair sticking up like he's just got out of bed, though it's well into the afternoon now. Hale shows him a piece of paper and Lucas peers at it groggily, then stands back to let him through. The door closes. I look around for Ingrid, but she's disappeared.

I should wait until Hale comes out. I shouldn't get involved.

But I'm not good at waiting. I bounce over and knock on the door before letting myself in.

"You can't just *take* it!" Pedro is more agitated than I've ever seen him, pacing up and down, running his fingers through his hair, while Hale packs a box on the bed.

Inside it is not just the dismantled drone, but also Pedro's phone and his telescope. Hale has a warrant and everything.

"Tell me again how you got this?" Hale says.

"We found it crashed in the street," Elena tells him. I send her a silent message of thanks for not involving me in this one. She knows I'm already in trouble.

"Uh-huh." His jaw works the gum.

"Why do you want *my* stuff?" Pedro says. I can tell he's trying not to lose his temper. "I bought that phone with my own money. I've got receipts if you want to check. The telescope is older, but it's mine too."

"That won't be necessary. Listen, guys," Hale sighs. I can tell he started out enjoying this but now feels more Bad Cop than Cool Cop. "This drone is Sequest property. You're interfering in their legitimate business."

Elena snorts in outrage.

"Legitimate business? You know what they're doing with it, then? Blasting infrasound over the whole town. Why, huh? Why?"

A flash of unease in my belly. Harold said to be discreet.

Hale folds the box lid over and puts his hand on it. "I don't know where you got that idea. It's just a delivery drone. It belongs to them."

"But my stuff doesn't! Who's asking for it?"

Hale sighs again and eyes the door. He wants out of here now. "The warrant came from the regional Police HQ out in Hastaville. I'm just executing the warrant, taking the items on the list. To be perfectly honest, I don't know why it includes some of your belongings, Pedro. I'm sure they'll be returned to you in due course."

Pedro throws out his hands in resignation. "They better be."

We watch from the window as he dumps the box in the boot of the car and drives off.

"How on earth did the police in Hastaville know you had the drone?" I ask. "That's what I don't get." I think of Ingrid, outside earlier, how she'd been listening in on us. Could she have reported it? But the others are skeptical when I share my thoughts.

"I can't see Ingrid cozying up to the police," Elena points out. "Those things must have trackers. Maybe Sequest checked the last known GPS and told them where to find it?"

"Probably. But now we know they have something to hide. Why else would the police come and confiscate not just the drone, but my other stuff too?"

He's right. This is serious cover-up behavior.

But what does Sequest have to cover up?

CHAPTER ELEVEN

"This place looks like a bombsite, Ansel Archer. Are you even listening to me?" Mom's rummaging around my room while I fire up my laptop.

"I'll tidy up, I will. I just have a load of homework to do first."

She peels a sock off the windowsill and dangles it in front of my face before dropping it in my lap. "Well. So long as you're actually doing homework and not chatting to Chad. If you're too busy to tidy up, you're too busy to chat, right?"

I raise my eyebrows innocently. "Of course! I've got a ton of Explosives Theory to do. Don't forget they're like five hours behind or something where Chad lives, anyway. He'll be at school, remember?"

I haven't told her about the drone. She's doing better now, after what happened—less pale and sad. It'd just give her something else to worry about, so I say nothing except to assure her I'm totally in homework mode.

Mollified, she leaves me to it, telling me dinner is in an hour.

I open up a tab for my homework, then click on FIN and see that the dot next to Chad's name is green, because of course he's online. They let them use their phones at his school (so unfair) and I swear he must never get any work done because at least half the time he'll pop up within minutes.

We all use FIN—kids, mainly, but lots of adults, too. The world outside Tremorglade might be a total basket case, but it's fun to have friends out there, and this is the best way to meet them. It's a pretty simple system—when you register it pairs you with someone in another part of the world whose interests are similar to yours. Elena talks to Trix in Rheitzland (she only knows a little Rheitzch, but Trix speaks perfect English), and I have Chad in the United Tannic Counties, all the way across the ocean. And today I want to ask him if he gets the doldrums. I've been assuming everyone does. But if it's just here . . . it might mean something.

I click on his icon and type:

Sel: Hey! Got a weird question for you.

Then I open up Happy Trappers in a corner of the screen while I wait for his response. The level twenty-one maze loads and I start to whiz around it as a couple of easy Rippers appear. I've zapped the first and am just about to ice the second when it freezes and I get one of the stupid survey questions:

What is your greatest fear?

I let out a growl of irritation—

Silent farts

—and click to resume the game. But it immediately flashes up again, the pop-up box right over the paused action.

What is your greatest fear?

I sigh. You can never get away with daft answers, though we like to try. It's smart. It wants your data, so it can tailor ads to you and show you stuff you're more likely to buy. But it's not as smart as it thinks it is. It can't make you tell the truth.

Spiders

The pop-up seems happy enough this time and I smile to myself—ha, suckers, I *like* spiders—and get on with the game. It feels like a victory to get one over on the data-gathering software, even if now I'll be bombarded with ads for bug-killing sprays.

Two minutes later, I flip back to FIN and watch the dots wave up and down as Chad types his reply.

Chad and I connected on FIN when I first started using it a few years ago. We have quite a lot in common—he's an only child, like me, and his dad died soon after he was born, like mine. Except his dad got the Rotting Plague, which we don't have here. I looked it up on Seekle—it sounds horrific and makes me glad yet again that we live here.

I don't exactly miss my dad, since I never knew him. But sometimes I like to imagine what he'd be like now, what we'd talk about. I think he was more chilled out than Mom, based on things she's told me, but I suppose bringing up a kid on your own doesn't leave much room for taking things easy, and maybe she was different back then. We don't have any living relatives in Tremorglade—my grandparents died pretty young. My mom's aunt might still be alive, as far as we know, but she lives somewhere down south, past the mountains, and Mom says that after the Disruption, contact with her petered out quite quickly. Mom said she got a few emails from her that sounded a bit offhand and terse, then they just stopped. I guess life has been hard out there and maybe she's concentrating on surviving. It's the same for all my friends—the Disruption split up a lot of extended families and people just . . . got lost out there. I guess it's one of the reasons why we're such a close-knit community here.

It's much harder for Elena, losing her mom, Valeria, only three years ago. It wasn't sudden—she was fading for months and months before then. The Wellness Center did everything they could—Dr. Adebayo especially went above and beyond to try to make her better. She had the idea of getting Elena's mom airlifted to one of the big hospitals in Hastaville, for more specialist treatment. But then Dr. Adebayo was suddenly transferred to Sequest HQ to start up some new project there, and the airlift never happened. Valeria died not long after. That's when Lucas, Elena's dad, started to get obsessed with moving away.

I feel like I can tell Chad anything. You have to be careful online—obviously, people might not always be who they claim to be—but I'm pretty sure I'm safe with Chad. FIN does ID checks, Mom knows about him, and there's no chance we could ever arrange to meet up, anyway. I think I'm fairly streetwise when it comes to the internet.

His connection isn't good enough to sustain a live video call, but Chad's sent me links to his blog, where he uploads stuff once in a while. He's got a massive bedroom about three times the size of mine. He lives in a place called Whipple Bay, which looks beautiful. Where we have the mountains, endless forest, a bit of sunshine, and a bit of drizzle, they have palm trees, alligators, beaches, and loads of scorching sun. Apparently, my grandparents went on their honeymoon there, way back in the olden days—Mom has a photo of them smiling and holding ice-cream cones, cuddled up on a deck chair. You couldn't do that now; no one sells ice cream on the beach, and it's best to keep moving if you're outside.

> **Chad:** Fire away.

As my fingers touch the keys, I pause. I'm suddenly aware that I'm always talking to Chad about myself these days. He's so willing to listen. I want to ask him about the doldrums, but it strikes me that it's kind of rude just to pop up with a demand for information when it's been more than a week since I last messaged him. Real friendship has to have some give and take, so I don't start grilling him right away.

> **Sel:** How's things with you?
> **Chad:** Okay, I guess. I thought I might be about to Turn because I got a fever, but it was just flu. My mom got the spare cage down from the attic and made me spend the night in it just in case, though.
> **Sel:** Ugh. Mean!

Chad: Yeah. Oh, and yesterday a Frozen
        Fever gang broke into our Wellness
        Center and stole all the meds, so
        we've got no tranqs, none of my
        grandad's blood pressure drugs, not
        even aspirin.

Sel: No way! So sorry. I wish you could
        live here instead.

Chad: Hey, me too! How cool would that be?!

I feel so bad for him. His house might be a lot bigger
than mine, but they're always on some alert or other to
stay indoors because of pirate gangs marauding with
Frozen Fever. You're burning up on the inside, but your
skin gets so cold it starts to produce ice flakes, and it
makes you aggressive and greedy. I can't imagine what
it must be like to live in fear the whole time like that. But
Chad never seems to stay down for long.

Chad: But you know what's worse? Bucky
        got in the pantry and ate a cake, then
        pooped everywhere in the night. The
        whole house still stinks.

I snort. Trust Chad to care more about that than a
Frozen Fever gang.

Sel:	You mean Barney? Or have you got a new dog as well? Exciting!
Chad:	D'oh. No new dog, still Barney. Stupid auto cat rectal.
	Argh!
	*Autocorrect, not auto cat rectal.
	😂 Oh the irony.
	So . . . what's this weird question then?

I take a deep breath.

Sel:	Do you get the Confinement doldrums?
Chad:	???
Sel:	You know when you feel rough, from dusk onward. I get headachy and dizzy.
Chad:	Sounds like you're coming down with something. Take some vitamins, maybe?
Sel:	No, it's a thing. Every Confinement night. People there don't get the doldrums?
Chad:	Never heard of them.

My heart beats faster. I've always assumed, because

people in Tremorglade talk about the doldrums, that it's the same across the world, but apparently not. And maybe the reason Mom doesn't remember them isn't because she's old, but because they didn't exist then. I flump back in my chair.

Chad: What's this about?

I fill him in.

Chad: What are you gonna do?
Sel: Don't know yet. But we can't just let it go.
Chad: Be careful. Can you trust them?
Sel: Trust who?
Chad: Like . . . Elena. You said she was the only other person who knew the passcode on your mom's cage. I've been thinking about that. Is she legit your friend?
Sel: Totally. 100 percent.

I try not to feel offended on Elena's behalf. It's not Chad's fault. He doesn't know her.

Chad: Well, don't do anything stupid, okay? You've already been in trouble. Don't

**give anyone another reason to make
your life harder.**

Sometimes I think Chad worries about me more than Mom does. He's out there where armed police regularly have gunfights with gangs outside his house, but it's almost like he thinks I'm the one in danger.

CHAPTER TWELVE

Ms. Boateng announces that normal classes are suspended this week because we're going to be involved in some research that our regional education authority is running, across all of its schools.

First, we go into a room one by one and Ms. Boateng shows us flashcards with random doodles on them. We have to say what we think they look like. I can't be bothered to make an effort, so just say they all look like doodles, which irritates her no end. Apparently, we'll get more flashcards for homework in a couple of weeks; we're meant to do them during Confinement night and bring our answers the next day. Trust school to find a way to ruin our one free night.

The next bit of the research turns out to be even less exciting. It's a survey, and not just a few tick boxes either. Everyone groans when Ms. Boateng hands out a twenty-page test booklet for us to work through in silence.

The questions are all about our so-called "well-being"— we have to decide on a scale of one to ten what our mood is like at various times during the month, how we cheer ourselves up if we're down, and how we feel about the prospect of growing up. I tick through in a bored stupor, and entertain myself by making up stupid answers:

> Are you a member of any clubs or societies in your community? How do you like to spend your free time? What do you do on Confinement nights?

> YES, I AM HEAD OF A SECRET SOCIETY OF CHILDREN THAT PLANS TO TAKE OVER THE WORLD. WE BELIEVE WE ARE SUPERIOR BEINGS AND WE OPERATE OUT OF AN UNDERGROUND LAIR.

I almost start to enjoy myself until I come to one question about my well-being on Confinement nights.

> When dusk falls, do you feel a) happy b) sad c) anxious d) afraid e) excited f) tired g) sick h) no change. Tick all that apply. Write down any differences you feel after dawn the following day.

Unease slithers in my belly as it occurs to me: this has nothing to do with school. This must be on behalf of Sequest.

I flick back through the paper, looking again at the questions. A pattern emerges. They're tracking what happens to us, mentally and physically, during Confinement nights. They know we won't feel well. They want detailed data on how the infrasound affects us month to month, to use for . . . well, who knows?

This is not just some idle survey. It's gathering the results of an experiment. On us.

I feel as though my eyes have been opened. We get exercises a bit like this every year, but now that I'm looking, I see Sequest's tentacles everywhere.

In PE, we have to take our heart and breathing rates before and after exercise, while the coach writes it all down. He claims it's educational, so that we understand how our bodies work, the way they respond to an increasing need for energy. But I notice he keeps the form with all the data. I bet it goes to Sequest.

The more I think about it, the more I remember. The school disco where they used strobe lighting and then checked our eyeballs on the way out. The time we had to walk through different classrooms, each with a weird smell inside. I can't even recall what the supposed reason was for that. Only that one of them smelled like sewage and a kid called Justin fainted, hit his head on a desk, and had to get stitches.

Elena's FIN friend Trix has never heard of the doldrums either, apparently. I'm no longer surprised. If you told me Sequest was reanimating the corpses of pigeons after harvesting their organs and secretly transplanting them into humans, I'd believe you. I'm all in.

We in Tremorglade are Sequest's lab rats. Worse, they can't be doing it without help from inside our community. Including school. Who here is in on it?

It's time to tell Mom. She deserves to know what's being done to us while the adults are Turned. I don't mention that Harold has encouraged us—she likes him, but she does think he's eccentric; she told me once to take everything he says with a pinch of salt. I fill her in on the infrasound drones, Hale confiscating Pedro's stuff, the weird questions at school.

She flips.

"Where is this coming from?" she demands. "This isn't like you, coming up with a load of conspiracy nonsense. Radiation beamed from the sky? Has someone been leading you on?"

"No! You're not listening to me, Mom. Infrasound, not radiation."

"Oh, I'm listening all right. You should have reported that drone, and you didn't, and now you've got your friends in trouble as a result. It's theft."

"But the survey, it's too much of a coincidence—"

She crosses her arms over her chest. "So let me get this right: you did some tests at school, and messed around—yes, Ms. Boateng did happen to mention that you wrote a bunch of silly answers—and now you're trying to justify it by making up a load of garbage about Sequest? You know if it hadn't been for them, I wouldn't be alive now?"

"I know, but—"

"You can't just go around saying this kind of thing with literally no evidence."

I almost tell her that the only reason we have no evidence is because the police took it, which probably means Hale is in on it. But somehow I don't think she wants to hear that.

"She's right, you know," Pedro muses the following day, at the café after school. He's bought me and Elena hot chocolates. "Evidence. We need more before we can challenge Sequest about it."

He's scrolling on the cheap phone he bought while he waits for his stuff to be returned. Hale won't tell us when that will happen. Apparently, Police HQ in Hastaville still has it—the forensics department. Like his phone and telescope are from a crime scene or something. I worry that he's being set up like in *Deadly Business*, but he doesn't seem worried about that at all. He just wants it back. Pedro's downloaded a special app on the new phone, so at least we can record the infrasound again. In terms of evidence, it's not much, but it's something.

"Okay, hear me out. What if they're *not* trying to make us sick with the infrasound?" he says. "What if the doldrums are just a side effect they're tracking?"

We consider this in silence. Elena slurps her hot chocolate, before wiping her mouth with her arm. Pedro passes her a napkin.

"We know the effect it has on humans. But what if it's not actually aimed at us?"

I gasp. "It's aimed at the pigeons!"

Pedro's lips quirk in amusement. "No, dork. Bless your heart."

Elena thumps her fists on the table. "Rippers. We don't know what it does to *them*."

I flush. "Oh. But they can't exactly tell us what they're feeling, can they?"

Pedro rubs his stubbly chin in thought. "No. But Sequest scientists aren't the only ones who can do experiments."

I'm not sure I like the sound of this. Experimenting on Rippers sounds like the kind of thing only trained professionals should do. Armed ones.

But Pedro's got that glint in his eye that Elena gets too, when there's nothing I can say to change her mind.

"Next Confinement, I'm going to be *your* lab rat."

CHAPTER THIRTEEN

JUNE—CONFINEMENT NIGHT

I suggest to Mom that we get her set up nice and early this evening, so I have plenty of time to check security. She doesn't need any persuading. She watches me pull the new, heavy crossbar down, and then gives the door a good push, testing all the bars round the cage before she's satisfied.

She bites her lip. "You'll be here all night, won't you?"

"Obviously," I say, feeling like the lie is written across my forehead. I'm not planning on going far, only over the road to Elena's, but I'm nervous about even doing that, now. I've checked everything about a zillion times and even asked Mika to do a quick sweep of our garden security before she got cracking on her own. But still.

She nods. "Okay. Good. Promise me you'll stay out of trouble?"

I wish I could explain to her that trouble seems intent

on finding *me*, and I can't ignore it. Instead I just nod. "Have a nice dinner."

We both regard it lying there unappetizingly in a wet puddle on the floor next to her. I put it there earlier, so my hands don't have to go anywhere near the cage once she's Turned. Which is ironic, really, considering tonight's planned activity.

I check the garden one more time, running my fingers along the wires and inspecting each individual stun pop, then hooking and unhooking the new graphene net to make sure it's not stuck. Next door, Mika gives me a friendly nod as she finishes up.

A gentle *ping* on my bracelet tells me dusk has fallen, and the familiar heaviness begins.

I let myself in at Elena's, setting my tranq down carefully against the inside of the door so I don't forget it. Our experiment needs Pedro to be fully conscious. I can hear their dad making a racket in his cage nearby but ignore that and take the stairs two at a time up to Pedro's room, where Elena is waiting, sitting on her brother's bed. I hear her singing as I reach the door, her voice sweet and clear. She stops when I go in, and Pedro's snarling fills the room.

I help her drag the stepladder in from a cupboard on the landing, placing it next to Pedro's cage. Then Elena busies herself with a pair of special headphones. Pedro made them himself last week, from separate bits he ordered off the internet, because he couldn't find any of the right kind in stock. These don't just muffle noise, they *cancel* the sound waves. And they should work especially well for the regular, low sound that's coming from the drones.

Pedro seems to be working himself up into a frenzy, biting at the bars, saliva spraying everywhere, muzzle crinkled as his lips pull back to reveal his gleaming, deadly teeth.

Faced with the reality of our plan, my throat goes dry.

Elena's hand waving in front of my face brings me back to myself. "Hey, wake up. I said, did you bring the meat?"

I hold out the carrier bag with the lamb leg in it.

She peers into the bag and wrinkles her nose. "That's *it*? It's tiny."

I shrug apologetically. "The butcher didn't have much left by the time I got there. Maybe it'll get stuck between his teeth and he'll be distracted trying to get it out."

"Yeah, right. He'll start flossing and that'll buy us some time." She sighs. "Here. Try these." She hands me the headphones, and I position them carefully over my ears, before turning them on.

Pedro's high-pitched yowling immediately quiets. Not a huge amount, though. I adjust the kit, trying to find the best fit, while he attacks the bars and paces around, tail swishing. His tongue occasionally runs over his fangs in a quick, restless sweep. Like every Ripper, he's just waiting for a chance to tear my head off.

I fiddle until the spongy earpieces are as tight as they can be. The yowling is less deafening, but by no means silent. I sag slightly in disappointment.

"I thought you said these would . . . ," I start, but then trail off. Although Pedro's tantrum is still distinctly audible, there's something else missing. It's as though my head has cleared. It's the exact sensation I get if I happen to be awake at dawn as Confinement ends. A lifting of pressure. An inexplicable increase of optimism. The doldrums have vanished. "Hey!" I find I'm grinning. "That's so cool!"

Elena smiles proudly.

"Your brother is a genius," I say happily. "We can get Pedro to make everyone a kit like this! He'll make a fortune! Everyone's going to thank us."

She takes the headphones back and rests them around her neck. "Now we get down to business."

I start recording on Pedro's phone, and prop it up on the other side of the room, checking that it can see the whole cage.

Elena clatters up to the top of the stepladder, just about level with the top of Pedro's cage. Pedro starts leaping to get to her, chomping at the air while unsuccessfully trying to cling to the bars at the top.

"Okay, Sel. Show him the food."

I fumble the lamb's leg out of the bag. Pedro ignores me, still trying to reach his sister.

"Wave it around a bit, get his attention," she says.

I draw closer to the cage, and, holding the leg where the bone sticks out, wave it up and down.

"Bring it closer. Nice and high, so I'll be able to reach his head." She lifts the headphones from round her neck.

The plan must have seemed rational when Pedro thought of it, but now . . .

"Elena, I'm not sure they're going to fit. He's got a really big head."

"Do it, Sel! Stop messing around."

I grip the lamb bone tightly with both hands. I need him to try to wrestle it off me for long enough that Elena can slip her arms through the top bars and get the headphones in position over his ears.

I bang it against the side bars close to his head, and for a millisecond he glances at it before resuming his attempts to get to Elena. I bang it again, and again, and again, to no effect. It thuds wetly on the bars.

And then, just like that, his teeth have the meaty end, and it slithers right through my hands.

"Sel!"

I stare at him gnawing it on the floor of the cage, well out of Elena's reach. "Oops."

Elena looks upset for a moment, and then makes a decision. She jumps down from the stepladder and barges me out of the way, heading to the cage door. She grabs a key from her pocket and inserts it into the padlock.

"What are you—"

She can't go in there with him. He'll kill her.

I glance in disbelief at the lamb bone. It's not going to last long. He's had two thirds of it already and is crunching on the last bit, facing away from Elena, his tail by the cage door. There's no way she'll get headphones on him before he finishes. And he'll savage her over a tiny bit of lamb bone anyway.

But she's already opened the cage door and slipped inside. I open my mouth to scream at her but stop just in time—I don't want him to turn around.

She reaches him just as he swallows the last piece and jumps onto his back, leaning over to fit the headphones in place. He jerks up to a standing position, lifting Elena with him, and I can only watch helplessly as the inevitable unfolds. She clutches a fistful of neck fur in one hand, reaching for the headphones with the other, but they bounce away and clatter to the floor. Pedro's head snaps round, missing Elena by millimeters, and he starts to buck and spin, trying to throw her off. There's no way she can cling on for longer than a few seconds.

Frantically searching around for Elena's tranq, I curse myself for not bringing mine upstairs. If I go to get it now, she'll be dead by the time I come back.

The headphones are lying right by the cage door.

Without thinking, I reach in and pick them up. They're flimsy and almost certainly useless in this situation, but they're all we've got. A stab of despairing, stubborn anger twists in my gut. If Pedro's going to eat us, he's going to have to do it wearing these.

Just as I step into the cage there's a horrible yowl of triumph as he throws Elena off, upward and to the side. Her body clangs sickeningly against iron and drops to the floor, unmoving.

Everything seems to slow down. I see it all in minute detail. The silvery, stiff fur standing up along Pedro's spine, the curve of his neck as he reaches for Elena.

I leap for him at the same moment he goes for her, coming at him from behind. I get a close-up view of his jaws closing on her shoulder, the teeth sinking through her T-shirt, blood instantly welling up. She screams in pain and terror. I land on his neck with my elbow glancing off his muzzle as he swivels around briefly. With all the strength I have left, I shove the headphones down over his ears.

He stops moving.

I lie half on, half off him, panting.

For one glorious moment, I think it's worked.

Then he throws me off with a quick, irritated shake, and I land on my back just outside the cage. He turns to finish off Elena.

Bracing for the sound of bones crunching, I start

to drag myself up ready to fling myself on him again, but then realize he hasn't gone for the kill. He's just . . . waiting. A drop of saliva lands on the floor next to Elena's head. Pedro's sides heave up and down, but otherwise he's still.

Then, very slowly, his haunches go back, and he lies down carefully, almost gently, next to Elena.

He doesn't pass out. But he doesn't get up, either.

The red stain on Elena's T-shirt creeps slowly outward. She hasn't moved.

"Elena," I whisper.

Her head rises, just a fraction, and I breathe again. She's watching him. After a few seconds, grimacing, she inches her leg sideways. Then she slides her bottom away, eyes on him the whole time. He watches her too, tongue lolling, alert but quiet.

She reaches the edge of the cage and, moving painfully slowly, neither of us daring to speak, I help her trembling body out into the room. The moment she's over the threshold, I kick the door shut and, shaking, latch it. After a few attempts, the key turns in the padlock.

Neither of us can speak. We can't take our eyes off Pedro.

While he looks entirely Ripper, his demeanor reminds me of Gunther, the grocer's elderly mastiff, who lies flopped on the wooden floor of the shop all day, watching the world go by.

We stay like that for what seems like hours. Elena's wound is painful but isn't bleeding anymore—looks like I stopped him before he got more than a nibble. Pedro sniffs and laps a little at the smear of blood Elena's left behind in the cage. Then he heaves a big, contented sigh, puts his chin down on his paws, and goes to sleep.

CHAPTER FOURTEEN

Pedro's video shows everything. And I mean everything. Mom is not going to be happy when she sees it, but when it gets to the end she'll understand. This is proper evidence, and it raises questions that Sequest won't be able to dodge. Also—and this is just a nice side benefit—it totally makes me look like a hero. And Elena, obviously.

Today's a school teacher training day, happily for those of us who have more important stuff to do. First thing this morning Elena was in the Wellness Center, getting stitches in her shoulder from Nurse Pete. She told him she'd been bitten by a stray dog. Somehow, she managed to keep the events of last night to herself while she was there, and by the time she arrives at the café where Pedro and I are waiting for her, she's desperate to tell the world.

I know Harold said to keep quiet about our

investigations. But the time has come to start making noise. This could change everything.

Our first stop is Tremorglade's community website—Tremorgossip. Usually it's just local news and notices, and people complaining about potholes, but Pedro uploads our explosive video, along with evidence from his infrasound app, plus a report that we spent all morning writing, about exactly what we did and why.

While Pedro emails the same thing to the two biggest national papers, the *National Times* and the *Sentinel*, Elena and I are tasked with handing a printout of our report to the Wellness Center, for them to pass up the chain to Sequest. They think they can ignore us, but we are going to get right in their faces, show them that we know what they're up to, and demand they tell us why.

Pedro said he felt fantastic when he woke up this morning. He doesn't remember any of last night, of course—no change there. He slept a little, according to Elena, who sent me home after I started falling asleep in her lap. At midnight he woke and howled his heart out along with the other Rippers. She couldn't bring herself to try going in the cage again, but she reckons she could have. The aggression we all thought was a major part of being a Ripper just wasn't there. The conclusion couldn't be clearer: the infrasound's making them angry, or scared, or both. But why on earth would anyone do that on purpose?

There's no one at the Wellness Center reception when we arrive so we sit on the squeaky chairs to wait. My phone beeps. It's Chad.

> **Chad:** Hey, Ansel! How u doing? Seen the trailer for Plague Terror 2 is dropping next month? Cannot WAIT.
>
> **Sel:** Hey yeah I heard! Bit busy rn. Speak later.

I smile to myself. When I tell him about this it's going to blow his mind. Even more than the *Plague Terror 2* trailer.

Dr. Travis's heels click as she strides to the reception desk, totally ignoring us, and starts filling in a form. Elena and I glance at each other, trying to work up the courage to interrupt, when Dr. Travis says, "What?" without looking up, in a tone that suggests we'd better have something serious wrong with us.

"Dr. Travis," Elena says politely but firmly, walking up to the desk and slapping our report down on it. "We would like you to send this to Sequest HQ in Hastaville, please. We've been conducting an experiment and have made some *remarkable* discoveries."

"Mmm hmm." She doesn't raise her eyes from the form.

"We've managed to calm down a Ripper," I blurt out. "Completely."

That gets her attention.

"You calmed a *Turned*, did you?" She can't resist a dig at my terminology.

Elena nods. "My brother."

"Would this have anything to do with the stitches that my colleague gave you this morning. Your . . . dog bite?"

Elena hesitates. "No. Completely separate incident."

"Really. And you did this how?" Skepticism pushes her eyebrows a surprisingly long way up her forehead.

"By putting noise-canceling headphones on him. It was . . . tricky."

There's a short silence. The eyebrows return to their usual position. A sigh. "Right."

"No, we did," Elena insists, jabbing at the paper. "You should read it. It explains *why* we think it works too. But you do have to send it to Sequest after. Our video will be on the news soon enough. Do you want to see it now?"

Dr. Travis goes back to filling in her form, pen scraping softly across the page. "I don't have time to watch Righteous Rippers videos, thank you. Put your letter on there." She indicates with the pen to a towering pile in a tray next to her.

"It's not for Righteous Rippers, it's important," I tell her. "Honestly."

Her mouth tightens into an impatient line and she

looks me in the eye. "More important than ordering Mr. Bates's heart medicine? Mrs. Juror's antibiotics? More important than requesting tests to establish whether someone has diabetes?"

I hesitate. "Y-yes?"

She snatches the paper and dumps it in the tray herself. "Can't wait to read it. Now, unless you have a broken limb or are bleeding to death, I suggest you leave."

"Do you think she'll send it to Sequest?" I fret, as we walk away from the Wellness Center.

"I think so. But even if she doesn't, they'll have to respond eventually, because of pressure from the media."

As we turn onto the next road, I spot something out of the corner of my eye. I nudge Elena, and she follows my gaze.

"Ugh. Ingrid."

"I swear she just came out of the Wellness Center," I say.

"I didn't see her in there."

"Neither did I. But the waiting room goes all the way around the corner. She might have been there the whole time."

"Don't worry about it. Who cares?"

"I guess. I just don't get why she's stalking me."

Elena snorts. "Haven't seen her with Fee and Loretta

lately. Maybe she thinks you'll be her new friend."

We walk faster, and by the time we reach home we've lost her.

Harold's excited when I phone to fill him in on what happened. But there's a horrified silence when I tell him that we've given our reports to the press and the Wellness Center. I hear the panic in his voice. "Oh, Sel, this is not being careful. Can you take it all back? We're not ready yet. There are still so many unanswered questions. It might have been a fluke. And if it's those wretched drones making Rippers aggressive in Tremorglade, why are they aggressive everywhere else in the world too?"

I hadn't thought of that. A tiny crack of doubt opens in my mind. But the effect of the headphones on Pedro was undeniable, and everyone will see it. "Well . . . maybe Rippers are just generally worse in other places, like everything else is."

There's silence down the line.

"Or maybe Sequest is doing it in loads of places. It could be we've uncovered an international scandal! It's fine," I reassure him. "We know what we're doing."

I'm on a high, we all are.

It doesn't last long.

The following day, we check Tremorgossip, looking forward to all the juicy comments on our post, but instead of the homepage, we're greeted with an error message. With spectacular timing, the whole website's screwed.

Pedro checks the emails he sent to the newspapers and finds them safely in his sent box. But then he makes an odd, confused noise. We gather round, peering over his shoulder at his phone screen.

"I don't understand. It can't be." His forehead is creased in bewilderment. "I sent them a link to the video—it was uploaded to the sharing site I normally use. But now there's nothing at the link."

"Upload it again," I suggest. "Use somewhere different?"

"I just did. Or at least, I tried. I picked another video-sharing site, but when I clicked the button to upload, the website downloaded some kind of malware onto my phone. The video's gone. Everything's wiped . . . " He trails off, gesturing hopelessly at the technology in front of him.

I'm starting to get a bad feeling about the whole thing, when there's a knock on their front door.

Pedro goes to answer it and when he comes back in the room, he's followed by Sergeant Hale, carrying a cardboard box. Elena and I stop breathing. Is he going to arrest us?

"Hey, kids, what ya doin?"

We're all frozen to the spot. He gives us a quizzical look, and then shrugs. "Well, okay. Here's your stuff back, Pedro. See? Told you it wouldn't be long."

When Pedro doesn't hold out his hands to take the box, but just stands there warily, Hale puts it on the chest of drawers. "Everything's in there, including your phone."

"So, Sequest isn't . . . you're not here to arrest us?"

Hale laughs. "No further action at this time. Why would I arrest you now? You learned your lesson, right?" He grins.

As he leaves, he gives us a friendly wink that turns my blood to ice.

Are they . . . playing with us?

CHAPTER FIFTEEN

Confinement rolls around again and nothing's changed. There's been nothing in the newspapers, no word from the Wellness Center about our report. Tremorgossip is still screwed. The parts Pedro ordered to make more noise-canceling headphones don't arrive, even though he bought them the day after last Confinement. There's a shipping delay. The entire universe is refusing to cooperate. Pedro spent a whole day changing all his passwords, and wiping and resetting his returned phone, taking it to pieces, just to make sure nothing has been done to it.

The paranoia has got to me too. I've started to feel like my school friends are acting distant somehow. I tried to tell a couple of them about what we found, but they were weirdly uninterested. Not avoiding me, exactly, but just . . . wary. Like I might infect them with something.

I feel like I'm being whispered about in the corridors, and not in a good way.

Harold's advised us to spend the rest of the month acting as normal as possible. We're not acknowledging defeat, but we are seriously spooked.

We don't feel like going to the Howler party today, but Harold persuades us, saying it'll cheer us up. There's nothing else to do, and we should probably act like everything's fine.

At first, the Howler party seems like it's going to be the same as every other one.

The sun has come out, and the cobblestones steam as the early rain lifts away. The air smells clean and fresh, until the barbecue is lit and then the scent of slowly charring corn-on-the-cob and sausages drifts on the breeze. There's rain forecast for the evening, but right now it's a perfect summer's day.

The town square is the farthest point from the forest, not far from our street. The ground starts to rise steeply here up to the mountains. Tremorglade sinks gently away in front of us, then the trees cover the distance up to the horizon. Birds are circling lazily above, early scavengers for dropped French fries and breadcrumbs. I follow their looping paths and hope none of them will be splatting tonight.

We all feel robbed when Confinement is on a weekend, or in the school holidays, like now. When it's not, we get the afternoon off school so we can prepare for dusk and go to the Howler party. The parties aren't compulsory, of course—we're not living in a dictatorship—but we're encouraged to go. Helps the bonds of community, and all that. Also there's always plenty of free food, so we rarely miss it.

Harold is sitting on a wooden fold-up chair next to one of the trestle tables, manning the drinks stall: tea, coffee, or his homemade punch. Elena and I keep our usual vigil next to the French fries and popcorn, munching our way through them while Mayor Warren makes his standard speech about the precious nature of Confinement responsibility, and what a privilege it is for the children to be entrusted with it. I mean, whatever.

Elena crunches anxiously on her popcorn, not saying much. Apparently, her dad had another job rejection today. Lucas never comes to the Howler parties anyway, which is probably just as well. I scan the crowd for Pedro but can't see him, though some of his friends are here, chatting and laughing in their usual group.

Mom's already gone home, even though it's only early afternoon. As always, she came with me and stayed for one drink, made small talk with as few people as she could as quickly as she could without seeming rude, and then left, pleading tiredness. She loves Tremorglade, loves our community, loves that everyone else wants to enjoy themselves before folks get hairy, but she can't bring herself to party.

Mayor Warren wanders around from group to group, stroking his mustache nervously like he's afraid it might fly off and leave his smile naked. I wonder if he knows about our video, if he's the one who made sure it didn't upload. The council is responsible for the town's internet, for the upkeep of cables and so on. A word from him could get someone hacked, I reckon.

But it's not him we need to worry about today.

"Heads up," Elena mutters into her drink, peeking over the rim. "Incoming."

Sergeant Hale is swaggering over to us, chewing gum, thumbs stuck in his belt. He nods at us casually as he comes to stand next to us, and there's an awkward silence.

Someone uploaded a video of him onto Righteous Rippers after the last Confinement and it's made its way around the kids of Tremorglade. *We* all know it was Justin, who Caretakes him since he has no children, but Hale has no clue and is desperate to find out who did it. I'm guessing he doesn't want to mention it in case we haven't seen it. I don't think there's any one of us who hasn't watched it about a hundred times. It won Ripper of the Month. It'll have been seen millions of times across the world by now. Chad says it's really put Tremorglade on the map.

The video begins with a shout of "Call the cops!" and an explosion of drumbeats that then settle into an intense, addictive rhythm. The visuals open on Ripper Hale in his cage, twisting and apparently spotting the camera. He's wearing his police hat, incredibly—someone's timed it beautifully, must have thrown it on him through the bars just before rolling the camera. It falls off almost immediately, but you have to hand it to the director, that is pure skill. It gets even better, though.

The video has been edited to add his school assembly speech over the top as a rap, so it looks like he's giving it as a Ripper. It's beautifully done. *Be calm, methodical, and responsible* he says as his claws swipe viciously through the bars just out of reach of the lens, blood smeared on his bared teeth, ramming the cage door with his head, yellow eyes rolling back in their sockets. *Some of you aren't taking this serious-serious-seriously* he raps, and then there's an instrumental break, during which he lifts a leg and pees up the wall.

"Hey, kids," he says now. "What you planning to get up to tonight?"

"Oh, you know. Catch up with homework. Chores. Clean the toilet, the usual," I say.

Elena smiles in agreement. "Yeah, I've got some explosives homework I'm really looking forward to."

His mirrored sunglasses give nothing away. I watch the gum stick to the roof of his mouth, drop, stick, drop as his jaw moves. There's a bubble of laughter building in my chest; I can't stop picturing the video.

Finally, he nods slowly. "Sounds good. I'm sure you've

learned from your mistake, Sel. But not everyone treats Confinement with respect. You hear about anyone behaving ... badly, it's your duty to let me know, yeah?"

It's hard to tell whether he's referring to our video of Pedro, or the Righteous Rippers one of him. Somehow, Justin has persuaded Hale it wasn't him who shot the footage. That it was someone unknown who picked the lock on the front door, broke in, made the video, and left again, locking it behind him.

Like I said, Hale is not much of a detective.

"What kind of bad behavior do you mean?" Elena blinks at him, her face upturned and innocent.

The gum squeezes, sticks, drops, squeezes, sticks, drops, faster. A one-shouldered shrug. "Just . . . doing stuff. Disrespectful things."

"We would never be disrespectful," I tell him. "Protect your future, right?" I add, quoting our school motto.

"Yeah, we take it serious-serious-seriously," Elena tells him as he starts to move on to another group. That does it—a totally audible snort-laugh escapes my throat. I turn it into a hacking cough so dramatic that people look around to see who's dying.

There's the tiniest hesitation in Hale's step, and I swear his ears go pink, but he walks away like he didn't hear it.

I'm not sure he's entirely out of range before we collapse into helpless snickers. Elena stops laughing long enough to take a sip of punch, but then catches my eye again and snorts it out through her nose. Then her face goes from amusement to horror as she stares over my shoulder. "Oh no. Dad."

I follow where she's staring. Lucas is marching into the square. As he reaches the crowd, he starts to bellow.

"Warren? Where are you, you filthy toerag?"

Silence falls. Mayor Warren looks around, as though Lucas must be talking to a different filthy toerag called Warren.

"You won't get away with it," Lucas thunders as he shoves his way through the crowd, until he reaches the mayor. "You! It's got to be you. You lying—" Then a bunch of curse words.

"Dad, no." Elena's mortified voice is too quiet to be heard by anyone but me.

Mayor Warren backs off slightly. "H . . . Howdy, Lucas. What seems to be the problem?"

"Don't howdy me. Why are you doing this to me?"

Finally I spot Pedro, making his way to his father's side, panting heavily like he's run to catch up. He puts a restraining hand on Lucas's arm. "Dad, don't."

But his father doesn't even seem to notice. He pokes a finger right in the mayor's chest. "You ruined my chances. You've been telling them all not to hire me, haven't you? This whole year. Every time. Every job. You made sure I didn't get any of them."

Mayor Warren is too shocked to even stroke his mustache, leaving it twitching convulsively. "Lucas, why would I do that?"

"Beats me. But you're in charge of this stinking place. It's you pulling the strings, isn't it?"

Pedro is tugging at his dad's arm. His normally placid face is strained with panic. "Dad, stop, please. Not here."

At that moment someone inserts themselves between Lucas and Warren. Harold's head barely reaches Lucas's chest, and I don't think Lucas even notices he's there until Harold speaks.

"You need to calm down. You're embarrassing your children."

Lucas looks down at the older man and some of the fight drains out of him.

Mayor Warren grasps the moment.

"Yes, go home. You need to take better care of yourself. I don't mean to be rude, but it's no wonder you're failing video interviews . . . " He gestures in Lucas's general direction. "Get yourself locked up early, sleep it off."

"You'd like that, wouldn't you?" But Lucas finally seems to realize he's not getting anywhere. He eyes Warren up and down with disgust, then starts walking away. He calls over his shoulder, "I fancy a change. Maybe I'll stay *out* tonight and have some fun. Might as well, since I'm stuck here. Whaddaya say?"

He doesn't wait for an answer, which is just as well,

because everyone's too shocked to reply to that one.

It takes a few seconds, and then the first couple of hushed voices become a hubbub of gossip. The mayor stalks off in a huff.

Harold checks on Elena. "Do you need help Confining your dad this evening? It sounded like he might . . . "

She shakes her head. "He wouldn't be that stupid. He's just mouthing off. You mustn't drag yourself all the way across town. Sel can help me if there's a problem." Elena notices her brother staring off into the distance. "You look like you've seen a ghost, bro. What happened?" She glances around then lowers her voice. "It can't be true, can it? Dad's being paranoid, right?"

Pedro doesn't answer at first. He seems shell-shocked.

"Hey." Elena snaps her fingers in front of his face. "You're scaring me. What's going on?"

"I don't . . . " He trails off, looking around him like he's just that moment landed in an alien spaceship. "There's something wrong with the internet."

Elena makes a confused face. "What's that got to do with it?"

I check my phone. "Tremorgossip is still down. But I've been on Righteous Rippers about ten times today and that's fine."

"Might just be yours. Do you think they're into your phone again?" Elena whispers to her brother. "You sure you completely reset it?"

But Pedro isn't listening.

"Here." Harold pours Pedro a glass of punch, which he downs in one go. "I think Elena and Sel should stay home tonight. Tranqs ready. Just in case."

We nod.

"You're still going to put those headphones on before you head for the litter box tonight, right?" I ask Pedro, pointing at the set slung around his neck. They're his only pair and he's carrying them with him everywhere now. It's highly likely they'll be destroyed—we're guessing the headphones will ping right off when his head balloons and stretches. But it's worth a try. We don't want to risk last month's fun and games again.

He nods distractedly and lifts the glass to his lips again to take a sip. He doesn't even notice it's empty. His friends glance over but none of them come to chat. Now I think of it, I rarely see him with them anymore. I hope all this stuff isn't messing with his social life.

The crowd has largely dispersed. Ingrid stands awkwardly by herself, casting furtive looks in our direction, but I'm certain she's too far away to listen to our conversation. It strikes me again how she's always alone these days. I guess she's too much even for Fee and Loretta.

Just then Pedro's phone buzzes. He checks the screen and sighs in agitation.

"What's up?" Harold asks, taking his empty glass.

"I've got to go. I'll see you for locking in, Elena. We need to talk."

We watch him head through the crowd. As he passes Ingrid, she catches his arm and says something to him. They exchange a few words and then he trots off down the road. Ingrid's gaze follows him until he's out of sight.

Elena screws up her face. "What's she up to?"

"I hope she's not trying to sweet-talk your brother," I say. "He shouldn't let her get under his skin."

"He won't," she says loyally. "He eats people like her for breakfast."

Mom goes into the cage early again, huddled in a blanket.

I click the sturdy new padlock while she watches, and then slot the crossbar down into place. It's definitely making her feel safer. "There you go. You're not getting out tonight. Promise."

My phone buzzes. It's Elena.

Need yr help urgent

My adrenaline spikes. Is her dad refusing Confinement like he threatened?

"Everything all right, Ansel?"

I swear Mom can sense a change in my mood by scent or something.

"Yeah, all good. Um, Mom, if you're okay I'm just going to check in with Elena for a sec. You know we go over each other's security now, just to be sure. But I'll come back right away, and I'll be just upstairs all night."

She gives a nod and the faintest of smiles. "Okay. See you in the morning."

I grab my tranq at the top of the stairs and sling the strap over my shoulder. The tripwires look good and taut as I skip over them, neon warning flags fluttering in the summer breeze.

I call out as I go straight in, not waiting for Elena's reply. I push open the door of her dad's room as I pass, fearing that I'd find her standing next to an unoccupied cage. But she's not there. Her dad is, though. He's lying on a bench next to the wall inside his cage, staring at the ceiling, under a threadbare blanket. He glances over at me balefully, eyes unfocused.

"Oh," I say, half in surprise, half in relief. "It's . . . it's good to see you."

He doesn't bother to reply, returning his attention to the ceiling.

I surreptitiously check the locks—all secured—and back out into the hallway, stumbling into Elena.

"He's there," I point back into the room, unnecessarily.

Elena's face is grim. "No, it's Pedro. He hasn't come back."

CHAPTER SIXTEEN

There's half an hour until dusk. Half an hour to find him.

He might still turn up, of course. But there's protocol to follow. Reluctantly, Elena buzzes the amber alert on her bracelet to get everyone watching out, and we grab our X50s, double-checking the syringes are full.

As we run down the front steps, Lucas's voice drifts out. "Where are you going?" Elena hasn't told him Pedro's missing, but he's obviously picked up on our panic, roused out of his stupor. We don't stop to reply. It's not as though he can help, anyway.

We have no idea where Pedro's gone. He doesn't answer his phone, though Elena keeps ringing it. None of his friends have seen him. So we split up—I go northwest, and Elena begins a sweep heading northeast. Harold will already know what's happened from the alert, but he'll stay at Shady Oaks with Dora—no doubt Ingrid has cut and run, as usual.

The sun is low and getting lower. Kids are mostly out on the streets now; they nod at me as I pass, looking relaxed, despite the amber alert. I suppose nobody really thinks they're in danger—Pedro's cut it a bit fine, that's all.

Except, he wouldn't.

Ahead of me a dark bank of clouds is approaching—the promised rain. It's so peaceful, it feels impossible that anything's wrong.

I check my watch. Twenty minutes to dusk. It's close—that moment between breaths, when the air has been expelled from human lungs, and is about to be drawn into Ripper ones. Even out in the streets, you can feel it. The change in the atmosphere, the rearrangement of particles. Transformation.

Pedro wouldn't hide from us, so he's got to be stuck somewhere. Or hurt. I just wish he'd told someone where he was going.

The thought hits me—he spoke to Ingrid just before he left the Howler party. He might have said something to her.

Of course, neither of us have Ingrid's number. Why would we?

Cursing myself for not thinking of it earlier, I break into a run, toward Juniper House.

A couple of Juniper kids I recognize—a skinny,

red-haired boy called Davide and his twin brother Philippe—are standing around on the porch as I jump over the marked wire at the edge of the property. They Caretake Bernice and Amy and tend to stick around like they're supposed to. Ingrid, on the other hand, will have finished with Dora as quickly as possible and won't have much to do tonight if she's alienated Fee and Loretta. I'm banking on her being at home.

"Ingrid?" I gasp as I take the steps up to the house two at a time, breathing hard.

"In her room," Davide replies, lifting his chin to indicate the first floor.

I almost knock her over halfway up the stairs.

"Where did Pedro go?" I yell.

She looks taken aback, her hand gripping the banister tight. "What? How would I know?"

"He spoke to you at the Howler party. Did he say where he was going?"

She shakes her head, brows furrowed. "Why, what's . . ." Then her eyes widen. "He hasn't come back? He's . . . *out*?"

I stare at her in disgust. Every kid in town knows by now. But then I check her wrist and see she isn't wearing her alert bracelet, despite it being mandatory. She won't have heard, sitting up there alone in her room. It's like she decided to opt out. Harold said he wasn't even sure she was going to bother to Caretake Dora anymore. That's why he's taken to checking on her himself, unofficially.

There's a familiar two-tone beep on my own watch and my stomach drops. That's dusk. Ingrid blinks at it like she doesn't know what it means.

"Yes, he's out," I snap. "You must know something. I saw him talking to you. Where did he go after the Howler party?"

Unpleasant noises filter up through the floorboards: Amy and Bernice on the Turn downstairs, safely behind bars. They're good people. Bernice was so moved by news of the last tornado out in the northern valleys that she's getting together food and clothing donations and she's planning to take them out there herself, once she can find a van to borrow for a few weeks. They'd do anything for anyone. But right now, they're no use to me.

Ingrid seems to gather herself. "I . . . don't know. It must have been one of his computer jobs—he said there was a problem with the internet."

"Yes, but *where*?" It's like talking to a toddler.

She reacts to the anger in my voice with her own. "I said *I don't know*. If I knew, I would tell you."

"What did you say to him? You grabbed him as he was leaving."

Her mouth sets in a hard line, her eyes flinty and stubborn. Frustration surges inside me.

"If he hurts someone, it's going to be your fault. I swear, if you don't tell me . . ."

My phone vibrates. It's Harold. I snatch it up, my eyes

not leaving Ingrid's face. Harold's voice is quiet, like he doesn't want to make too much noise. Fear shakes every syllable.

"Sel, I can't get hold of Elena, but I've sent an alert. Pedro's here. He's right outside."

I leave Ingrid frozen halfway up the stairs and sprint, the first few spots of rain cool on my skin, my X50 banging against my back, urging me faster.

There's a steady drizzle by the time I reach Shady Oaks, a couple of minutes later. Scudding clouds hide and reveal the full moon, so that its white glow ebbs and flows, a pulsing lunar heartbeat. The grounds here are lit by LED lampposts. A few lights are on inside the building. Nothing is obviously amiss. Except . . . I was expecting a bunch of twitchy-looking kids with X50s to be standing around. Anyone who can be spared is meant to come and help in a situation like this. That's what the alerts are for.

Then I realize. My bracelet never went off, except to announce dusk. I check it now, wiping the rain from its plastic face, and I'm right—I didn't notice before because I was there with Elena when she sent it. And there was no alert that Pedro was at Shady Oaks . . . I only know because Harold phoned to tell me. There's nothing on my bracelet to say there's a problem at all. No wonder everyone seemed so relaxed. No wonder Ingrid was clueless. I press the alert from my own device now, but just get the loading symbol, going round and round. Pedro's comment about the internet comes back to me. Is the whole network glitching?

Moving warily across the lawn toward the entrance, I don't see any smashed windows or broken-down doors. My sneaker slips on something soft, and I lift it slowly to check the underside. A dark glob of goo slides from the rubber sole onto the grass, rejoining a pile of what looks like scrapings from a butcher's-shop floor: blood, fur, a coil of intestines that glisten wetly, still warm. What's left of a fox, maybe, or a squirrel. Or part of something bigger. Hard to tell. Either way, it's likely the gruesome signature of a Ripper on the loose.

I curse quietly. The wind breathes across my neck, raindrops rustling the thick bushes all round Shady Oaks.

My phone vibrates—Harold again. "Sel, he's in the bushes somewhere." His voice cracks. "I'm sorry. I'm out of shots. I thought I'd got him but I must've missed because he just kept going."

"Are you safe? Are you inside?"

"Yes, yes, I'm right here. Behind you."

Harold is at his window, gesturing madly at me. I spin to scan the foliage, trying to hold my phone to my ear and lift my tranq at the same time. I hate the feeling of the hands-free headset on my ear so rarely use it, but I wish I had it now. My phone slips through my sweaty fingers and lands in the fleshy remains on the grass. I bend to pick it up, causing the butt of my X50 to swing around and hit me hard across the cheekbone. I avoid looking back at the window to see Harold's reaction and shift my attention to the bushes dotted around the gardens instead. There are a lot of leaves and they're all moving in the wind and the rain, which is driving harder by the minute. For some reason, my last target test score flashes into my brain. It doesn't fill me with confidence.

Harold reads my mind. "Want to swap? I'm coming out. I'll use yours."

"No, no, I can do it." Shame courses through me. Harold's white face looms behind the glass. His mouth is an O of horror and I give him a reassuring thumbs up before realizing that he's trying to draw my attention to something behind me. Through the drumming of rain, I can hear movement, close.

I turn very slowly, and there he is.

Pedro, slinking between bushes, nose to the ground, nostrils dilated and drawing air in hard; he's got the scent of something. Me. He raises his head; the fur on his muzzle is covered in blood. He's definitely been feeding. Please let it only be a fox.

The main entrance door bangs open behind me. Harold's voice. "Hey! Hey! Over here!" Oh, no. The old fool's trying to distract Pedro.

"Harold, *don't move*." Out of the corner of my eye, I can

see him standing there with a bundle of netting and . . . a broom? He can't possibly think he's going to fight off a Ripper with those.

Dread seeps through my veins. Pedro glances between Harold and me, deciding. His inhuman, yellow eyes are flecked with gold. I don't see even the faintest trace of my friend's soul, or whatever it is that makes him *him*. Only a savage hunger and hostility. But there's something about the way his subtle fur coloring suggests the familiar arch of his brow, and I find myself croaking, "Hi, Pedro," in case he recognizes me, too, even though I know he can't. "Did you forget your headphones, buddy? It's me, Sel."

Faint notes float on the air—someone's playing music in town, and in the midst of my terror my brain helpfully identifies it for me as "Moonlight Disco." *They're playing your favorite song, Pedro.*

His lips draw back revealing pointed teeth, and he releases a low, purring growl. I've never heard a sound like that from a Ripper before, one that reverberates through every cell in my body and turns my insides liquid. It's not a warning. It's a murmur of pleasure, in anticipation of the kill.

"N-n-nnno!" I shift the X50 around in an uncontrolled jerk until it points at his chest, but the barrel is bouncing along with my heartbeat and shaking hands. "It's me. Don't . . . Pedro, don't—" My voice gives up, the words swallowed, my tongue thick and useless in my mouth.

His shoulder muscles twitch, tensing in readiness.

Harold picks that moment to advance with the broom, hobbling forward with a reedy war cry.

My finger, stiff and numb, struggling to find the trigger, presses down. Nothing happens. With a gently dawning, strangely sweet, sense of inevitability, I notice that I never actually took the safety off. The blood in my veins slows to a trickle. We're both going to die.

But in that instant, my hair ruffles as something whizzes over it, and "Moonlight Disco" reaches a peak. A drone. It pauses, hovering just over the Ripper's head. Pedro's attention snaps to the movement and sound. His muzzle swivels up, nostrils flaring as though he can smell something special.

Finally my fingers relax enough to slide the safety off, and I refocus on Pedro, quickly wiping water from my eyes with the back of my hand. The drone is making small darting movements, like it's teasing him, and it's working—his eyes are following it. I finally get off a dart and, to my elation, it plunges right into the side of Pedro's neck. It's only then that I see the gash at the back of his head. The fur is flattened around it, glistening and sticky with dark blood, like it's been smashed against something hard. He's badly injured.

The effect of the tranq is supposed to be almost

immediate, and it was with my mom, but now it's as though Pedro doesn't even feel it. He jumps for the drone and it skirts upward out of his way, then zooms off into the darkness, with him in pursuit, just as Elena appears, right in his path. They're clearly both as startled as each other. Pedro hesitates for the tiniest moment, but it's all the time Elena needs. She swings her tranq up and points it at him, just as Pedro springs at her. His powerful legs carry him several feet in an instant, but she's ready for him and sends a volley of darts into his chest—at least three or four hit their mark.

He doesn't break his stride.

In an instant, he's on top of her, knocking her to the grass with ease. But then he's gone, galloping after the drone, leaving Elena winded on the grass in a hit-and-run.

We're all paralyzed in shock and confusion.

He had us and left us alive.

I run to her, but she's already clambering up.

"I can't believe he just . . . ," I say, almost laughing with relief. "How did you do that? That thing with the drone?" I expect her to show me a remote control or something, but there's nothing in her hands except the tranq.

Her expression is utterly bewildered as she stares after him into the darkness. "That wasn't me."

Harold catches up. "It wasn't? Then who—"

Elena shakes her head. "Never mind. We can't lose him. Come on. There're streets full of kids just down there. I don't think that drone will entertain him for long."

Harold throws the bundle of netting to me, pulls a flashlight from his belt and hands it to Elena. "Go. Don't wait, I'll catch up."

It's easy to follow Pedro's path through the long grass in the moonlight—his heavy paws have flattened a wide swath. To our relief, he hasn't headed into town. The drone has led him to the river—the faint strains of "Moonlight Disco" are coming from a little way upstream. He's taken a straight line to the bank, and for a horrible moment I think he's jumped off, straight down the waterfall to certain death. But then the path bends sharply, along the bank on this side of the river. We follow the sound, and the trail of flattened grass. Then the music shuts off abruptly ahead.

Over the thundering of the water, a shout from Elena. "Here!"

When I catch up with her, her flashlight is aimed at the sky, and for a moment I wonder if Rippers have suddenly learned to fly. But then, through the illuminated raindrops, I spot him. He's hanging by one leg from a rope slung in a tree, the remains of broken sticks in the dirt where he's set the trap off. Pedro is swinging upside down over the river, thrashing wildly and snarling, biting at the air in an attempt to sever the rope, as the river thunders past underneath him.

Relief floods through me. We got him. I silently

bestow endless thanks on the person who decided to set up the trap and sent the drone. There's no sign of it now. But there's another shout from Elena, who doesn't look relieved at all. She's grabbed the net from me and is frantically untangling it.

Then I see why. The branch the rope is looped over is breaking. It's far too thin to bear the weight of a Ripper, much less one that's thrashing around, struggling for its life. As I watch, I can almost see the sinews of the branch thinning and tearing apart.

I search around and pick up a long stick with a gnarly knot near the end, and hold it out over the river toward the rope, trying to hook it and pull it toward us, but it's not long enough.

I strain toward the juddering rope, but it stubbornly jumps around inches away from the stick. Elena finally shakes out the net, wraps part of it around her wrist, and flings the rest as far as she can toward Pedro, but he's on the out-swing and it misses him by a hair's breadth. I give up on the stick, flinging it to the ground behind me, and help her drag the net back out of the river's clutches— the current is hard and fast, tugging against us viciously. Elena tries again, waiting for her moment, and this time it catches around Pedro's forepaws and head. As he swings away again, Elena is yanked forward and I grab at her, my heels skidding ruts into the mud.

I've got her, and she's got him—just. But he's bucking

and twisting in panic, snarling and yelping in outrage.

"Stay still," she screams, though he can't understand, let alone cooperate.

There's a crack, sharp and audible even over the water's rush, and just like that, he plunges into the river, taking the net and half the branch with him. The force pulls Elena over, her head and chest dragged under the surface of the water, leaving me desperately clinging on to the waistband of her jeans, sliding on the mud. Then all at once, the resistance disappears. Pedro and the branch sweep away at speed, leaving Elena holding the broken net.

He's gone.

I don't remember Harold helping me drag Elena out of the water, coughing, distraught, and shaking with exhaustion. All I see now, whenever I close my eyes, is the bulky shape of Pedro being rolled over and over by the current, downstream to where the riverbed falls away in a hundred-foot vertical drop, and the waterfall snatches him over.

CHAPTER SEVENTEEN

I can't believe this day is happening. Pedro's memorial. They're not calling it a funeral, because they've nothing to bury. The waterfall, and the rocks at the bottom of it, took that away from us.

Mom waits while I climb the steps up to Elena's house. We're walking over there with them.

I give a polite knock on the open door, then head into the house. In the living room, the top of her dad's head is visible over the back of the sofa, and the black shoulders of his suit. He's ready, at least. I wasn't sure if he'd be up to it. He's got the news on. Floods and hurricanes across the rest of the country again. The presenter is ankle-deep in water, lashed by rain, shouting at the camera about how this is the third straight month of emergency.

"Good morning," I say, and immediately feel like I've been crass. It's not a good morning. He doesn't respond.

I take the stairs quietly up to Elena's room and raise my hand to knock, but then I hear music coming from Pedro's door opposite and walk in there instead. For the tiniest of moments, part of me thinks maybe he'll be in there. He'll grin at me and say surely I didn't really think he'd actually gone?

The curtains are shut, making the room gloomy. Elena's sitting on Pedro's bed, hunched over his mini Bluetooth speaker, the one that he used to take with him so he could listen to decent quality music when he was out on jobs. It's playing a song I recognize as one of his favorites, though I can't remember what it's called. No lyrics, just a thumping bass and electric guitar soaring over it.

I sit next to her and can't think of anything to say. Sergeant Hale has already informed them that his "investigation" is over. What a joke. He says there couldn't have been a drone playing music, and even if there had been, a Ripper wouldn't follow it like that. His bosses out at HQ have told him so.

He seems to think *we're* hiding something. That maybe we're lying because we were involved in Pedro staying out, and now we feel guilty. According to Hale's report, Pedro decided to ignore Confinement, for unknown reasons. I watched Hale carefully as he was speaking to us, and I still don't know if that's what he really believes because that's what he's been told, or if he knows exactly what's going on. One thing is for certain: Sequest's fingerprints are all over this.

As the track comes to an end, Elena switches the sound off but carries on holding the speaker, stroking it with her thumb like it's a little pet. When she turns to me, her eyes are puffy and dull. I go for a hug, to let her cry on my shoulder, but then she surprises me, and holds me off gently. Her voice is steady and clear.

"Somebody stopped him from coming home. He must have been held somewhere and then let out, or broke out, after he'd Turned, at dusk. Did you notice he was wounded? He had a horrible gash on his head, he was bleeding. Someone did that. And we know who they were working for." Her jaw tightens, as if the images are floating through her mind. "Sequest killed him."

I hesitate. "But ... who around here would hurt him? And if they wanted to kill him, why didn't they just do it when he was still human, instead of letting him Rip out? And who sent the drone? Whoever it was, they saved us."

She shakes her head. "If his human body had been found, there'd be a murder investigation. If he'd gone missing, everyone would have torn up the whole town and the forest looking for him. No. Someone wanted us to see him die. An accident. They wanted it shut down quickly. It was choreographed."

Realization dawns. The trap over the water that

wouldn't hold his weight. The drone wasn't sent to rescue us. It was sent to lead him to his death.

"Whoever was controlling that drone knew exactly what they were doing. They knew how to make him ignore the three juicy living steaks right in front of him."

"The music . . . ," I offer. "Pedro's favorite song?"

"Yeah, partly. But I don't think that would be enough. It would have needed some other bait too. A pheromone, maybe—he was sniffing at it. And the way it was moving around above him . . . Trying to get his prey drive to kick in."

I think back to the way the drone was darting around. It reminds me of the way I tease Harold's dog, Eddie, with the ball before I throw it, to get him psyched up enough to fetch.

I shiver. An image of Pedro tumbling over the edge of the waterfall flashes into my head yet again.

Elena gets up, puts the speaker carefully on the desk. She closes her eyes, breathes in deeply. "It's time to go."

Funerals and memorials are supposed to help the people who are left behind deal with their grief, surrounded by friends and family. Pedro's memorial is dignified, somber, and yet feels to me like a sick joke.

It can't be real.

After the service in the town square, people drift

away, murmuring condolences to Elena and her dad. Lucas accepts them with an expression of such restrained agony that it's hard to look at him. Elena told me he's fallen apart. He blames himself for causing a scene at the Howler party. There's been no more job searching. Not a trace of his previous anger. He's just . . . given up. Retreated into himself.

I tell Mom I'm going to hang around in case Elena wants to talk, and she heads home after giving me a long squeeze and telling me to take all the time I need.

"Howdy, Sel." I surface from my misery to find Mayor Warren in front of me. The *howdy* is at least a subdued one, for him, but it still annoys me. "I'm sorry for your loss too. I know what a good friend Pedro was to you."

I nod and swallow hard. I don't want to hear anything from him right now. I figured I had nothing to lose and went to see him yesterday, after Hale ended the investigation. I started asking why the alerts hadn't been working that night. He shut me down right there and then. He'd checked, and the alert system was running fine. Not only that, but he'd heard alarming reports about my behavior recently, and that of Elena and Pedro—that we'd been throwing around "wild allegations" and being lax about security. And just look where it had led.

I should have known it was pointless. He and Hale are pretty tight.

The warning was clear: we must stop causing worry

and panic in our community, especially at a time like this.

The thing is, nobody's worried—that's the problem.

Now I watch him walk off, only to be replaced by something worse: Ingrid approaching. I check behind me—Elena is deep in conversation with some other kids and hasn't noticed my plight. Bernice is hobbling away back to Juniper House on Amy's arm—she broke her ankle on an unmarked tripwire someone left out in the grounds. At least it wasn't attached to a stun pop. But it's meant she's had to delay her goodwill trip to the northern valleys. I watch them go, ignoring the urge to call them back to protect me from Ingrid.

No, I've got to handle this one. I brace myself, plant my feet and wait.

Ingrid stops in front of me, hands shoved deep in her trouser pockets. She's wearing a smart black suit, and her hair is pulled neatly back into its ponytail. She seems to roll the words she's going to say around her mouth before she says them.

"We need to talk. You, me, and Elena."

I laugh bitterly. "No, we don't. Can't you leave us alone, even now? We know you've been spying on us. You and your minions. Where are they, by the way?"

Her mouth opens and then closes again, her face flushing a deeper pink. "I'm not friends with Fee and Loretta anymore." No denial of the spying, I notice. It occurs to me that Sequest's spies might well include children, to do their dirty work for them during Confinement nights. Letting my mom out, for example. It would explain a lot. "I can't talk to them. They don't get it. You know things. I want you to tell me."

"Oh, I bet you do. So you can report back, hey?" I turn away in disgust, but her hand is still on my arm, and she pulls me back around to face her. I glance over at Elena, who's still not looking this way. I don't want a fight at her brother's memorial.

I lower my voice. "Go away. Unless you want to make a confession. What did you say to Pedro at the Howler party, Ingrid? Hmm? Did you tell him to go somewhere? And then make sure he couldn't come back in time?"

Ingrid looks horrified. "No! Nothing like that." Her gaze sweeps the people around us, briefly. "We were arranging to meet up the following day, to . . . to talk about stuff. Honestly. Trust me."

It's such a barefaced lie it almost makes me laugh. "Oh, come on. You're the last person he'd confide in."

"*Trust* you, Ingrid?" Elena is next to me. I wasn't aware of her approaching, but I'm guessing she heard the last exchange. She seems exhausted but combative, like her anger is all she has left and it's looking for something to do. I really hope she's not going to start an actual fight, because I don't have a hope of holding her back. "I was just having a little chat with Justin," she says, crossing her arms. "He was telling me how he was at Shady Oaks on the morning of the last Confinement, painting the hallway baseboard for Harold. He saw you coming out of Dora's room, stuffing something under your top. And the funny thing was, Dora was in the kitchen at the time. Care to explain? Should we ask Hale to search your room at Juniper? It wouldn't be the first time you've stolen, would it?"

Ingrid's eyes flick toward Sergeant Hale a few feet away. His face swivels in our direction, mirrored shades revealing nothing. She doesn't answer.

Elena nods. "Thought not. Come on, Sel. Let's go see Harold. He says he's got something to show us."

CHAPTER EIGHTEEN

When we arrive at Shady Oaks, Harold is waiting outside for us. We follow him across the lawn, up the gentle slope toward the hedge that marks the property boundary. He's very slow, and almost turns his ankle a couple of times, reaching out to hold my arm for support. He's pale and trembling, utterly shaken.

"I don't normally go up here," he pants. "But I couldn't find the pruning shears, so thought maybe someone had put them in the old shed by mistake."

We pass a small cluster of trees and come to it, up against the hedge. Just on the other side is Warren's place. The shed is clearly not being used anymore. The door is hanging off by the bottom hinge, and there is a bulge in the side where planks have splintered outward, as though it's been hit forcefully from the inside.

I've been in the other, newer shed just outside the back

door of Shady Oaks before, when Harold asked me to fetch his rose gloves. It's full of thick cobwebs and cluttered with junk, but it's made of painted steel and doesn't let the rain in, unlike this one.

Elena and I step up to it warily, as though whatever caused the carnage might still be in there, even though it's obviously empty.

Through the doorway, the walls are splattered with dark stains, and there are more stains on the floor. Might be mud. But I think it's dried blood. Elena reaches out and touches one of the nails. There's a piece of silvery fur caught on it. It looks very much as though something has fought its way out of here. It wouldn't take much—the wood is old and thin.

I imagine Pedro, unconscious, bleeding from his head wound, dragged in here and left until dusk. I feel sick.

"You were right, Elena," I say. "He was here. Someone shut him in, knowing he would break out when he'd Turned."

She holds the fur gently between her fingers, biting her lip hard, obviously trying not to cry again. A rebellious tear escapes down her cheek and she quickly wipes it away with her sleeve before stowing the fur in her pocket. Something else to remember him by.

Harold's voice shakes with indignation. "How could they do this? He had his whole life ahead of him. His whole life." His voice breaks.

A wave of anger and grief is building in my chest, threatening to overwhelm me.

"Someone in our community is a killer." Harold reaches for my arm again and I let him hold on. He leans against me heavily and I worry he's going to collapse. I lead him to a nearby bench and then at his suggestion, Elena and I search the area for any more clues.

After a while, Elena shouts, "Hey! I've got something!"

I run over to where she's crouched by the hedge, reaching under it. When her hand emerges, she's holding a shiny black rectangular object, covered in dirt but still instantly recognizable by the bullet-hole stickers on the back. Pedro's phone.

The battery's dead, of course. We can barely keep still while we wait for it to charge, back in Harold's room. Finally it has a few percent and we try switching it on. For a moment nothing happens, then the logo appears. Never has a start-up process taken so long. But finally, Elena opens his text messages.

There it is. The last one. Tuesday at 12:14 p.m. The one he got at the Howler party. It's from a number that doesn't seem to have been in his contacts.

I hold my breath as she clicks on it.

We read the message, and the name at the end of it.

*Howdy, Pedro, we need to talk. Can you come
straight from the party? Warren*

There's something inevitable about it, but at the same time I'm shocked to the core.

Eventually, I say, "Warren? Mayor Warren?"

"I don't know any other Warrens, do you?"

None of us do. And the *howdy* nails it.

Elena's still scrolling through Pedro's phone. "Okay, but there's an entry for Mayor Warren in Pedro's address book, and it's a different number."

"New phone?"

"Could be."

I try to imagine Warren as a cold-blooded, calculating killer. Luring Pedro to the shed, knocking him unconscious, and shutting him in. Setting up the trap and flying the drone to get him there. The picture isn't convincing. I once saw him get stuck in his own deck chair. Warren and Hale would be the two finalists in any incompetence contest. But maybe it's all an act.

Elena is eyeing Harold's tranq, clipped onto the wall next to her. She touches it lightly with the tip of her finger, and I see an idea start to form. She stands up.

"Dad called Warren a liar. Let's find out if that's true."

Then she yanks the tranq off the wall and strides out of Shady Oaks with it.

CHAPTER NINETEEN

I can barely keep up with Elena. When she sees I'm trying to stop her, she starts to run. People gawk as she speeds past—you're not allowed to carry tranqs outside of Confinement. Why would you, when there are no Rippers about?

Unless you wanted to kill a human being.

As we reach the path that leads up to the mayor's house, she swings around and points it at me.

"Sel, you need to stay back."

When Ingrid pointed her tranq at me, I was afraid she'd pull the trigger. But now that my best friend is doing it, it's so much worse. I've seen that look on her face before. Nothing's going to stop her—not even me.

A few people are on their phones, I guess calling the police station, but Elena's already marched up to the front door and pressed the bell.

When Mayor Warren opens it, she sticks her foot in the gap.

His palms go up right away. "Whoa, whoa, what's this! Elena!"

"Why did you text Pedro just before he disappeared?" she says, the tranq aimed right at his belly.

He hesitates. "Young lady, you need to put that down. I know you're having a hard time right now—"

"*Why?*"

He cracks, slightly, and a hiss of desperation leaks out. "I didn't! I don't know what you're talking about! Please, Elena! Put that down."

"You're working for Sequest, aren't you? Why didn't the alerts work that night? What's going on?"

He's sweating now, his forehead shimmering. "You're grieving, Elena. You're not thinking straight."

She tilts her head to one side, considering. "Yeah, you could be right. If only there was something that could calm me down. Some kind of sedation, maybe . . . " She holds out the tranq in front of her as though measuring its size. "Worth a go, huh?"

She reverses the tranq, pointing it at herself, her arm only just long enough to reach. As I cry out, and the mayor lunges forward to grab her, it's too late.

There's the mundane click of the trigger, and the *thunk* of a Ripper tranquilizer dart in her thigh.

» » »

We're in one of the treatment rooms at the Wellness Center. I watch Nurse Pete check Elena's drip and then take her oxygen level and pulse.

"You are one lucky duck," Pete tells her, "to get a faulty dart."

"Luck had nothing to do with it," she tells him, fiddling with the strip of tape holding the needle in her hand.

He taps it away. "Leave that alone, it's just in case you need any drugs. But your vital signs are looking good. You gave us a bit of a worry!"

That's putting it mildly. She should be dead several times over.

"Now, I think we can probably let you go home, but Dr. Travis just needs to sign off."

I wait until the door closes behind him before losing my cool.

"What were you *thinking*?" I seethe. "I thought you were going to . . . and then I thought you'd . . . I practically had a heart attack."

"I *knew* they were duds, Sel."

"But . . . how's that possible?"

"We just pick up random tranqs from Sequest each month, right? When we drop off the old ones. We choose the box ourselves off the shelf before they sign it out. So that means that this month, they're *all* duds. That's how they made sure no one could stop Pedro."

I consider. "I suppose."

"See? I knew there was no danger."

"You didn't *know*. You *thought*. That is not the same thing. And you didn't think to tell me this plan before you shot yourself in front of me?"

She has the grace to look slightly sheepish. "It only just occurred to me in Harold's room. Sorry about that. But don't you see? Now they've had to admit there was at least one faulty dart. Even if they try to say it was only that one, it's enough to knock people's confidence in the system. We need more people asking questions, and that will happen now."

I don't know about that. Most of the chatter outside while I was waiting was about how Elena must be mad with grief.

"You really scared Warren. I swear he peed himself."

"Of course he was scared—because he knew I was about to expose his lies about the tranqs."

"Or because he didn't know the tranq was a dud."

She makes a dismissive noise. "Pah. He knew all right."

The door crashes open and Dr. Travis comes in with a face like a slapped buttock, followed by Nurse Pete.

She lifts Elena's wrist and listens to her pulse. "Huh," she says, grudgingly. "Normal."

"Well," Pete says brightly, "that's good news, isn't it?"

Dr. Travis narrows her eyes at Elena. "There's no trace of tranquilizer in your system whatsoever. I don't know what you were playing at, but you can leave. You're fine."

She doesn't add "unfortunately" but her tone says it. I guess she's annoyed she can't pump Elena full of drugs or slice her open.

"Excellent!" Pete beams. "Thank goodness for that. And how are *you* feeling, Sel?"

Elena turns to me in surprise. "Why, what's wrong with Sel?"

Apparently I fainted at the mayor's place. They had to carry me here. "Nothing," I say quickly. "I feel great."

Pete lays a hand on my shoulder. "Just a touch of a panic attack, I think. Some relaxation techniques would be beneficial for you, Sel. Breathing exercises."

I nod in thanks, but honestly my breathing is fine. It's the constant threat of death that's the problem.

CHAPTER TWENTY

I never used to dread Confinements. It's always been my favorite night, even though I feel under the weather. And this weather's a doozy. My limbs are leaden, my stomach is roiling, there's a buzzing in my head like a persistent fly. I wish I could wear Pedro's headphones, but they're gone, along with him. Maybe it's just the infrasound that's giving me intense vibes of approaching doom.

Or it could be that I've been talked into doing something even more stupid than shooting myself with a tranq.

In some ways Elena's bizarre stunt was a triumph. It was a scandal—people were asking how many faulty darts there might be. Could they trust Sequest to keep them safe? We started to hope that it would set off a cascade of investigations that would give us our answers. Then Sequest did something we didn't expect; they apologized.

Apparently, mistakes were made by an employee at HQ in Hastaville, and that person has been fired. New, unbreakable systems have been put in place. A new batch was sent out; a fully checked set of darts arrived at Sequest on the drone, and everyone collected their allocation.

All done.

Simple as that. Unbelievably, it's dying down. When Elena tried to show people the text on Pedro's phone, it was gone. Of course.

Mom thinks Elena is just struggling with her grief. I haven't tried to persuade her again—maybe it's for the best that she believes Sequest, for now. I don't want to put her in danger. With every day that passes, I'm more convinced that Harold is right about the lengths they will go to, to keep their secrets.

And Elena? She's grounded, for this and every Confinement for the foreseeable future, and they've taken her tranq away. To add insult to injury, her next-door neighbor Asim has been told to take over Caretaking her dad. Lucas is quiet as a mouse anyway, these days.

It's been decided that maybe it's best if I don't have access to tranqs right now either. Guilt by association. And it probably doesn't help that everyone still thinks I messed up with Mom's cage lock. Our reputation in this town is at rock bottom.

But I'm not grounded, which is why I'm out right now.

Of course, Elena wanted to come with me, grounding or no grounding. What persuaded her not to in the end was realizing even the other kids think she's a danger to herself and others. For once, they might actually rat her out.

That means tonight's job is all mine. We haven't told Harold our plans, being pretty sure he won't approve. We promised him we'd lie low for a while. Not give Sequest any more reasons to pay attention to us. He actually begged us. I think he might be regretting he ever encouraged us in the first place.

The thing is, Elena reckons if Mayor Warren is up to his neck in it with Sequest, then there'll probably be evidence in his house. Documents. If we could get those, we'd be in a much stronger position. There's only one night we can do that—when he's locked up.

Of course, there's a slight chance I'll get more than I'm bargaining for.

Someone was flying that bait drone. It would be difficult to control it from Sequest HQ in Hastaville, which is quite far away, but it's in the same time zone as us, so everyone there would have been Turned, too, unless they hired an Immutable to do it. Or a kid. No, it's much more likely to have been someone nearby. We've all been assuming that Mayor Warren is just your average guy, not Immutable like Harold. His assigned Caretaker is a kid that lives nearby, Yoona, but she tells us she's never actually seen him Turn. No one has.

Just how much of a liar is he?

As I stroll through Tremorglade to Warren's house in the dark, trying to look casual, I'm desperately hoping there's a caged beast in there that wants to rip me apart, because the alternative is even worse.

It's nearly midnight as the white walls of the mayor's house appear. Dim lights mark the pathway up to the front door. I glance around, in case any late-to-bed kids are watching, and lift my face up to the sky, searching for any telltale red lights above, straining my ears for the distinctive buzz of propellers. If they've got drones for playing music and baiting Rippers, they've almost certainly got drones that can watch me. All is silent. The full moon bathes everything in a ghostly glow.

I shake my head to dislodge the doldrums, to no effect. The gnawing sense of dread isn't going to shift, either. Now I know what's causing it, I feel like I should be able to dismiss it, but I can't. My body is overruling my brain.

A howl pierces the night, instantly joined by others. Midnight. The cacophony surrounds me, and I can't tell if there's one coming from the house in front of me too. They go at it for a full minute. I've heard it plenty of times before, of course, but it never fails to send a chill down my spine: mournful, despairing, agonizing, beautiful.

It trails away gradually, and the gentler noises of the night return.

Stepping over the explosive bunting, I make my way up the gravel path. The stones crunch under my shoes, and I slow, treading more lightly. Bypassing the front door, I head around the side, where we've noticed there's a bathroom window that never seems to be quite shut.

Up close, it's above my head, and smaller than I thought. I can probably just about get through, but it's not going to be fun. Music is playing inside.

With a final check around, I find the crack at the bottom of the window and pull up. It sticks, then suddenly gives, sliding wide open. The music immediately pours out— "Eternal Melons" by Fruit Basket. It's either incredibly loud or playing really close to the window. Lifting my chin, I peek through. The moonlight is on this side of the house, and I can clearly see the white bathroom tiles and a bath with a shower curtain drawn across. Underneath the window, a toilet. After a moment's thought, I take off my sneakers and hide them behind a plant pot farther along the wall.

It takes me a couple of attempts to hop up high enough to get my elbows onto the sill, my feet scrabbling at the whitewashed brick. Painfully, I shift my chest through the opening, and stop to listen.

"Eternal Melons" is still blasting out, but not from the bathroom—from farther inside. He must have it turned right up.

Halfway through, at the point of no return, I realize it would have been better to go feet first, although I'm not sure how I'd have managed that. My shorts pocket catches on the window latch and I spend an awkward few seconds trying to unhook it. When it releases, I slip and have to brace my shins against the window frame in order not to slide headfirst into the open toilet bowl.

My hands grip the edge of the bowl as I slowly bring my feet through the window, effectively doing a handstand on it. At this point, it becomes clear that I should have thought this through more. I've never been any good at gymnastics, and as my toes come over the sill, I lose control and let go of the toilet seat in order to avoid doing a backbreaking somersault onto the bathroom floor. My cheek scrapes against the sticky porcelain, and my hand hits the tiles with a sickening jolt that sends agony from my wrist through my entire body. For a moment I lie curled on the floor, nauseous with shock. When I tentatively move my arm, waves of pain radiate through it. I think it's broken.

The temptation to lie here on the floor until morning is so great that I close my eyes and imagine that it won't matter. He'll find me when he comes for his morning pee and I'll come up with a totally plausible explanation and he'll find it perfectly reasonable and not bother mentioning it to Mom and everything will be fine.

A noise from just beyond the bathroom door makes

me scramble to sit up, and then crouch, the adrenaline releasing me from thoughts of my wrist, for now. I might have imagined it. The music is loud enough that it's hard to tell—the relentless drum beat and soaring vocals obscuring everything—but this sound is on a different register, somehow, off the beat of the music. A thud that doesn't belong.

The bathroom door is open a crack, and I put my eye to it. The hallway is in darkness, save for a dim nightlight plugged into a socket close to the floor. Why would you bother with a nightlight here, when your cage is in the basement, as Yoona told us his is?

I slip out, my feet sinking into the thick carpet.

At one end of the hall is the front door, letting moonlight through an arch of colored glass at the top. Next to that, stairs up to the first floor. I poke my head through a door into an empty living room. A book lies open on the arm of the sofa—*Ten Habits of Successful Leaders*—beside a plate with crumbs on it and a mug containing dregs of cold coffee. Back out in the hallway, the kitchen is through an archway. I can see a tiny, pulsing light on the dishwasher.

Next to the kitchen is another door, open, with steps leading down. That's where the music is coming from— it must be deafening down there. But farther down the hallway there's another closed door, and this one has a bright light under it. My breath catches. His study, I think. Did it have a light on when I peeked out of the bathroom earlier? I think it might have. I'm not sure.

Yoona told me a while back that Mayor Warren has a similar attitude to my mom when it comes to people watching him Turn. He doesn't like it. Yoona strictly has to check he's locked in at least half an hour before dusk, and then get out of the house. She has to leave Warren's mustache-care kit just outside the cage so it's within easy reach for the morning, before he'll even consider leaving the basement.

I never thought much of it, until now. I watch the light under the door for a while, to see if there's any movement, but there's nothing. He might just have left it on.

Thud.

I glance up at the ceiling. Was that above my head? Someone moving about upstairs? It's impossible to tell— it could just as easily be coming from a cage below.

I'm starting to despise "Eternal Melons." He's got it on repeat. Must be the mayor's favorite song.

There's no point just standing here trying to identify strange noises. It makes sense to check out the basement cage first. If there's a Ripper in there, then I'll just check the study and leave. If not . . . well, I'll leave then, too. Fast.

I don't have to worry about making any noise as I tread down the cold stone steps, but nevertheless I move slowly, brushing the wall with my left hand, my right wrist dangling uselessly at my side, throbbing reproachfully. A faint breeze wafts against my bare legs, the bass drum beat vibrating through my feet. There's a light switch on the wall at the top, but I don't touch it. It's just possible he's sitting down there in the dark, 100 percent human. It would be a weird thing to do, but then again, this *is* Warren.

My eyes slowly adjust to the cool darkness. It's not totally black— a chink of light is coming from some kind of vent near the ceiling at the other end of the room. I can barely hear myself think. The speaker is a big one, on a shelf just at the bottom of the stairs. My entire body vibrates with the bass notes. The cage is on the other side of the room, a neat stool to one side with a small box on it. A tingle runs from my feet up to the very ends of my hair. My breath catches. Even from here, I can see the door is wide open.

The cage itself is fairly standard but decent quality. He's got one of those fancy remote-controlled locks, so Yoona's role is really just officially confirming he's all set.

There's something lying on the floor inside. I hold still and try to breathe without disturbing any air. Seconds pass agonizingly, and the shape doesn't move. It doesn't look big enough to be a Ripper.

I've come this far. I can't run away without checking properly.

I shift forward slowly, the floor freezing my feet through my thin socks. I'm right outside the cage now, and the shape still hasn't moved.

The small box on the stool is Warren's mustache kit,

like Yoona said. A trimmer, a teeny-weeny little pair of scissors, a pot of expensive-looking wax.

As I get closer, the shape resolves into a lumpy, ripped blanket. My trembling hand reaches out to lift a corner of it. There's nothing underneath. Just the blanket, all bundled up. I let out a long, shaky breath, and step out of the cage again. Leaning against the wall, I try to think logically.

Whatever he is, Ripper or Immutable human, he's probably still inside the house. The front door was shut, and when I was on the ground floor, there were no signs of broken windows. No alerts, either. He might be prowling the house as a Ripper, but my instincts are telling me he's human. If that's the case, he wouldn't want to risk being spotted around town. And there's that light under the study door.

Either way, it's pretty important I don't meet him right now.

At least I don't need to get through the toilet window again—I can just use the front door. Then I can run. Elena's expecting me at her house, to report back.

I push off the wall to make for the stairs.

As I put my foot on the bottom step, a shape fills the open doorway at the top of the stairs.

The hallway's dim nightlight provides enough illumination that I can see the outline of what's coming for me, and learn that my instincts suck.

The good news is that tomorrow morning, the mayor won't know I was here.

The bad news is, that's because he'll have entirely digested my body by then.

My hand automatically reaches for my tranq and finds only my T-shirt. Agony shoots all the way up my arm in protest at the movement.

He's seen me, already halfway down the stairs, not even wasting time on a growl. Flailing out with my good left hand, I heave the speaker off the shelf and send it flying into him. It bounces off his head and hits the wall, crashing to the floor, and yet somehow "Eternal Melons" still plays, albeit quieter.

He springs for me, and I hurl myself to the side, his jaws missing by half an inch, his hot, stinking breath passing across my face. Even at this urgent moment, some tiny part of my brain registers that the furry pattern under his nose is exactly the same as the mayor's mustache. Stumbling, I run for the cage, blindly grabbing the only object in my path—the stool—and throwing it behind me before crossing the threshold. I turn to swing the door shut behind me and see the stool crushed in his jaws and spat out, the three metal legs twisted out of shape. Before I can get the door totally shut, a huge, hairy paw reaches in and swipes. I cry out in pain as the tips of claws scrape just under my knee, and yank the cage door as hard as I can against Warren's front leg, throwing all my weight on it again and again. The Ripper roars in anger, claws extended, still trying to bat at me. Something sharp is under my foot—the mustache kit is lying scattered on the floor. Seizing the tiny scissors, I start stabbing them into his leg, ignoring the searing agony up my arm, putting every ounce of my strength into it. But I don't think I'm even reaching the skin through all that thick fur.

His head is pushing farther into the cage, trying to follow his paw, forcing the door open wider. I change tactic and aim the scissors at his face. The point punctures the softer skin around his nostril and I drag it down. It's no more than a scratch, but a droplet of blood wells up and he yelps, withdrawing for a second. The cage door clangs shut and, seizing my chance, I fumble for the latch, pushing it down into place. It's not much. Just a piece of metal a few centimeters long—the heavy-duty electronic lock does the real work. I spot the remote lying just in front of the cage, dive to the floor, and reach out for it, but he instantly goes for my arm and I snatch it back, empty-handed. I need to divert his attention.

The blanket. I grab it from the floor, dab it against the blood oozing plentifully from my knee, and start to feed it through the bars on the other side. "Hey! Smell that! Lovely blood!"

He immediately goes around that side and tugs on the blanket, shaking it in a frenzy to destroy. I slide back to get the remote, listening to his snarls and the sound of cloth ripping. My finger hooks it and starts to pull it toward me, just as his back foot kicks out and sends the remote flying across the room, well out of reach. He shreds the blanket, and then turns back to me, shivering with frustration. If anything, the blood has got him more excited.

I hold the tiny scissors in my dripping fist and make feints toward the bars.

He watches me for a few moments, yellow eyes narrowed as if to say, *Really?* Then the lips draw back from his teeth and he lowers his head, surging forward. He's going for brute force.

Bang. The impact on the cage door makes the iron bars sing.

The latch won't hold for long on its own. There's a thick bar that slides into place when you press the remote, but it's tucked deep inside the lock mechanism and there's no way to make it work manually.

He takes a little run-up this time.

Bang.

The cage judders violently. The latch is bent out of shape. It's still holding, but only just. I brace myself against the door, wrapping one arm through the bars, and one through the door itself, holding them together with my body.

Bang.

It slams open, yanking my arm nearly out of its socket, throwing me off. A moment later he's on me, that breath on my face again, my hands grasping into the fur of his neck, hopelessly trying to keep him away. The nightmare darkness of his wide-open mouth fills my vision.

A sudden white light blinds me just as his body knocks me to the ground, crushing the air from my lungs. My face is full of fur. Some part of me marvels how soft it is, like Mom's, even as I wait for the jaws on my neck.

And I'm still waiting.

He's a dead weight. Squashed underneath, I can feel him breathing, in and out, his belly squeezing me into the floor.

This is the second time I've been trapped under a Ripper, and yet . . .

I'm alive.

Painfully, I heave my shoulders to one side, poking my face out to take a gasp of air. Emerging from the darkness of fur, I blink against bright light. The bulb in the center of the ceiling is swinging slightly.

Bringing my left hand out from under him, it brushes against something sticking out from his neck. A tranquilizer dart.

A face looms over me, blurry. My savior starts to tug the Ripper off me, grunting with effort, as sparks appear at the edges of my vision, patches of darkness swimming in and out. My tongue feels like a useless lump of meat in my mouth, but just before I pass out, I think I manage to say her name.

"Ingrid?"

CHAPTER TWENTY-ONE

Elena's face is priceless when she opens her front door to Ingrid's hammering, to find the two of us together. To her credit, she adjusts pretty quickly, and asks no questions while they help me upstairs, and she sets about washing and dressing my knee. It takes quite a long time to stop blood soaking through the pads, but eventually the gash is hidden under a bandage, throbbing.

My wrist is swollen and hurts so much it's making me nauseous. I guess it could have been a lot worse. But there's no way I can avoid getting it seen at the Wellness Center. I won't be able to hide it from Mom, either, which means I need to think up a plausible story that doesn't involve breaking and entering, and nearly getting killed.

Now I'm sitting on Elena's bed slumped against the wall, with her beside me and Ingrid standing awkwardly in the doorway, clutching her backpack, like she might need an escape route. My memory of the last couple of hours is already a little hazy. But I sort of remember Ingrid dragging me out from under the unconscious Ripper, and watching her heave his hind legs and tail the rest of the way over the threshold so she could shut the cage door on him. She even had the presence of mind to remove the tranq dart from his neck, conduct a fruitless search of his study, and straighten the place up before leaving, putting his speaker back on the shelf. Although if he touches it, it will definitely fall apart. With any luck, when he wakes up in a couple of hours, he won't have a clue anything happened.

I'm shivering a little as the shock slowly ebbs away. I can't wrap my head around the fact that he was out of his cage. Yoona is one of the most responsible people I know. Which suggests that someone let him out on purpose. That person could easily have opened an external door, too, but they didn't. It's as though someone laid a trap for me. But we didn't tell a single person I would be there.

I don't know what it means.

"All right, Ingrid." Elena points to the space on the bed on the other side of me. "Talk. Seems like you earned the right."

Ingrid swallows hard and doesn't take her up on the invitation to sit down. She looks more scared now than she did in the mayor's house. "So I followed you tonight, Sel. I knew you wouldn't give up just because Elena got grounded."

"You knew we wouldn't give up . . . what?" I ask, reluctant to let go of my habitual suspicion.

"Investigating Sequest." She snorts at our expressions. "Come on, the whole town knows about it. You haven't exactly kept it quiet. And, well . . . I've been thinking about them too. You wouldn't talk to me, so I had to make do with spying on you."

I eye her warily. She can hardly be surprised we didn't want her around.

"I need to talk to you about what happened last Confinement. When your brother . . ." She trails off. I feel Elena stiffen next to me.

"I'm sure Sequest had Pedro killed. I think they realized he was close to figuring something out, and they stopped him telling anyone."

My gaze flicks between Ingrid and Elena and back again. "What did he find out?"

Ingrid chews her lip. "I don't know, exactly. But I think maybe it's related to something I found earlier that day. I told Pedro at the Howler party that I had something to show him, because I didn't know what to make of it. He's . . . he was always kind to me, despite everything. We arranged to meet up later, but he never . . ." Her face crumples for a moment, then she gathers herself. "I'll show you what I never got a chance to show him."

She retrieves a plastic folder from her backpack and takes out some papers, passing them over to us.

The very first piece of paper has *Sequest, Inc.* in small letters as a header, some kind of code and PEDRO TORRES at the top, plus a date from about six weeks ago. And then other stuff that, as I read, shifts my world on its axis.

```
Seekle searches include:
Infrasound; Fen Zhao next movie;
quick-drying deodorant.


Sites frequently visited: Razz
Clothing (browsing age 14 sweaters
and hoodies, most likely birthday
present for sister—see report
FX643b); AllComputerParts.com
(motherboards, wireless chipsets,
dual band antennae).


Torres continues to show great
interest in Sequest activities
and has continued to monitor
Tremorgossip. 16 attempts to upload
comments onto the site blocked.
42 attempts to access the source
code for the website via hacking
successfully rebuffed. Continued
high-level monitoring is required;
further action may need to be
```

```
taken. The social manipulation
team has successfully isolated him
from his own-age peer group—they
believe he has been attempting to
break up existing relationships
and gossiping, and as a result have
distanced themselves from him.
```

I can't process what I'm seeing. "How ... what *is* this?"

"It's a report. Sequest was watching him. And messing with him."

Elena takes the paper with trembling fingers, silently rereading how they stole her brother's friends from him.

"There's one on you, too," Ingrid tells her quietly. We read Elena's, which tells us, among other things, that she is resisting all inducements to drop her obsession with Sequest, and that she spent four hours on Happy Trappers in a single session.

I hardly dare ask. "Is there one on me?"

Silently, Ingrid gives me the next page.

```
KJ224z
ANSEL ARCHER


Seekle searches include: how to
remove bloodstains from clothes;
cute dog videos.
```

Sites frequently visited:
Righteous Rippers;
WorldsFunniestAnimalVideos.com.

Archer is increasingly suspicious of
Sergeant Hale, a common expression
being that he is "in on it." He
shows great fondness for crude
jokes and takes any opportunity
to refer to body parts and bodily
functions with juvenile humor. This
is in line with expectations. He
responds to empathy shown to him
and the offering of private/personal
information by revealing his own
private thoughts in return. This
will no doubt continue to prove
useful.

Archer wishes to remain in
Tremorglade and has no desire
to visit the rest of the world,
unlike his constant companion,
Elena Torres (FX643b).

Obtaining data from Happy Trappers
has been more problematic, in that

his juvenile humor prevails in
first responses, and the team's
view is that subsequent responses
may be an unreliable indicator
of his true feelings. Data so far
gathered from this subject should
be considered substandard.

A heavy silence has fallen over the room. I think of all the searches I've done, the messages I've sent, all being read by someone at Sequest. Like the one last night telling Elena I was on my way to the mayor's house. That would explain my furry welcoming committee. We'd already sussed that Sequest was experimenting on us, but this takes my breath away. They're deeper into our lives than we ever imagined.

Elena is simmering with rage. "We've *all* been hacked. Where did you get these? Wait, was it the Wellness Center?"

"Nope. That's the thing. I found them in Dora's room."

CHAPTER TWENTY-TWO

"I knew it." I slap the bed. "I *told* you she was shady, Elena." Then my thoughts finally catch up. "Hang on. They're into all our computers?"

Ingrid shrugs. "And our phones, apparently. They know what we search for on Seekle. They see what we type in those ads on Happy Trappers. They even listen in on our conversations on FIN."

"Is there one on you?" I ask Ingrid. "Can I see?"

"Yes," she says, flushing slightly. "You can read it later." She rushes on, "There were more, too, in the pile. It was stuffed behind some books on her shelf. I didn't take many, hoping she wouldn't notice. I saw more names, though, when I was riffling through. People from our class—Justin was there, Mika, Rudy, Asim. Loads."

"But . . . *why*? What's the point of it all? Why do they care so much about what websites I visit, or . . . " I hold up another page and pick a random line, "what novelty socks I order off Sock Emporium? What do they think it means?"

"It must be part of their research," Elena says, sniffing her tears away. "It's not just the physical stuff. They're interested in our minds, too. Although I don't know what deeper meaning your sock choice could have, other than your terrible fashion sense. And we all know that already."

I ignore the habitual tease and reread the report on myself. A horrible creeping sensation climbs over my skin. I think of all the things I confessed to Chad. And all the things he confessed to me. All that time they were listening in. And then a far worse thought strikes me.

"Oh no. It's *them*. Happy Trappers. FIN." Fizzing with adrenaline, I jab my finger into the report. "Think about it. Those stupid survey questions on Happy Trappers. Why are they even there? Most of them don't make sense if they're for ad targeting. They're not just reading our responses, they're asking the questions."

"You mean . . . ," Elena says, catching on slowly. "Trix might be . . . one of them?"

The thought horrifies me. Could Chad really be working for Sequest? Could he be . . . fake? I've been chatting to him for three years.

"I mean . . . that would be . . . a lot," Ingrid says. "It's not possible, surely."

We sit in silence for a minute.

Slowly, a few things start to swim to the surface of my brain, out of the depths. Chad getting his own dog's name wrong and claiming it was autocorrect. I scroll to our last chats on my phone.

Chad: **Hey, Ansel! How you doing?**

I could slap myself. It's right there. I'm *always* Sel, except with Mom. My email is sel@tremorglade.net, my username on Happy Trappers is SuperSel, my FIN ID is TremorgladeSel. Hey, I never said I was imaginative.

For all he knows, I could be Selwyn, or Selgi, or . . . I don't know, anything. And yet, Chad knows my full name, even though I'm certain I've never told him what it is.

But I wasn't paying attention then. I am now.

Elena pulls out her own phone. "Only one way to find out. A test."

"I'll try it with Herman," Ingrid says, already swiping her phone open.

As they consider what to type, my thoughts are spinning. "Remember who encouraged us to use the app? Three years ago?"

Elena snaps her fingers. "It was in that Wellness Center leaflet we were given."

"But FIN has been around for ages—it didn't just start three years ago."

"Yeah," Ingrid says slowly. "But just as we were starting, the app was down for a while, do you remember? Site maintenance, they said."

"I bet that's when Sequest took it over! They must have been doing it since then."

It's scary how easy it is for Ingrid to slip Herman up. He doesn't correct her when she gets his age wrong.

"Okay, that's definitely weird. He didn't even seem to notice," frowns Elena, leaning over to read Ingrid's screen.

"Nope. And thinking back, sometimes he sounds almost like different people, you know? Sometimes he's really chatty, and other times it's like talking to a robot. Information only, no frills. I wonder if it's more than one person?"

Elena breathes in deeply. "Trix's turn." She brings up FIN. The green dot says her pal is online. "I can't think what to say."

"Think of something she told you a while ago," suggests Ingrid. "Something she should remember. And ask her about it."

Elena bites her lip, thinking.

Elena: Hey, Trix!

Trix replies almost the moment she presses send.

Trix: Hey! How is your dad doing?

"We talk about my dad a lot." Elena starts typing. "But not today."

> **Elena:** Fine. My friend just broke his wrist, and I was remembering that time you broke your arm. Which one was it again?

The green dot turns red.

"Oh, she's gone." Elena frowns.

We wait, but five minutes pass and Trix hasn't come back.

"Why's she gone?" Elena frets. "I guess it was a slightly weird question. Maybe I've accidentally tipped her off." Then her phone beeps.

> **Trix:** It was the left arm. Why?

"Yeah, it was," she tells us, sounding relieved. "I remember because she's left-handed and she got let off schoolwork because she couldn't write for a while. About six months ago. Shall I try something else?"

But Ingrid has leaped up, grabbing Elena's phone. She holds it out to us triumphantly. "She totally had to go and look that up."

Elena hesitates. "Maybe she just went to the bathroom?"

Ingrid shakes her head vigorously. "No way. She had to go right at that moment? Seconds after she'd said hi, all ready to chat?"

"Maybe she has diarrhea?" I suggest, part of me still holding out a vain hope we might be wrong.

Ingrid is pacing round the room, talking loudly in her excitement. "No. She does not have diarrhea. If anything, she's constipated. Because she's *full of it*. Guys, they're all fake." She suddenly stops and then slaps her forehead. "Of *course*! That's what Pedro meant! When he said there was something wrong with the internet . . . he didn't mean just on some client's computer. He meant *all of it*. That's how Sequest has a stranglehold on Tremorglade." She gestures at our phones.

In that moment, it all falls into place.

That's why Sequest has always seemed one step ahead of us. We were never going to be able to spread the word about them on Tremorgossip, or any other place online, because they've got it all sewn up.

And they haven't been spying on us.

We've done it for them.

CHAPTER TWENTY-THREE

I'm home in time to have a quick shower before letting Mom out.

I sit for a moment dripping on my bed, reading and rereading my own report, unable to stop even though it hurts me, like picking a scab. It's the words "in line with expectations" that really get to me.

I stuff it under my mattress before heading downstairs.

All I know is, whatever it is they expect from me, I want to be the opposite.

Mom instantly spots my arm, despite me trying to hide it under my bathrobe. It's swollen and all shades of unhealthy colors. I end up showing her the knee bandage as well, just to get it all out of the way at once. Of course, she immediately starts interrogating me but, to my relief, eventually seems to buy my falling-down-stairs explanation. Unfortunately, after that, she's convinced there must be something wrong with my balance and starts going on about getting me a brain scan. The last thing I need is Sequest having direct access to my actual brain. Eventually I persuade her I fell because I was texting, but she insists I go to the Wellness Center, right now, to get properly checked out.

I stop myself from messaging Elena and Ingrid to tell them. No more using our phones. At least, not for anything we want to keep from Sequest.

I cut across the park, scattered with randoms who have no idea that their every move is being logged. Just before we left Elena's last night, Ingrid gave me her report too. She didn't look me in the eye when she handed it over. The top sheet is headed *INGRID ROSSI: PW477f.*

I sit on a bench to read it.

> Rossi's resentment of Ansel
> Archer (KJ224z) shows no sign of
> abating. Since the commencement of
> experiment 242.b* eighteen months
> ago, she continues to be receptive
> to suggestions that Archer is, as
> she writes in her electronic diary,
> "evil." As intended, she believes
> that the many unflattering rumors
> and jokes about her spreading on

Tremorgossip are instigated and
propagated by Archer.

Experiment 242.b? The asterisk directs you to a
footnote on the last page of the report, and I jump to it.

Experiment 242.b: a Dr.ed clip
of CCTV was anonymously emailed
to Rossi, which claimed to show
Archer in the grounds of Juniper
House at the time the owners' cat
was killed. Footage was amended
by our image manipulation team to
strongly suggest that Archer was
the culprit. Once we confirmed the
video had been watched, the email
was deleted remotely to prevent it
being disseminated more widely.

My jaw drops open. I flick back to the main report text,
unable to stop reading.

Since that incident, Rossi has
been unable to persuade anyone
else to believe her account,
hampered by the general dislike
with which she is regarded in

the community, and also our
deletion of the email. Despite the
anonymous origins of the video,
she appears never to have doubted
that its contents are genuine—
no doubt due to the hostility
our Psychological Shaping team
had been carefully building
between the two subjects in the
preceding months. Her failure to
apply scepticism in this case is
fascinating, and testament to the
excellent work done by the whole
team. Rossi has much to teach us
about the components, causes, and
effects of hatred in the human
brain. This will certainly provide
a fruitful source of further
data, with an expanded range of
subjects.

I have to read it a few times to understand what they're
saying.

For the past couple of years, they've been setting
Ingrid and me against each other. There's no way to tell
exactly how they first "suggested" to her that I was a
nasty piece of work, out to get her. But they made it look

like I killed Hinky. Since then, they've been putting lies about her online, and we've all repeated them. They've been whispering in our ears and taking notes on how we tear ourselves apart.

They sound so horribly *satisfied* with themselves. What reason can they possibly have for doing this to us? How is it for our health? Do they think they'll find some kind of cure for hatred or something? Give me a break.

I think giving me this is Ingrid's way of apologizing, or at least explaining, why she's been the way she has.

But I've been just as bad, spreading those lies about her. We'll have to rub out everything we thought we knew about each other and rewrite it.

But we'll do it. More than anything, I'm determined there won't be "further data" like they plan.

It's got to stop.

Dr. Travis is running behind, as usual. I sit alone with my throbbing wrist, increasingly nervous. Ingrid reckons Sequest doesn't know she has those reports. If they did, she reasoned, she'd already be dead, like Pedro. Is this what Pedro discovered? I'm guessing it is. Somehow, he must have given away what he knew. We just have to make sure we don't do the same. Which means no telltale internet searches. No texts. No calls. We'll have to talk only in person, when we've checked no one's listening in.

"You, *again*."

I jump out of my chair when Dr. Travis speaks, right in front of me. She looks about as keen to see me as I am to see her.

Her gaze runs over my hideous wrist, and she sighs before turning wordlessly away to walk down to her clinic room. I follow her, and, as she unwraps my bandage to check my knee, quickly tell her my story of having been bitten by a dog.

She examines it carefully, then her eyes flick up to meet mine. "A dog? And would this be the same dog that bit Elena recently, I wonder? Sounds like it needs to be put down."

"Uh, maybe. I don't know whose it was, must have got loose. It was just wandering around and I tried to pet it. Stupid, really."

"These look like claw slashes. Not a bite."

I swallow. "I'm up to date with my tetanus jabs. So I should be okay, yeah?"

She frowns but brings her attention back to my knee. "It doesn't need stitches, and it's clean," she adds grudgingly. She puts on a fresh bandage, telling me to keep an eye out for any signs of infection, then moves on to my wrist.

"And how did you do *this*? Quite a night you had, it seems."

"Uh, I, uh, fell down some stairs. Running away from the dog. Is it broken?"

"Just sprained," she says dismissively, as though someone as incompetent as me could hardly be expected to achieve a proper fracture. She types on her computer for a minute before spinning the chair to fetch a splint from a cupboard.

"Wear this, if you like. You'll need to rest it as much as possible until the swelling goes down. I suppose I'd better prescribe you some painkillers. Give this to Mrs. Folke at the pharmacy."

She hands me the paper and I read the words on it suspiciously. Are these really painkillers? Why did she mention Mrs. Folke and not the other pharmacist? Is she in on it too? I hate the way this whole thing is making me suspicious of everybody.

"Thanks," I say, weakly, and start to get up.

"Oh, hang on," she adds, checking her screen. "You need an extra blood test. Might as well do that now."

"An extra one?" I go very still, poised half out of the chair. "W-why?"

An irritated tut. "How would I know? I only get the request. It just says 'increased monitoring protocol.' Probably because you're getting close to Turning age, you know. It's not that unusual."

"But . . . how did they know I'd be here today?"

She huffs in amusement. "They didn't. Just a coincidence. If you hadn't been here already, you'd have gotten an email invitation to come in."

I swallow. I really don't want her to stick a needle into me. I'm still half crouched out of the chair. "I actually don't have time today."

"Don't be silly, it'll only take a minute." She pulls open a drawer and starts rummaging to gather what she needs.

I glance at the door. Sometimes she locks it when she has a patient, to avoid being disturbed. I can't remember if she did this time. I wonder if I can get there before her.

"Dr. Travis, I really don't want to." The fear in my voice makes her look up.

"What? You've done this hundreds of times."

"I know. But I—can I just go?" I stand up slowly, starting to back across the room.

Her frown follows me to the door, but she doesn't try to stop me. She sighs. A despairing wave of the hands. "Of course, Sel, you're free to leave."

I'm halfway down the path from the Wellness Center when I stop dead. I can't believe I didn't see it before.

She just lied to me.

Ingrid is surprised to see us again so soon when she opens her bedroom door at Juniper House. "What?" she says bluntly.

"No idea," Elena chirps, going right in and flumping onto Ingrid's bed without an invitation. "Sel wouldn't tell me until we got here."

I wanted to blab my news right away, but there were delivery drones all over the place on the way, and call me paranoid, but I feel like any of them might be able to listen.

I follow Elena in and perch on Ingrid's desk, pushing aside a couple of Explosives Theory textbooks.

Ingrid looks both ways down the empty corridor, then closes the door. "People will get suspicious if they see us meeting up. We're supposed to be mortal enemies, remember?"

"This is important," I assure her.

"At least you remembered not to text me. We can't be sloppy anymore."

We all glance toward the window, half expecting to see a drone listening outside. There's nothing, but I get up and close the curtains anyway.

Ingrid leans back against the door and crosses her arms.

"Okay, spill."

I take a deep breath. "I think we're stuck here. In Tremorglade, I mean. All of us. No one can leave."

Blank stares.

"Okay, so: example. Bernice's broken ankle. She fell over a tripwire, right?"

Ingrid stiffens. "That wasn't my fault. Davide and Philippe do all the security here."

I wave her defensiveness away. "I know. But Bernice

also had loads of trouble getting a car for her trip to the northern valleys, yeah?"

"Yeah. She eventually persuaded Nurse Pete to let her borrow the old ambulance, but then the battery died just as she was about to set out. After that got sorted it had two flat tires and she had to order them in—a special size or something."

"And then she broke her ankle. Don't you think that's weird? Isn't that a lot of bad luck?" I ask.

Ingrid shrugs.

"Haven't you noticed that lately, the few times anyone around here decides to leave Tremorglade, it never actually happens? They never make it. *Something always happens.* Sequest isn't just experimenting on us. They're keeping us here."

Ingrid laughs skeptically. "That's wild."

"Think about it. Who's actually left Tremorglade in the last few months, that you know of?"

"Well . . . ," Elena hesitates. "Okay, not many, for sure."

Ingrid blinks. "One or two?"

"Yeah? Come on, then. Who?"

"Well, I can't immediately . . . " Ingrid says. She's staring into nothing, racking her brains. "Wasn't your friend Eira going to move to Dageford, Elena?"

"She was. But her parents changed their minds. Something about a house sale falling through."

I click my fingers. "I'll tell you who was the last person

to leave. Dr. Adebayo. On that passenger drone Sequest sent for her." We all remember it, because it was such a unique event: everyone came out to watch her go. It landed in the town square, she got in and waved. We watched until it became a black dot and disappeared over the treetops.

Elena's eyes narrow as she thinks. "She got called out to Hastaville suddenly to work for them on some kind of research project. Three years ago, was it?"

Ingrid nods slowly. "Yeah. Three years ago. Just when it looks like Sequest started messing with us."

None of us can recall a single other person who's left Tremorglade since then.

"And Dad," Elena breathes. "All those jobs he got rejected from."

"I bet they interfered to make sure he didn't get them," I say. "If you think about it, it wouldn't even be that hard for Sequest to keep us here. Most of us wouldn't dream of leaving, anyway. But if anyone does—if they search online for holidays or jobs or whatever . . . Sequest knows about it, and they make sure it doesn't happen. Set rogue tripwires. Drain car batteries." I swallow. "Even kill, if they have to."

"That research Dr. Adebayo was recruited for," Ingrid breathes. "Do you think . . ."

I finish the thought for her. "We're it."

We sit with that for a moment. We all really liked Dr. Adebayo. It seems impossible that she would agree to have any part in this. I can still see her face in the window of that passenger drone. Excited. Happy.

Elena draws in a sharp breath. "Just after she left was when they said Mom couldn't be sent away to that big hospital for treatment after all. Did they . . . do you think they stopped it happening?" She twists the duvet next to her, knuckles white.

There's a sensation like ants crawling up my spine.

In three years, they must have done an awful lot. We're only just starting to scratch the surface.

"I want answers," Elena says grimly.

"Well," Ingrid says, thoughtfully, "it's Thursday today."

We look at her blankly. "So?"

"Dora will be out at her book club."

Harold shifts from foot to foot on the threshold of Dora's room, wringing his hands. Eddie is oblivious to his discomfort, trotting excitedly around between the rest of us as we search, tail wagging briskly. "You really mustn't."

"No, we must," Ingrid retorts. "Go back in your own room, if you like."

"Don't break anything," he says. "Please put all her books back *exactly* where they were. She'll know."

"There's no CCTV in here, is there?" I ask, suddenly worried, scanning the ceiling for anything that might be a camera.

"No. We don't need it," he says primly. "We *usually* respect each other's privacy here."

I don't remind him how often he's found Dora in his room, poking about.

Despite all the evidence we've shared, Harold refuses to believe Dora has anything to do with Sequest. I can tell he's also having trouble accepting that Ingrid is now part of our team. In fact, I think he's half a breath away from accusing her of having planted the reports.

"It makes no sense," he says for the third time. "Dora doesn't use a computer!"

Ingrid grunts. "Maybe she didn't write them—maybe they're reports *for* her. Either way, it's not good, is it?"

She reaches down briefly to scratch Eddie's ears, and he leans into her blissfully.

Harold tuts. "Look, I don't know how she got hold of them but there's no way she'd be involved. She must have picked them up by mistake. You barely know her, Ingrid," he adds with a sniff. "It's not as though you bother spending any time with her when you Caretake. None of you know her like I do."

I slide my hand under a chair cushion. Nothing there.

Harold points a finger in the air, a sudden idea. "Someone working for Sequest must have hidden them in here!"

Ingrid rolls her eyes. "Yeah, right. It would totally make sense for Sequest to hide their top-secret stuff in some rando old lady's room, for her to find when she's picking out her next bedtime read."

We share an amused glance, a tiny connection between us, just for a moment. It feels nice, but weird, like when my braces came off and it took me a while to get used to how smooth my teeth were. I'm starting to see Ingrid for real, not as Sequest wants me to see her.

And she's right, of course, in her sarcastic way. All the same, I can't help but admire Harold for defending his friend. Especially as I've never seen Dora be much of a friend to him in return. It crosses my mind that maybe he's in love with her. If that's the case, I can only pity him.

We give up shortly after that. There's nothing else behind the books on the shelves where Ingrid found the first reports, and we soon run out of places to search. Maybe Dora's being more careful now. Maybe she noticed some of them went missing.

We head back over to Harold's room, closing the door behind us and whispering, despite the fact that Dora's not due back for at least another hour. Harold opens a packet of ginger nut cookies.

Elena grabs one and talks with her mouth full. "You have to promise not to tell Dora anything we talk about, Harold. Right?"

"Of course." He sniffs. "I'm not going to put her at risk. That's what I've been telling *you* not to do, blabbing to everyone. Fat chance you ever listen to me, apparently.

And by the way, Sel, that was *extremely* silly of you, going to Warren's house. When I said you should be discreet, I didn't mean break in under cover of darkness. If I'd known, I'd have told you not to do it."

"Which is exactly why we didn't tell you," Elena retorts.

"Well, we didn't find anything," I admit. "But no one's come knocking at my door to arrest me. The thing is, it's all got to come out somehow. *Everyone* needs to know what's going on. We have proper evidence, with these reports. We just need to get them out there."

"Yes, but look what happened when Pedro tried to post on Tremorgossip," Elena points out. "They've got a stranglehold on the network. On our computers, our phones."

"We . . . uh . . . we photocopy them and post them everywhere around town?" I ask.

"And who's to say you didn't type them yourselves as a prank, hmm?" Harold replies.

He's right. Our reputation—Elena's, mine, Ingrid's—is at a low point right now. Sequest has done a pretty good job of making us look completely untrustworthy.

"Might as well just ask them to kill you," Harold adds. "Your power right now is that they don't know—yet—what you've just discovered. You can't squander that. You have to use it at the right moment."

"Power? We have no power," Ingrid says, her voice dull, defeated. "We can't even use our phones or computers without those stalkers seeing what we're doing. They know everything about us."

"Not everything." Harold takes another ginger nut and crunches it thoughtfully. "They're clever. Manipulative. They have a lot of private information about us. But we also know they're sloppy. Your FIN so-called 'friends,' for example, have screwed up more than once. They're the weak link. They don't know you've found out about them. Or Happy Trappers. That gives us an opportunity."

"To do what?"

"Lead them astray."

"How?"

"Make them think you've given up. That you've realized you were wrong. It was all a horrible mistake because you're just silly teenagers. And then . . . boom."

"Boom? We're going to blow them up?"

"Metaphorically speaking. Next Confinement night, when there's no one in authority paying attention . . . that's when you finally make your move."

"Which is?'

"Remove yourselves from their control. Physically come out of their network, so that you can expose them. I can't do it. But you can."

"*Remove* ourselves? How?"

"Leave Tremorglade."

CHAPTER TWENTY-FOUR

Remi.

Remi Colletto. That's whose name has been rattling round my head. Remi, who went into the forest with his family for marshmallows and songs around the campfire and never came back.

Maybe it was a bear that killed them. Maybe it was Sequest. Maybe it was a genetically engineered bear sent by Sequest.

But they're all dead. That's the main point.

Only a week to go until we follow their example. A week to go until next Confinement.

I'm lying on my bed playing Happy Trappers when Mom calls me downstairs. Even though I know it's Sequest's stupid game, it's still addictive. And I don't want to disrupt my normal routine in case they notice. I just answer the pop-ups with my usual dishonesty.

I thud down in my slippers and find Mayor Warren at the door. When I see what he's holding, I freeze.

My sneakers.

For some reason, even when I couldn't find them the morning after last Confinement, even after Mom quizzed me on the last time I saw them, my memory drew a blank until this moment. Maybe it was the trauma. But it's only now I see them in his hand that my brain chooses to flash up a looped GIF of myself dumping them behind a plant pot next to his house, before pitching myself through his window.

"See what Warren found!" Mom says, her head tilted questioningly at me.

"I don't think . . . Are they mine?" I say, peering as though they're not in focus. "No, they look similar but they're not—"

"Well, they have your name in them," Warren chirps.

Oh yeah. Mom and her insistence on naming all my possessions so they don't end up in lost property. Of all the ways for her to be proved right.

"How in the *world* did they end up in Warren's garden, Sel?" she frowns.

My mind is drawing a blank. "I. Have. No. Idea." I shake my head, smiling sheepishly, as if to say it's just a funny old world, in which sometimes our shoes make their own way to the other side of town. "But at least I can stop wearing my old ones now! They're way too small."

Mom always keeps my last pair, in case of this sort of loss, seeing as we can't afford to buy multiple pairs.

They're both staring at me.

There's a few seconds' silence that feels like years. In my head, I can see Warren pretending to show Pedro something in that shed, hitting him—

"Uh, thanks," I say, grabbing the sneakers. I want to run back upstairs but I can tell Mom is already hugely embarrassed, and that would just about finish her.

Mayor Warren rubs at his mustache, which I can't help noticing looks slightly less groomed than usual. I guess his little scissors are bent after I stabbed him with them.

"How's the arm?" he asks.

Not trusting myself to speak, I half lift it in a shrug and wince. It still really hurts, even in the splint and the sling.

"Well," he says, "I shall keep an eye out for any other possessions of yours that have somehow made it onto my property."

He walks away down the path, whistling a tune that gives me a sudden flashback to his basement—"Eternal Melons," the song that was banging out in his house that night. When he reaches the road, he stops and turns back. "Bit of advice, Sel. Look after the things you care about, or you might lose them for good."

It's the kind of benign, meaningless phrase he comes

up with all the time. But as Mom shuts the door, I can't shake the feeling he isn't really talking about my sneakers.

At first, even starting up FIN makes me want to puke. When I initiate a chat, the reply dots going up and down look sinister, a snake twisting and slithering its way into my home. The first time, I shut the laptop before Chad's words can appear.

But as the days go by, it gets easier. I tell him I'm starting to wonder if my imagination hasn't run away with me a bit lately. I ask him how likely he thinks it is that Sequest is doing experiments on us.

Chad: Honestly? I don't think so.

Honestly? Like you would know what that word means, Chad.

After a while I find it fascinating, watching him take the bait. Encouraging me every time I express a doubt. He asks how my friends are, and I tell him Elena is feeling brighter, coping better with her brother's death. That she reckons he just got too absorbed in one of his hobbies and forgot what the time was, forgot about Confinement.

Chad laps it all up. I can almost see him smugly passing on my responses in one of those reports. I begin to enjoy myself in a way that surprises and slightly disturbs me.

I feel smart, calculating. I take a brittle pleasure in the turning of the tables. All this time he was lying to me and I believed every word. Now I get to lie to him and watch him get suckered. Make him sweat a little.

I ask him if he's ever thought about working for Sequest when he grows up. He says he's never considered it, but they'd certainly be a good option.

Elena and Ingrid disapprove when I tell them. Elena chastises me, "Don't make him uncomfortable, Sel. We don't want him thinking too hard. We want him relaxed and confident."

The thing is, I don't want that. As the next week passes my anger grows. I want Chad, whoever he is, to be afraid. I want him to feel the same creeping terror and dread that's tortured me. I want him punished for being part of the system that killed Pedro. I want him hurt, the way he's hurt all of us in Tremorglade. Sometimes I scare myself.

But Elena is right, of course.

I rein it in, reminding myself that if I screw this up, we lose our chance.

Once we're free of Tremorglade, our voices can finally be heard. Online. In the streets. National newspapers. Anything we can think of. And Sequest will be powerless to stop us.

» » »

We all have our blood tests without fuss this week. I apologize to Dr. Travis for running off last time, and tell her how great I think blood tests are, and how I bet Sequest is doing amazing things with the results. She studies me briefly, one eyebrow raised. "Okaaaaay."

Stick that in your stupid report, I think.

I find myself wondering if she knows Chad. Is there some chatroom where she and Warren and Sergeant Hale and Dora and probably half of Tremorglade discuss us with their Sequest handlers?

Elena and I meet up less often than usual, as if we're going off each other a bit. And since we can't talk on the phone, I've never felt more lonely. We stagger our visits to Harold in case anyone's watching. We don't try looking in Dora's room again—Ingrid, Elena, and I all reckon it's too risky, and Harold, unbelievably, just thinks it would be an invasion of her privacy. I'm glad not to run into her when I'm at Shady Oaks, at any rate.

The night before next Confinement, Mom and I eat dinner together and linger over apple crumble and custard, the kitchen warm and smelling of cinnamon. I wish I could talk to her about it all. But she still wouldn't believe me; and if she *did* believe me . . . well. I've no doubt now: Sequest would kill her.

She thinks I've forgotten all about my strange obsession, moved on. I can sense her relief. She's happy.

Tomorrow, I'm going to destroy that.

As she hugs me, I breathe in her familiar scent, and squeeze my eyes shut to hold back tears. There's no choice. It's our job to protect her now. To protect everyone.

CHAPTER TWENTY-FIVE

Confinement rolls around again. It's sunny, but with the half-hearted warmth that tells you it's one of the last times you'll truly feel it on your skin before autumn dies into winter.

The new school year started this week, and I'm so jumpy in physics that when Ms. Boateng unexpectedly calls on me to answer a question about the mechanism used in stun pops, I leap to my feet, knocking over my chair, heart belting at my ribs, and everyone laughs.

My bag is packed. Over the past twenty-four hours I've pilfered bits and pieces from the cupboards and the fridge, plus a big bottle and a flashlight. The bike ride to Hastaville will be the longest I've ever done, according to the maps: some thirty miles or more, north along the forest road until the trees end, and then taking the westward fork a few more miles into the plains. Elena estimated we can cycle eight miles an hour, though I'm not sure she's fully taken into account how rough the road is, how likely my bike is to fall apart after ten minutes, how unfit I am, and how sore my right arm is. By doing it on Confinement, we not only have the best chance of going unnoticed, but also we'll get one full night in the forest before anyone starts to wonder where we are. Will that be enough?

I've been thinking a lot about the people out there, in Hastaville and elsewhere. I know they have their own problems. Big ones. But I'm guessing they don't know what's going on here. I'm guessing they don't know that Sequest is experimenting on us, supposedly for everyone's benefit.

When we tell them, I hope they believe us.

I hope they care.

Because if we're going to put an end to it, we need their help.

I manage to hold it together when I say good night to Mom. I fidget around making sure her clothes are folded nicely. The meat is on the cage floor. I thought about leaving the bar up and the key in the new padlock, so at least she can get out by herself tomorrow, but that would just make her suspicious, so I've asked Rudy to check on her in the morning, making up a vague excuse about having to go out early. I hope he remembers. I'd have asked Mika, except our stupid basement isn't accessible for her because of the death-trap stairs.

I dwell guiltily on how Mom will feel when I'm not there at dawn, her anxiety creeping up slowly. She'll ask around. Then go searching.

And then there's the fact that I might not come back at all, if it goes wrong.

I force myself up the stairs, back to my room to pick up my bag.

Ping

That's dusk.

My stomach lurches.

Carefully, I remove my bracelet. I stuff it in the middle of the pile of laundry under my bed. That should take a while to find. Harold thinks they can track us with them.

Ingrid arrives on her bike almost immediately—Harold's Caretaking Dora tonight, so Ingrid can come straight over. Ten minutes later, Elena joins us. We don't say much, our nerves too jangled to waste energy on unnecessary words. We show each other our bracelet-free wrists.

"Phones off," Elena reminds us. "And hoods up. We don't want to be spotted by any drones away from our bracelets."

Just as I'm about to switch my phone off, it vibrates, and a logo starts flashing on the screen.

"Don't answer," Elena says quickly. "Just switch it off."

But I hesitate. "It's Harold."

Elena watches the flashing logo uneasily. "What's he doing calling us now? He knows the plan. Maybe he's butt-dialed you?"

He hasn't. The logo means it's not a voice call. He's pressed his emergency button.

He wouldn't press it without a good reason. If he'd done it by accident, there's an easy way to cancel it too— three long presses straight after.

He doesn't cancel it.

As we approach Shady Oaks at speed, then throw our bikes down on the lawn, there's an increasing tingling in my stomach that I tell myself is the infrasound.

He probably just forgot to tell us something.

But then I see the blood.

Something's been dragged through the double doors. It's left a smear all down the corridor up to the path. My feet slow, not wanting to take me to see what's inside, but Ingrid rushes ahead, slamming through the doors and sprinting down the corridor to Harold's room. Elena's right behind her. The door of Dora's room is open. As I pass, I glance inside.

Her cage is empty.

As I tear my eyes away from it, Ingrid bursts back out of Harold's room into the corridor. "He's not there. Harold? Harold?!"

We all start yelling our lungs out until Elena calls us around the corner, where the fire exit leads out to a secluded, neglected part of the garden. The fire door's been propped open, and I can hear barking from outside. Eddie.

Within a few moments I identify it as coming from the new garden shed. When I open the door he doesn't come out, so I step in toward the back, pushing away the cobwebs. The barking is coming from a cardboard box—someone's put a toolbox on the lid. I lift it up and Eddie bounces out, and goes pelting through the door, making for a thick bank of bushes up against the wall of Shady Oaks.

There's a low moaning coming from somewhere behind them.

"Here!" Harold's voice is reedy and exhausted. "Oh, Eddie! Thank goodness you're all right! I thought she'd eaten you."

Ingrid jumps in and immediately gets caught on a load of brambles, yanking furiously at her limbs to force her way through. Elena and I try to help her by holding them back, getting scratched up everywhere in the process. Eventually I remember there's a machete in the garden shed, and after hacking away for a minute we reach Harold. There are cuts all over him; blood has seeped down from his eyebrow and been wiped across his eye, making it look like he's been punched in the face.

With difficulty, we help Harold limp inside and sit him down in his bedroom. We start attending to his cuts and our own with iodine and cotton wool from the first-aid box in the kitchen. "She tricked me," he keeps saying. "I can't believe she tricked me!"

Apparently, some of the things we said about Dora kept bothering him. He decided to look around her room for himself. And that's where she found him, earlier this afternoon.

"I'm guessing she wasn't too pleased," says Elena, finishing with Harold's face and casting a critical eye over the scratches on his hands.

"She *attacked* you?" Ingrid says, reaching for one of Harold's juice concoctions in the box under his bed, and popping the cap. "Hey, can I have one of these?"

"Leave that alone!" he snaps, so harshly that we all jump. "You may not. Listen to me."

"Wow, pardon me for being thirsty," Ingrid grumbles. "Guess I'll have water." She fills a glass from the bathroom tap then plonks herself down again. "Carry on, then."

Harold closes his eyes briefly. "She hit me with something from behind. Next thing I knew, I was lying in her cage. I believe she was planning to join me in there when it was time for her to Turn. That way, she'd get rid of me, and it wouldn't even look like her fault. Eddie must have been making a fuss, so I suppose that's when she put him in the shed too. I pretended to still be unconscious, and when she opened the cage to get in just before dusk, I took my chance. Tackled her."

I try to imagine Harold bringing Dora down like a fullback, and half wish I'd been there to see it.

"We grappled for a while, but I couldn't get her into the cage. Then it was too late—she started to Turn, and I just ran, to raise the alarm. But I realized I wasn't going to be fast enough. So I hid in the bush before she came outside and pressed my emergency button." He blows out air through pursed lips. "Thank goodness I got you here before you started out along the forest road."

"Yeah. But, if you're okay now, we really need to get going," Elena frets.

Harold grabs her arm. "Not yet."

"You think maybe Dora went in the forest?" I ask.

"I don't know. But that's not why I wanted to stop you. Before you go, you need to see what I found."

CHAPTER TWENTY-SIX

Harold reaches into his pocket and shakily unfolds a crumpled piece of paper. We gather next to him.

It's a map of Tremorglade and the surrounding area. The town is not much more than a dot, with the forest around it. I've seen it all before. Except for one thing: a thick black meandering line encircling the trees, up to the mountains.

"What's that?" I ask.

"Maybe it's where the infrasound zone ends?" suggests Ingrid. "The outer range of their experiments?"

"It's more than that," Harold says grimly. He turns the map over. There's a key on the back. He pokes a bloodstained fingernail at it.

DEFENSE WALL

"Defense? Could that be left over from the Disruption?" Elena wonders. "Maybe they built a wall back then, to keep people out? I don't remember learning about that."

"That's because they didn't," Harold says. "It all happened too quickly. A project like that takes time. And do you notice anything missing?"

We stare at it for a while. Then Ingrid gasps.

"An exit. There's no gap. The road goes right up to the wall and stops."

He nods. "I think it does." He looks up at us. "We're not just isolated and tricked into staying. We're actually, physically trapped."

"There must be a way out." Elena traces her finger along the line. It's solid. "Could we climb it?"

"If the point of it is to keep us in, I'm guessing not," I say.

"No," agrees Harold. "I expect it's huge."

I've never wanted to leave Tremorglade before. But now I feel like I'm slowly suffocating, that wall closing in, growing in my mind until the sky is shut out.

"So we're stuck here," Ingrid says. "We can't communicate with the outside world, and we can't get out."

"Not necessarily," Harold says. "I think there is a way. And you'll need to do it tonight. Let me show you." He gets up stiffly and puts the map on the card table where we can all lean over and see it more easily. "Listen. I know this is scary stuff. But I have absolutely no doubt of your ability to pull this off." He lays a hand on my arm. "You're brave. You've already shown you're willing to go into places and do things that most people wouldn't even consider."

I snort. "You mean when I broke into Mayor Warren's house? That was stupidity, not bravery. And if there was any, I used it all up that night."

"Sometimes there's a fine line between the two," he says, smiling. "And I think you have plenty left. You went into the shed just now to rescue Eddie from that box, fighting your way through all those cobwebs. I know what a big deal that was for you. You're always telling me how terrified you are of spiders." He winks, and puts a finger on the map, and starts telling us what we need to do.

I don't hear a word. I feel dizzy, but it's not just the doldrums. I can hear my own heartbeat in my ears, a roaring white noise as a wave of horror rises in me.

I bend over, throwing up my entire dinner into Harold's wastebasket. The others stop and stare at me in surprise.

"Ew. Gross." Ingrid wrinkles her nose.

"Sel, what's up? You've gone pale," Elena's voice breaks through.

"Spiders . . . ," I whisper.

"Where? And anyway, so what? Don't be such a wuss."

Harold lays a hand on my arm. "It's all right, Sel, there aren't any in here."

I shake him off. My breath is coming fast, as though

I've been running. "And I . . . I never told you Eddie was in a box in the shed."

The others just look at me, uncomprehending.

He laughs. "Yes, you mentioned it."

I shake my head, adamant. "I didn't. The only reason you'd know that is . . . is if you put him there yourself."

He takes a step back from the table, shocked. "I what?"

Elena looks concerned. "You know he wouldn't do that, Sel."

Ingrid puts her hands on her hips. "Okay, can we forget about Eddie for a minute and focus on—"

"And it's not just that. He thinks I'm scared of spiders."

Harold takes another step back from me, like I might hit him. "You . . . you're always saying it."

Elena and Ingrid are worried I'm having a breakdown. Elena sighs in frustration. "Sel, we don't have time for this. Can we just—"

"I've *never* said it. I *love* spiders. They're amazing. Their webs are the strongest . . . for their size, they're—" I force myself to stop. I'm babbling, yelling at Elena. "The only reason he might think I'm scared of them is because I wrote it in those survey answers on—"

"Happy Trappers," Harold finishes for me. Too late, I realize he hasn't been backing away from me, but toward the door, where his tranq is hanging on the wall. He unhooks it carefully, takes the safety off, and points it at me.

"Oh dear. I had really hoped to avoid this."

CHAPTER TWENTY-SEVEN

I want to lie down and cry at my own stupidity. Elena and Ingrid don't seem to have absorbed the truth yet.

"How do you know what Sel wrote in Happy Trap . . . " Ingrid trails off as understanding dawns.

"Wait a minute. It's *you*?" Elena finally says.

"Are you going to kill me?" I ask. My voice is weirdly steady, awaiting the inevitable.

"Of course not," Harold says, but he doesn't move the tranq. "I just need you to hear me out." He reaches behind him with one hand and turns the key in the door, then pockets it carefully.

"So put it down, Harold," Elena says slowly. "And explain. We're not about to run off."

"Move back a bit, please, all of you. To the other side of the table." We do so, and he relaxes his grip on the tranq slightly, holding it across his body instead.

"Now, you mustn't do anything stupid. Just listen."

"Well, talk, then, instead of threatening us, you scumbag." Ingrid doesn't bother to conceal her anger.

"First things first." He moves to grip the tranq under one arm, and dips a couple of fingers into his shirt pocket without taking his eyes off us. Then he chucks something small onto the table. Elena picks it up.

"A memory stick?"

"I was going to pretend I'd found it in Dora's room, but you might as well know it's mine. Tonight, I finally managed to bypass the encryption for the most damning evidence and downloaded it. That's when I found out about the wall. They hid that from all of us. But now we have it, this is much better than just telling people. There's more than enough evidence on that to destroy Sequest, if it got out into the world."

"But . . . you're working for Sequest?"

"Yes. No. I was. I mean, technically I still am. Oh dear." He's sweating, frustrated at his inability to find the words he wants. "The most important thing you must believe is that I didn't kill Pedro. It's not *me* running Happy Trappers, or FIN for that matter, but I have limited access. Listen, this is all very awkward. But it shouldn't make any difference. It mustn't. I know this makes it harder for you to trust me now."

"Ya think?" Elena says. She's looking him up and down as if she's seeing him for the first time.

"Which is exactly why I was trying to avoid confessing. But I'm on your side. I want the truth to get out there." He gestures wildly. "But my only communication channel goes to Sequest HQ, and I'm not fit enough to run. I need you." He smiles hopefully, like we ought to be flattered.

"Think about it: it was me who set you on this path in the first place. I'd been hinting for ages that you and Elena should look into Sequest, but you never took me seriously." I notice he doesn't mention Ingrid; I guess she wasn't part of the original plan. "So I worked out how to give you a nudge. I crashed one of their precious drones in your tree, to make sure you'd find it."

"*You're* in control of the drones?"

"They're mainly automated, but I used to have supervisory access. Not since I crashed it, obviously. They took it off me after that and gave the job to one of their Immutables at HQ. Luckily, they thought I'd messed up accidentally."

I throw up my hands in disbelief. "Why didn't you just fess up? Why go to all the trouble of pretending to find out with us?"

His face crumples. "I knew you'd think I was a traitor. Especially after they killed Pedro. I couldn't bear . . . " He gulps. "I thought I could push you in the right direction, help you leave, and you'd never find out I'd been a part of it. You just needed my guidance. I kept begging you to keep it quiet, but you're not very quiet, are you?" he adds reproachfully.

"Why were you even working for Sequest in the first place?" asks Ingrid.

He sighs. "Three years ago, they asked me to help with an experiment they wanted to do here. It didn't sound bad. A little bit of infrasound for a while, to study whether they could use it to trigger Rippers to return to a human state, and a few other interesting things, that's all. Like those." He gestures vaguely to the box of juices under his bed.

"Your punch?" Elena shrieks. "You've been *drugging* us?"

"Nothing harmful. Careful doses of various things, depending on the brief each month. I was to take notes on who had some, occasionally try to get certain people to drink it."

He seems taken aback at our horrified faces.

"Honestly, the whole point was to do something *good*, believe me. Make breakthroughs that would benefit the whole world. The thing is, people get in the way of their own well-being. They behave irrationally, in ways that harm themselves. Sequest needed to understand and test how our bodies and brains work, in order to help us overcome all sorts of things—not just physical diseases, but grief, boredom, aggression. They think they're close to finding out how to cure those things! Wouldn't that be wonderful?" He seems desperate for us to understand. "But it's impossible when people won't cooperate. So they had to do something radical. And they put quite a lot of pressure on me to say yes. They'd already recruited a few others here to help out, but I was in a unique position."

"Because of being the only Immutable," I say.

"Exactly. I'm the only adult who can observe things on the ground on Confinements, see how children actually cope with the doldrums, that sort of thing. And frankly some of the others are useless the rest of the time too. They don't use Warren for anything much because he always messes up. That night, Sel—when you texted Elena that you were on your way to his house, a shift supervisor at Sequest panicked and decided this was an opportunity to take you out. So he unlocked Warren's cage, thinking he'd eat you and put a stop to any more nosiness. Emails were flying the following morning, I can tell you. The supervisor got the sack, of course. They don't encourage people to use their initiative."

"They can unlock our cages all the way from Hastaville?"

"They can hack into any electronic lock here." He catches my eye and has the grace to look slightly shifty. "Yes, they let your mother out, when they realized you'd found their drone. It's just as I warned you at the time: they wanted to trash your reputation, to minimize the chances of anyone taking you seriously."

I *knew* getting that flashy cage was a mistake.

"So Warren's in on it. Who else? Hale? Dr. Travis? Dora? How many?" I ask.

He inclines his head. "Not Dora. I meant it when I said she had nothing to do with it. She does, however, insist on nosing about in my room, and found the reports. It seems she'd been onto me for quite some time, slowly gathering evidence, though she clearly hadn't figured out what to do with those documents, bless her. She knew enough to try to keep you lot out of it, though, for your own safety. She just didn't bank on Ingrid's thieving ways." He laughs, as Ingrid flushes. "But actually, Dora solved a problem for me. I'd been wondering how to get those reports to you without arousing suspicion."

I gasp. "She tried to warn me, that time she told me not to Seekle anything . . . She suspected Sequest would be watching everything I did on the internet." Oh, Dora.

"Have you killed her?" Ingrid thunders.

"Good grief. How could you think that? No! I just let her out as an excuse to get you here, make it look like an emergency. I had to come up with something on the fly. I think she killed a fox on the way out. Just as well I put Eddie in the shed, isn't it? *I* wouldn't kill anyone," he insists. "Some child will tranq her, no doubt, if she does go into town." My blood chills at his casual dismissal of the danger she poses to herself and everyone else.

"I guess Sequest must pay pretty well," Elena sneers. "For you to betray everyone."

He looks horrified. "No, it wasn't like that at all, at least for me! The others were happy to do it for the money, but I thought I was doing something wonderful, at first."

"So you didn't take any money, then?" Ingrid interrupts, but he makes like he doesn't hear.

"They said if the experiment were to end prematurely, millions of people elsewhere in the world wouldn't get the treatment they need. I thought the potential good outweighed the . . . small amount of suffering here."

"Just a minute," Ingrid says, crossing her arms over her chest. "Something about this doesn't add up. You were happy for us to be treated like lab rats. You were still on board even after they killed Remi and his family. You must have known about that." He opens his mouth to object, but Ingrid presses on. "In fact, you enthusiastically joined in, with your toxic Howler party punch and who knows what else. But then you suddenly have a massive problem with it. I don't buy it. What changed?"

He purses his lips in disapproval of her attitude. "Let's just say I came to my senses. Regardless, I think it would be much better if you escaped, the three of you. Teach them a lesson."

Elena puts my thoughts into words. "Except now we don't trust you one bit, you sicko. How do we know you're not sending us out there so Sequest can do the same thing to us that they did to Remi?"

Eddie pokes his nose toward a plate of chocolate cookies and Harold nudges it away with the end of the tranq.

"No, Eddie! Chocolate is poisonous for dogs!"

The little terrier flumps down at his feet again in a sulk, looking as betrayed as we feel. "Eddie doesn't know what's good for him, and what will kill him. Like you, apparently." His expression darkens. "Fine. If this is what it takes to get you to leave, I'll tell you. Back in the spring, I saw something on the system. Just briefly, before it was deleted. Something I wasn't meant to see." He glances away, unable to bear our scrutiny.

"What did you see?"

He licks his lips. "The end."

He seems reluctant to elaborate. We wait.

"They're wrapping up the whole experiment, in just a few months' time. And because its existence is so sensitive, they're going to make sure news doesn't get out. If you know what I mean." He gives us a significant look. We return blank stares, until he capitulates, and explains. "They're going to kill you all."

The air seems to have been sucked out of the room.

Ingrid finds her voice first. "They can't."

"I couldn't see the details. But it'll be the whole works. Armageddon." Harold fiddles with the tranq nervously. "When I saw that, I knew I had to do something. I can't let them kill you. You're my friends, believe it or not."

There's a long silence, and then Elena slaps her forehead. "Ohhhh . . . Now I get it. They're going to kill *you* as well, aren't they? No plans to send a drone to bring out their loyal workers, eh? *That's* why you have a problem with it. They tricked you. You and all the other people here they conned into this sick project. You're just as trapped as we are."

From Harold's deeply uncomfortable expression I know she's hit the nail on the head.

"That's a very hurtful way of looking at it," he insists. "But it makes no difference, does it? If you want to save the people you love, then leaving without them for now is the only way. Tremorglade is a closed system."

There's silence for a moment as we digest this. If he wanted to send us to our deaths, he's had plenty of opportunities to do it before now. He's right. It's the only way to save people.

"We're trapped inside a massive wall, according to you. How are we supposed to escape?" I say.

"That's what I was about to show you. You're not going to hurt me now, are you?" He glances warily at Ingrid, who seems like she might. She shrugs and turns away. He hooks the tranq back on the wall, then picks up the cookie plate, pops one in his mouth, and starts to crunch noisily. He holds the plate out to us and we just regard it dumbly. This doesn't feel like an appropriate time for cookies.

"Just take it, will you? I need both hands for this."

I grab it, and he slides both his hands under the bedside table. In a smooth movement, his bed rises silently, and the floor underneath it opens up to reveal a large console, with two screens. "My little work station."

Elena raises an eyebrow. "Guess we know why this place is so expensive, huh?"

"They fitted this just for me," Harold says, with a touch of pride, and in this moment, I think I see how they got to him. It wasn't enough to be liked—loved, even—around here. He needed to feel important.

He touches one of the screens, and it flickers to life. A map of Tremorglade appears, with the wall marked on it. "Now, this will be slightly tricky." He taps the map and it zooms in. "The road leaves town there, as you know, and goes straight north. It used to be that when it came out of the forest, it forked east toward Yojay, and west toward Hastaville. Now, the wall blocks it before the fork. The river, however, runs northwest. It goes through a gap in the wall quite a few miles away from where the road leads. And it's closer—only fifteen miles or so from here, though the going will be a little slow—there's no path. So your bikes are no good, I'm afraid. But it's a more direct route to Hastaville. This is where you get out. By river."

"In a boat, right?" I croak, hopefully.

He shakes his head. "No, you'll have to swim it."

It's the worst possible thing he could have said.

"And since your little adventure in Warren's house, spy drones will be keeping an eye out, for you in particular, Sel. Probably armed ones. Looking for any break in your habits. You coming here isn't particularly unusual, but they'll certainly take an interest if they spot you heading into the trees. Don't go straight from here. Throw them off the scent by walking somewhere more crowded first. Hoods up. When they can't find you tomorrow, we don't want this to be the last place you were seen."

I can't help thinking it sounds like he's covering his own back, rather than taking care of us. I glance toward the window, imagining cameras hovering up high, out of sight, but watching. My throat is dry. "Armed? They're going to gun us down?"

"I doubt it. How would they explain your bullet-ridden bodies lying in the street tomorrow morning? No, they'll use tranquilizers and make it look like an accident. Delinquents messing around and taking risks. You do have a reputation for that kind of behavior, after all."

This doesn't make me feel better.

"So we go somewhere more crowded. Then what? How exactly are we supposed to make it into the forest without them noticing?" Elena asks.

Harold rubs Eddie under the chin, then looks up at us with a casual shrug. "We'll need a distraction."

CHAPTER TWENTY-EIGHT

Ingrid wants to lock Harold up in Dora's cage before we leave, but he points out that he needs to have access to his console to organize the diversion for us, so we leave him free.

It's not that we trust him.

What choice do we have?

I wish we could take Eddie with us. If we survive this, Harold's going to prison and Eddie is coming home with me. *I'd* never shut him in a box in the dark.

We walk out of Shady Oaks casually, like we're just going for a stroll, leaving our bikes on the lawn where we abandoned them earlier. Harold will have some questions to answer about those, but that's his problem. It's ten o'clock—peak hanging-out time for the children of Tremorglade. Without our bracelets, it's impossible to tell if anyone's encountered Dora and raised the alarm, but I don't think they have. People are chatting, messing around. We get a few odd glances as we pass, but probably only because we're walking with Ingrid. A few weeks ago, I'd never have believed it myself.

The moon is flitting behind thick strands of cloud, hiding and reappearing, playing with us. We stick near to the last row of houses before the trees, approaching the forest road.

Then Elena taps my arm and whispers, "Don't look, but there's one coming."

I hear it before I see it. It passes over our heads and its blinking red light catches my eye. A drone, just above lamppost height, skimming away from us along the street. It looks like a normal delivery drone—no one else pays it any attention, but collectively, we shiver. It's headed in the same direction we're going. We watch as it skirts a rooftop and slows, hovering. Is it following us?

The Confinement sense of doom is worse than ever. I tell myself it's not a sixth sense, it doesn't mean something terrible is going to happen—it's just the infrasound making me feel that way. But it's no good. I start to tremble. Harold's been lying this whole time— why should we think he's stopped now? I'm not sure that everything he said really adds up. If we go into the forest, we might never come back. Our bodies will be found in a few days, or weeks, mauled by wild animals. Quite possibly by Dora, if she went that way.

Just then, it happens.

A kid I recognize from the year below us is playing skittles in a front garden with a girl who is probably his younger sister. He stops suddenly, straightens, and checks his bracelet. Up and down the road there's a collective shift in body language as everyone gets the alert.

Then another one.

And another.

And another.

A girl close to us, about to win the jackpot in her group's game of marbles, curses loudly and spits on the grass before joining her friends as they start running up the street, accompanied by the rattle of safety catches being thrown off tranqs.

Kids are coming out of houses, dragged from their sofas, from their pizzas and movies, by the series of alerts Harold sent. Harold picked six different areas across town to make sure there are kids moving in every direction, so that we won't stand out.

They stream past us, our classmates, neighbors, friends, scared but for the most part willing to do what needs to be done. I feel a surge of pride in them all, and the prickle of tears.

"Look." I follow where Ingrid nods discreetly. The drone has doubled back and is heading for Shady Oaks. Another one breaks out of the alley opposite—we hadn't even noticed it was there—and buzzes off after it.

Heads down, hoods up, we start to move more quickly, half walking, half jogging, up to the start of the forest road. We don't break pace but glance around as we reach it, scanning the skies, straining our ears for drones. I spot one high up over the trees, in the distance, a tiny pinprick of red light, coming this way fast. But it whizzes far over our heads, into town with the others. Have we fooled them? I remember that Harold said some of them can recognize us, and quickly hunch over, keeping my eyes on the ground.

Our feet pound the rough gravel toward the trees. We've already agreed we should go deeper into the woods for a short while, well away from the edge of town, before turning ninety degrees westward to find the river, and following it downstream. At some point we will meet the wall, though I'm hazy on how long it might take us in this direction. A few hours? All night?

As we go deeper into the forest, the dense canopy blocks more of the moonlight and we struggle to see where we're putting our feet. The road is in disrepair here, potholed, strewn with large stones and branches. Judging that we've gone far enough this way, we leave the road and follow Elena's compass west. None of us want to risk switching on our flashlight yet.

"Do you think they have infrared cameras?" I whisper. "Will they be able to track our body heat?"

"No," Elena says, with a certainty she can't possibly

feel. After all the technology Harold described, infrared seems kind of basic.

After that, we walk in silence. The occasional rustling bush and snapping twig tell us nocturnal forest creatures are watching our progress. We move as quickly as we dare, nervous energy spurring us on.

Harold's betrayal sits on me like a dead weight, and though I know I need to focus on survival, I can't help but dwell on it. His friendship was a lie. That first day when he fell over right next to me in the grocery store, was that planned? Did he pick me out because he thought I'd be easy to manipulate? The offers of money, that I thought so generous. Was that out of guilt, or—nausea rises in my throat at the thought—was he *buying* me? His ticket out of here? Did he think so little of me?

Whichever way I look at it, there's no avoiding the fact that he thought—no, still thinks—he's better than us. More deserving of the truth, of being treated like a human being. I don't doubt he was happy to carry on, until he realized he'd be counted alongside us, marked for destruction.

My whole life, I've felt incompetent. But never worthless, until now.

After half an hour, in which we might have gone slightly astray arguing over the compass, we come to the river, looking down on it from the top of a steep bank. Upstream somewhere, there's Shady Oaks, and the waterfall. We head in the opposite direction, switching on the flashlights. Remi floats into my mind, and I wonder how far he got. I shake the thought from my head.

"Stop." The tension in Ingrid's voice makes me freeze. I start to whisper to Elena to stop too, only to realize that she already has. None of us are moving, and yet footsteps are still crunching through the undergrowth. I swing my flashlight wildly in the direction of the noise. A pair of golden eyes reflect back.

A low growl.

"Dora."

Ingrid's way ahead of me. She points Harold's tranq at the eyes, and lets off a dart, but Dora ducks low at the same moment she pulls the trigger, and it sails over her head. After that, there's an empty click. Ingrid curses. Dora's haunches wiggle slightly—she's preparing to spring.

"Run."

I don't need to be told twice. Keeping my eyes on Ingrid's back, I follow her weaving path as she jumps fallen branches, avoids holes, Elena's panting breath just behind me. I risk a glance back. Dora's nowhere near as fast as Pedro, but she's gaining, pausing briefly to jump obstacles, clearing them with ease.

I bash my right arm on a tree trunk as I pass, and pain courses through it. I cry out and stumble.

"Come on!" Elena yells in my ear.

Suddenly there's a new voice. Two voices, talking.

Except they seem to be coming from above, getting louder. People have found us. They must be from Sequest. Panic and terror wash through me.

And then I hear the words. "Oh, Henry, my answer is yes! Poor as I am, I am yours forever!" as something swoops down fast toward my head. I duck instinctively, but it moves past, whirring: a drone, lights flashing. It ignores me and dips in front of Dora. She skids to a halt and yowls.

"My dearest Margaret!" the drone gasps delightedly in an upper-class man's voice. "Then we shall be married today!"

Finally the penny drops. It's playing one of Dora's audiobooks. The drone begins to dart about in front of her, toying with her, just as that one did to Pedro the night he was killed.

"Harold must have sent it," Ingrid yells. "Come on, let's go."

We run again, leaving Dora behind, swiping ineffectually at the drone. When I glance back, I can't see her—the happy voices grow fainter, leading her away.

We slow our pace, breathing hard, taking shaky swigs of water from our bags.

"I don't get it," I say. "I thought Harold said he didn't have access to the drones anymore."

Ingrid shrugs. "I guess he figured out how to get back in the system."

I let it go but can't quell a gnawing sense of anxiety. Is there something important we're not seeing?

Maybe it's just the infrasound. Above me, there's only solid black emptiness, but I can feel those drones. I know they're up there somewhere, their malign sound waves pulsing through me, plucking at my nerves with their song of fear. Helpless, my body resonates along with it.

CHAPTER TWENTY-NINE

I've no idea how long we've been out here now, but my legs are telling me we've walked a thousand miles. The river is a constant static rush next to us in its deep gully, nearer than before, as the ground we're on slopes gently down. When I go to look over the edge, my breath catches. It flows so fast here, and it's so wide. Not ideal for someone who failed to attain a single swimming certificate. I even had to be rescued from the baby pool once after I slipped and knocked myself out.

The sky seems lighter. Dawn isn't far away. My heart starts hammering. We're still not out. They'll be searching for us soon.

And still we walk. My feet rise and clump down automatically. If I stop, I'm not sure they'll start again. I'm having a snack—beef jerky from my pocket—when Ingrid whispers, "Hey, there's a building over there."

As I peer through the dense tree trunks in the brightening light, I see it too. A stone structure.

We move forward cautiously. As we approach, the structure reveals more and more of itself. It's not a building: we've reached the wall.

With shaking hands, Elena flicks her flashlight on, and its light sweeps back and forth across the dirty gray stone, up and down. Harold wasn't kidding. There seems to be no end to it.

Ingrid marches across in front of me. "We need to get down to the river."

Reluctantly, I follow her, and we stand at the edge of the steep incline. The river is below us, not far, but it's steep enough that we can't just walk down it without slipping and rolling all the way into the river. Trees dot the slope, their roots bulging out at intervals, and Elena suggests we climb down backward holding on to them. We can't quite see through the vegetation to the point where the river goes through the wall yet.

Elena doesn't hesitate, clambering down, grabbing onto roots as she goes. It doesn't look too bad. Ingrid follows, keeping pace with Elena. I'm somewhat slower with my bad arm, which throbs at every step I take. My sneakers slither through the dirt, and I make my way down with a mixture of climbing and sliding chaotically. By the time I join them at the bottom, my knees are a scratched, bleeding mess.

We've made it. This is the place Harold said is the only way out.

But as I take it all in, my heart immediately sinks. The river is a rushing white noise, streaming past us up to the wall. I had imagined a tunnel with the river murmuring politely along the bottom of it, where we could doggy-paddle to the other side. I thought I might not even get my hair wet.

No such luck. The gap itself is invisible, because the water fills it entirely, churning and throwing itself up the stone in its hurry to leave. With the recent rains, the river is swollen and boisterous. The tunnel is more like a hole in a dam. We stand watching it for a few minutes, unwilling to be the first to point out the obvious. We're going to be smashed repeatedly against the wall and held under water. We're going to drown.

The others take their hoodies off and stash them under a bush. I follow suit, my fingers stiff and clumsy. "I'll go first," Elena says breezily. "I'm a pretty good swimmer." She pretends not to notice that I'm staring in horror. "Whoever goes next should leave it ten minutes to give me time to get through and find a spot to help them out of the river on the other side."

Ingrid turns to me. "Wanna go next? I don't mind."

I don't want to go at all.

"Okay," I hear myself say. "Is this a good time to remind you I can't swim? I feel like it's relevant."

"Hey," Ingrid puts a hand on my shoulder. "You can do this. Big breath before you go in, kick hard with the current. We don't know how thick the wall is. It might take a while to go through. Just don't panic, let the flow take you out."

My legs have nothing left. All I'm fit for is to lie down and sleep for a hundred years.

A faint buzzing. Without a word, we all take cover, ducking into the undergrowth. It grows gradually louder, then the drone bursts across the sky in a gap between the trees, soaring overhead and veering toward town.

"Delivery, I think," Elena says. "But we'd better go before the next one." She puts her backpack down, takes off her socks and shoes, then ties her hair up like she's going to do a couple laps in a pool. She's got the memory stick sealed up tight in a freezer bag, zipped in her shorts pocket.

"Be careful," I say, pointlessly.

Elena sits on the riverbank and dangles her legs in the water. "Whoo. That's some current," she says. She bites her lip, working out how to get in and what position to take. "Headfirst, I think. Dive down as far as I can, so I'm less likely to get bashed against the top of the gap."

"See you on the other side," Ingrid says quietly. I study her face. I don't see spite there anymore, almost as though it's been scrubbed away. It gives me a surge of hope. We're already beating them.

One second Elena's there, the next she's gone. The river snatches her away and throws her toward the wall. At first, I can see the red of her T-shirt under the surface, but as she reaches the gap it's subsumed into the froth and churn. I can't tell if she's gone through or not. The roar of the water fills my ears, my head. I lose track of time for a while, straining my eyes into the foam, and startle when Ingrid says, "Okay, that's ten minutes. Your turn. Remember, dive down. Big breath first."

My legs tremble and Ingrid has to help me sit down on the bank. The water is freezing. I've read that people can die just by jumping into really cold water—their body forgets how to breathe for long enough that they panic and drown. I'm already panicking.

"Ready?" Ingrid puts her hands on my upper back. "Want a push?"

"No!" I twist around and clutch at her in terror. Now the moment's come, I'm falling apart.

She lets me hold her for a few seconds and then gently unpeels my fingers.

"You can do this."

"I can't."

Her lips purse, and for a second I think she's going to get angry. But then she says, "Listen. When I saw what those stalker weirdos wrote about me in their report, something finally clicked into place. My grudge against you was only helping *them*. It was hurting you, and it was hurting me even more. As soon as I let go of it, they lost part of their control over me. They can't use it anymore, to predict me, or persuade me to do things. It was the first step in being free of them. Your fear is the same. If it stops you from leaving, it's working for them."

I nod, miserably, but don't move.

"Do you want me to go next instead?" she suggests. "Then there'll be two of us to pull you out."

The thought of being left here alone is unbearable. I don't think I'll ever actually do it if Ingrid isn't here making me. I finally shift toward the edge, bring my knees under me. "I'll go."

"Okay, good. Breathe slowly with me. In, out. In, out. Clear your mind. Arms over your head to shield it—oh, well, one arm, anyway. Just protect the bad one as best you can. And aim for the gap. The water will buffet you around a bit, but stay focused."

"A bit? It looks like a washing machine on spin cycle over there," I snap.

"So at least your clothes'll be clean for once," she bats back, and a tiny bit of tension leaves my chest in a laugh. "I'm going to count to three, then you're jumping in. Take a big breath when I say three, and I'll tap you on the back a second later. Not push, tap. You're going to do it yourself. Okay?"

I nod again.

"Ready? One. Two."

I realize I've forgotten to take my shoes off.

"Three."

The shock of the freezing water hits me like a ton of bricks. I meant to dive, but it was more of a bellyflop. The current gleefully grabs me and drags me under straightaway. All thoughts of aiming at the gap desert me. I have no control here, no power. The river throws me about, turning me over and over until I have no sense of which way I'm facing, or even which way is up. I'd closed my eyes, but when I open them all I can see is a mass of underwater murkiness, the odd rock looming out of the blackness. My bad arm scrapes against a sharp point and then my back slams into something solid, so hard all my breath escapes at once in a cloud of bubbles. I'm twisted and thrown again, and my face breaks the surface—a flash of daylight, the gray of the wall right next to me; that must be what I hit. I've missed the gap and have no idea where it is. I gulp in a lungful of air and try to get my bearings but I'm pulled under again, as though some huge creature has grabbed my feet and yanked me down. My arms are windmilling—I try to raise them to protect my head but the river pulls against them, whipping them away.

Without warning, everything goes black, and I think for a moment I've passed out. But a smooth curved surface rushes past my side and I realize I'm inside the gap. The wall forms a tunnel above me. Underneath me. Around me. Hope rises; I'll be through any second.

It goes on. And on.

My lungs are bursting. Every bump knocks air from me until there's no more to take. I can't see anything but blackness, and now I can't tell if I'm being swept forward through the tunnel or just tossed around in circles endlessly inside it. I open my eyes wide, desperately searching for a glimmer of light, a clue as to which way is out. There's nothing.

Everything in me is screaming for air. The pain in my chest is now the only thing I can feel. My hands and feet don't belong to me. I can't kick. My thoughts are slow, muddled. I'm an observer, watching myself from a distance, a tumbling object in the blackness of space, a microscopic dot in the vast universe. The pain starts to go away, replaced by a creeping sense of peace as I watch myself getting smaller and smaller. It's curiously beautiful.

And then something hauls me into light so bright it hurts every part of my body. I'm tossed onto a hard surface, and repeatedly hit. The peaceful feeling disappears and I spew out the river, convulsing over and over until I finally lie back, every molecule of my body in agony.

My eyes flicker, burned by the light. A face hovers over me. Elena comes into focus slowly. I lift my head, despite the pain. My top half is on a muddy bank, my bottom half still in shallow water, which is streaming over my ankles. I let my head slip back onto the mud.

"Well, that wasn't efficient or elegant, but you're here now," she tells me, relief making her jovial. Her hand strokes my hair.

I try to speak, to tell her what it was like floating free through space, and how beautiful it was, but what comes up is another load of water from my lungs.

CHAPTER THIRTY

We wait, Elena close to the wall, me farther up in case she misses Ingrid. We stand in the water near the bank, up to our knees, as far out as we can without losing our footing and being swept away. Unbelievably both my sneakers are still on my feet, though they've definitely lived a lifetime over the past twenty-four hours and must be ready for shoe heaven.

There's not much to see from here, apart from the wall—grassy slopes rise gently up either side of the river and it's impossible to see much of the surrounding countryside. I'm bursting with curiosity but keep alert for any sign of Ingrid.

Elena's getting worried, I can tell. It's fully light now—Saturday morning. We don't see any drones this side of the wall, which is just as well as there's very little cover.

My relief at being alive leaks away as the minutes pass. How long has it been since I came out? Feels like at least an hour. I glance at Elena, and she gives me a helpless look back. We both know we can't stay here forever.

"Sel, I think . . . " She trails off, unwilling to say it.

"Not yet."

She bites her lip, pained. "They'll know we're gone, now. They might have noticed Harold downloaded that stuff onto the memory stick. They might have forced him to talk. It won't be long before they figure out what we've done. Where we are."

"Just a few more minutes."

But I know she's right. If we stay here, we might as well not have bothered.

Then I see an auburn flash in the water. "There!" I yell, pointing. Ingrid's head is above the surface, and I can see her arms flailing, trying to move toward the side. I wade awkwardly through the water, splashing toward her, but Elena's there already. She makes a grab and catches hold of Ingrid's T-shirt as she passes, stretching it as the water tries to pull her away. I reach them and grasp Ingrid's arm, and together we help her out.

"What took you so long? We were really worried," I chide her, sounding exactly like Mom.

She catches her breath and waggles a finger at the sky. "Drone," she gasps. "The next one came and just hovered over the gap. Like it was guarding it. I hid."

Elena looks scared. "Do you think it spotted us going out?"

She shrugs. "Don't think so. It arrived just as I was going to go, ten minutes after you left, Sel. Maybe they just finally realized that was the only place we might get out. I gave up waiting in the end. Chucked a rock at it." She grins proudly. "Knocked it right out of the sky. It landed in bits, half of it in the river."

I high-five her, laughing.

"We'd better get moving right away, though," Elena points out. "If they notice they've lost a drone there, they'll figure it out."

We drink from the river, get to our feet, and start walking in the shadow of the wall, following it around, relief feeding new energy to our exhausted bodies. The air is too chilly to dry our soaked clothes.

Finally, the ground drops away to our left, giving us a spectacular view of a valley. We stop, shivering. Spread out below us, tucked into the undulating landscape, is a city. I've seen cities in pictures and on the news, of course, but it still takes my breath away. The reality is bigger than anything I've imagined. Red brick and glass and concrete. Tiny vehicles move steadily along the crisscrossing streets: so many of them. A flashing blue light weaves through the traffic, and a faint siren filters up toward us—a reminder that these streets are filled with danger and crime. Nevertheless, my heartbeat quickens in excitement and hope.

"Hastaville," Elena breathes.

An hour or so later, just before we reach the outskirts of the city, we pass a lone, pretty cottage with a line of washing hanging outside. It has a thatched roof and a trail of clematis climbing up over the front door. The curtains are closed.

"Hey, look." Ingrid points. A row of shoes sits under the shelter of the front porch. "Come on."

Adrenaline surges again—are we really going to steal them? Our first act now we're out of Tremorglade is to commit a crime? On the other hand, the soles are flapping off my sneakers. Besides, this must barely even qualify as a crime in Hastaville.

I follow Ingrid to the front porch, expecting someone to open a window any moment and shout at us. We grab what look like the closest sizes. I yank a pair of shorts and a T-shirt off the line, then glance up. I could swear I see a curtain twitch.

"We've got to go!" I hiss. We run, and don't stop until we're well out of sight of the cottage.

"That was *perfect*, practically a shopping mall," Elena giggles quietly, then rolls her eyes at my disapproving glare. "We're not going to get far with bare feet, are we? How do I look?" She smooths her hair.

The truth is, we're scruffy and dirty, but at least now less damp. In a city, hopefully we won't stand out too much. My nerves jangle as I think about what might lie ahead. We might have been in a prison, but it was safe. Sort of. Out here, things are different. This is a notoriously violent place. I'm conscious of my arm throbbing at my side, useless. Not that I'd be much good in a fight anyway.

One minute we're on grass, the next it's concrete. In between a couple of warehouses, up an alley, and we're in the city. The smell of exhaust fumes hits me right at the back of my throat. So many cars, revving and honking. As we walk along the busy streets, nobody gives us a second glance. I try not to catch anyone's eye, but can't help taking sneaky peeks. Hastavillians look...ordinary. No different from Tremorgladers. No one tries to rob us. No one pays much attention to us at all.

The houses are packed in more tightly than in Tremorglade, but what strikes me most is that there's not a single bit of neon bunting to be seen. In Tremorglade, the morning after Confinement, we roll and stack it all neatly, but we don't completely remove everything. It would take *ages* to set up from scratch every month. I observe as much to Elena.

"Maybe they don't need to pack it up." Elena talks quietly out of the side of her mouth. "Maybe they didn't even set up in the first place. Don't forget, not everywhere is as organized as Tremorglade. They might not even bother with the external security, just the cages. And in some places they're even slack about those. We're basically in the Wild West now."

As we walk along, it doesn't *seem* very Wild West. A guy selling fruit and vegetables, topping up his outside displays, gives us a brusque nod as we pass. A toddler pulls a frazzled dad toward a candy store. I gasp involuntarily when a woman hurries out of a shop just in front of me holding a knife, but then she stoops to cut the strings around some of the stems in a bucket of flowers. POPPY'S PETALS says the sign.

We've agreed to head straight to the library, as Harold said. Apparently there's free internet there, and we'll be able to upload the data from the memory stick. I'm not entirely comfortable still following Harold's instructions, but it does seem more sensible to use the library, rather than go around talking to strangers in a town with Hastaville's reputation.

All the same, I marvel at how relaxed and full of life the streets are—people walking along minding their own business, talking, laughing, window shopping. We're on the alert for armed gangs, but the farther we go, the less we worry. People don't seem hostile at all, even if they're not exactly friendly. Mainly they don't seem interested in us. There are definitely fewer bears and pirates than I feared. We don't appear to be in any danger at all.

And so I forget what Mom always says: "Don't judge on appearances."

They can be deceptive.

The library in Tremorglade is tiny, with an aging carpet and a musty smell. Hastaville's is something else. Long, wide steps lead up to a pillared facade, and gleaming glass doors rotate to let us in.

Inside, it's busy, with lone browsers at the rows of tall shelves or tapping away at computers dotted in little nooks here and there. We wander aimlessly for a few minutes, checking out the labels at the end of each shelf. Biography, History, Pets, Fiction A–Aq, Hobbies. I've never seen so many books all together. My fingers run along the spines, then I become aware that I'm being watched. A blond woman in a yellow dress stands just a bit farther down the shelves. When I spot her she quickly smiles, and goes back to browsing. Maybe she doesn't think I should be stroking the books. I fold my arms and move on with Elena and Ingrid.

"We need to find a free computer," Elena whispers.

"Wow," Ingrid says, and nudges us to look up.

I hadn't noticed the vaulted ceiling until now, but it's beautifully painted with woodland images, creatures peeking from between trees. I spot a Ripper or two here and there. We stand with faces upturned, gazing at it.

"Can I help you?" We spin around. A man in his early twenties is standing beside us, hands clasped behind his back. He laughs. "Sorry, didn't mean to startle you. Only you seem a bit lost."

Elena switches on a radiant smile. "We're from . . . uh . . . out of town, just came to do some, er, research. We were . . . admiring your ceiling."

"Ah yes." He smiles back. "Rather lovely, isn't it? If a little on the scary side. Are you looking for anything in particular for your research?"

"Just wondered if we could use one of your computers. We want to Seekle something."

"Excuse me?"

"You know," Ingrid says slightly impatiently. "Search for something on the internet."

"Are you a member?"

"Uh, no. Like I said, we're from out of town."

"Oh, yes. Well . . . I'm afraid the computers all have a passcode, generated from members' library cards. Sorry about that. Perhaps you can find a book to help you." He gives us an apologetic smile and walks off, only to be accosted at the other end of the stacks by the woman in yellow, who talks to him in a low voice.

"Great. How are we supposed to upload the stuff?" I ask.

Elena peers around after him. "Maybe we could wait for someone to leave, and hope they forget to log out?"

With no better idea, we station ourselves where we have a view of most of the consoles, trying not to look like we're waiting.

"Where did you say you were from?"

The man is back, having arrived behind us suddenly.

Without thinking, I say, "Tremorgl—" then try to swallow my own tongue.

The librarian's brows furrow slightly. "The wildlife sanctuary?"

I stare back at him.

Ingrid jumps in. "Sorry, my friend misheard you. We're from Kinettia." She smoothly names a city a hundred miles west. "He meant we came to see it. The . . . the wildlife sanctuary. We heard it was nearby and thought we'd include it on our visit. Is that . . . what's behind the big wall?"

"Indeed." The man nods. "Well, I'm sorry to have to disappoint you. They don't allow people in there. Rare species and all that, mustn't be disturbed. There's no way in—they just keep an eye on things with drones." He takes our astonished expressions as disappointment. "But there are plenty of other things to do and see around here. And . . . my usual boss is off sick today, but there's someone in from head office who just said I can let you use one of our computers. So follow me!" He beams, and strides off, leading us to the back of the huge room, where a door says STAFF ONLY.

It opens into a small office, where a computer sits on a neat desk. Another door leads out through the opposite wall, a discreet CCTV camera lodged above it.

"I'll find you some leaflets with local places of interest." He leaves us and shuts the door.

"*Wildlife sanctuary?*" Ingrid hisses. "What the—"

Elena sits at the computer and the screen flickers on. She takes out the memory stick, and feels along the edge of the attached keyboard for the slot, then pushes it in.

A few clicks later, a single folder pops up, labeled "Tremorglade."

"*Yes.* Right, let's see what we've got."

She clicks on it and we watch the screen.

I'm expecting files with photos, videos, charts, reports, all the things Harold promised would send shockwaves around the world when we upload them.

There's nothing.

"Did it get damaged in the water?" I ask, holding my breath.

Elena shakes her head. "It's fine. It's just . . . empty."

We stare a bit longer in the hope that something will appear, but it doesn't.

"Harold *is* useless with computers," I say. "Or at least . . . I think he is." The sense of missing something important, temporarily pushed away by the novelty of the city, returns with a vengeance.

"Let's just go online and see what we can find," I suggest. Elena's fingers patter over the keyboard, and up pops a blank white screen with an unfamiliar logo on it.

"What on earth is that? Where's Seekle?" she mutters.

Nevertheless, she types "Tremorglade" into the search box. The list of results come up but can't be right.

```
Tremorglade Wildlife Sanctuary


Tremorglade, an abandoned town at
the edge of the Hasta mountains,
is now a secure sanctuary for rare
animals in danger of extinction,
which also pose a risk to public
safety. The animals are allowed
to live out their natural lives,
observed at a distance by trained
scientists. The sanctuary is owned
and maintained by Sequest, Inc.
Visitors are not allowed due to
the inherent dangers posed by the
creatures, and there is no viewing
by the public.
```

She clicks on the Sequest hyperlink, but the only results for the company relate to Tremorglade. There's nothing about Wellness Centers at all. It's all this wildlife garbage.

"Animals?" Ingrid breathes. She starts to pace away from the computer, then circles back, fists clenched. *"Animals?"*

At that moment the librarian returns, and hands me a small stack of leaflets. "Here. There are a couple of really good museums and a number of interesting walks in the area. These explain the geography and history, and the local legends you were so fascinated by on our ceiling— the werewolves."

"The whatwolves?" I ask.

He laughs. "Oh, very funny. Not what, where!" He looks from me to Elena and Ingrid and back again. "Werewolves. You know—full moon, big claws, rahhh." He hooks his fingers in the air.

We blink at him. "You mean Rippers?" I say.

He hesitates, bewildered. "*Werewolves.* Ancient legends about people who would turn into fearsome wolf-like creatures once a month. I love those stories. We have a whole load of them if you fancy a read."

Stories?

There's an awkward few moments while his smile falters, not knowing how to respond to our complete failure to understand.

"Uh, anyway, did you find what you were searching for?" he asks, checking his watch.

"Need a tiny bit longer," Elena tells him in a strangled voice. "If you don't mind." As he turns to go, she adds, "The . . . wildlife sanctuary. Didn't it used to be a town just a few years ago?"

He nods. "Oh, it was an isolated community once. But

they moved the last few people out and built the wall in order to accommodate the animals, ooh, about . . . let me think." He taps his chin. "About twenty-five years ago. Before I was born, anyway. It's been there all my life."

The door clicks gently closed after him.

CHAPTER THIRTY-ONE

I'm not sure that I'm breathing. We're short of sleep—is it possible I'm dreaming?

An absurd idea whispers into my brain. I lean over Elena and type into the search box:

Corpus pilori

My whole body is tingling. I think I'm beginning to see the shape of the truth. A truth, at least. But it's too big for me to name. My mouth is dry. The others are both frowning at the screen. It tells us there are no results and asks if we meant *"Helicobacter pylori"* instead, a stomach bacterium that causes ulcers.

All of a sudden, I know why the streets of Hastaville are so tidy the morning after a Confinement.

"There are no Rippers," I say, woodenly. "No Confinement."

"What are you talking about?" Ingrid sounds half angry, half scared. "Of course there are."

"Not out here."

"Sel, we've come outside a wall, not gone through a sci-fi portal." She sounds irritated, but I can hear doubt underneath.

"No, no." I'm struggling to explain. "We picked up a few clues, but we didn't follow through. The world is . . . it's nothing like we've been told it's become since the Disruption. You saw Hastaville. Where're all the Frozen Fever gangs? The acid rain? It's . . . nice. What Sequest has done . . . it's not just a few fake webpages, or apps, or planting ads for electronic cage locks . . . It's *everything*. And not only for three years. We assumed that on the basis of a couple of little things, and never questioned the timing after that. But you heard him. Tremorglade has been enclosed since our parents' time. Ever since the Disruption. In fact . . . I'm not sure there ever was a Disruption. At least, not as we know it. The world just carried on as before. It's Tremorglade that changed."

"That's not possible." Ingrid's statement sounds more like a plea. "They'd have to . . . "

"Make a whole separate internet for us," Elena says, slowly. "The news. Movies. Songs, even. A whole fake environment. Just for our parents, then for us. A whole, vast operation to convince us that Rippers are everywhere."

"But they aren't," I add. "The experiment isn't the infrasound. That's just a tiny part." I slap my hand to my forehead. "*That's* what Pedro meant when he said there was something wrong with the internet. I think he was on the verge of figuring it out. That's why they killed him."

Ingrid reaches out to the wall to steady herself.

I can see it all now. As though the pieces of my life have been put together wrong, and they've just rearranged themselves into the true picture. It's so surreal I almost want to laugh.

"Guys." Ingrid is staring at the door on the other side of the room. "That camera over the door just swiveled."

We regard it warily, but it doesn't move again.

Elena talks out of the side of her mouth, quietly. "Did you see that woman out there in the yellow dress? I think she told the librarian to bring us in here."

Ingrid nods. "He said his normal boss isn't in, that someone's here from the library head office instead." She glances to the door. "Guys. I think he's wrong about where she's from."

I whisper. "And . . . back at the cottage where we got those clean clothes. I could have sworn we were seen. But no one came after us."

It's as though all those clothes and shoes were left there for us. We were so grateful for them at the time that it didn't occur to us to think it was strange. A little too easy.

And now we're here, it's hard to avoid the idea we were expected.

We all realize at the same moment, but it's Elena who whispers it.

"This is a trap."

We were *sent* here, to the library.

By Harold.

"We should go." I press on the door handle, but even before I try it, I know it won't budge. Rattling doesn't achieve anything. Elena tries the door on the other side of the room, with the same result.

A few minutes of impotent panic follow, as we each attack the door handles with increasing desperation.

Finally, there's a click and the door to the library opens. Our guy is back, with a friendly smile. "Hi! Me again. I've been told to take you to—"

Ingrid kicks him in the groin and he drops to his knees with a sound like a slow tire puncture. "You're not taking us anywhere."

Elena drags me staggering through the door behind her, trying to avoid stepping on the curled-up librarian. We half-walk, half-run through the library, our stolen shoes slapping loudly on the shiny floor. Heads turn as we weave around surprised browsers until we reach the main aisle, in sight of the door. A man pushing a trolley full of books stops right in our path. "Can I help—" Ingrid gives the trolley an almighty shove and it topples over, spilling its contents across the aisle.

"Hey!"

Elena drops my hand and leaps over the trolley. I follow with somewhat more difficulty, skidding as my leading foot crushes the spine of a huge tome lying open upside down, losing my balance, arms windmilling and catching the open-mouthed man hard under his chin.

"Sorry!" I yell.

We're outside, blinking in the sun. Ingrid doesn't hesitate, making for the other side of the road, where an alley leads between a butcher's shop and a nail salon. There's a deafening honk and a screech of brakes as a van jerks to a halt a hair's breadth from me. For a moment I am very still, the adrenaline of the near-miss sending shockwaves down my body. It's so close I can feel the heat from its engine.

A shout from behind. The woman in the yellow dress is standing on the library steps, yelling and pointing at us. People in the street have stopped to stare—a woman has dropped her groceries, a little dog is barking frantically at the end of its leash. Another shout: Elena. My legs spring back into action and I dive down the alley in time to see Ingrid round the corner out of sight at the end, Elena close behind her.

Running footsteps behind me, more shouting. My

legs are slow, stiff, protesting at the sudden speed after so much abuse. Hobbling, I finally round the corner after the girls, and am brought to a halt.

I'm in another narrow alley. Ingrid and Elena are right in front of me, but they've also stopped running. Ahead of them are four figures in white hazmat suits, blocking the way. Back the way we came, more hazmats are jogging awkwardly toward us. Behind them, a glimpse of a yellow dress. A cross voice.

"Oh, for goodness' sake, who authorized the protective clothing? Look what a public spectacle you're causing. They're children. They're not infectious." A sigh. "Get on with it."

"Please," says one of the hazmats in front of us, approaching slowly. "We aren't going to hurt you."

His words are slightly undermined by the enormous needle he's holding in his white-gloved hand.

"You keep that away from us," warns Ingrid. "I've got a black belt in tae kwon do."

"Yes," says one of the others from behind the blank helmet. "We know."

That's when the net comes down.

CHAPTER THIRTY-TWO

I wake up in my own bed.

Sitting up with a gasp, my heart pounding, half relieved that I seem to have dreamed it, and half terrified because I'm sure I didn't. There's a nauseating sense of wrongness, but when I look around, I see nothing out of place.

My posters are on the walls, my computer in its usual place on the desk. Mom's tidied up, though. A lot. All my drawers are shut properly, for once, with no stray socks sticking half out. The curtains are closed, but the light is on. The familiar blue star lamp is on my bedside table, though my phone isn't next to it.

Everything is as it should be, except it's not.

My hands slide over my duvet—the zigzag pattern I've had for years—and it's . . . smoother, silkier than it normally feels. I touch my hands to my face in case they're numb, but they feel normal—warm, a little dry.

When I pull back the duvet, I'm wearing my favorite pajamas. The ones that used to belong to Pedro before he grew out of them. Except . . . the hole in the fabric, next to the seam at the elbow, is gone. I check the other arm in case I'm remembering wrong, but that, too, is perfect. The design is clearer, brighter somehow, like it's gone back in time to before its first wash. My arm feels a lot better and the swelling is barely visible now, just a dull ache reminding me of that close call with the mayor's toilet.

I slide my feet onto the carpet, and that, too, is softer. My toes sink in just a little farther than usual as I walk across the room. My sneakers, not a scuff in sight, are neatly placed on a chair. I touch the desk, squeak my finger along the surface. Everything is *really* clean. I feel out of sync. I've no idea what time it is. The curtains are thick, and I can't even tell if it's daylight. I grasp both sides and pull them apart, then stagger back in shock.

Instead of the road below, the front gardens and Elena's house opposite, there's just more of my bedroom wall. I touch it. It's definitely there. My fingers pick up the trace of a line, a slight indentation, and follow it along. There's a gentle hiss and the wall opens up.

My body tenses, half expecting a row of machine guns to be revealed, or a noxious, fatal gas to puff into my face. But then I realize it's much worse than that.

A black screen flickers on.

There's the Sequest logo, and the jingle from . . . oh, no. It's the *Your Changing Body* video.

I run to the door. It's locked. I hammer my fists on it. "Let me out! Let me out!"

But then there's a voice from the TV, and I look back. It's not the *Your Changing Body* presenter; it's someone else. I struggle to remember where I've seen her before, then it hits me. It's the woman from the library, the one in the yellow dress. Except now she's wearing a lab coat. That doesn't mean she's a scientist, of course. Actors can stick on a lab coat when they're pretending to be one. Usually they wear glasses as well, like being shortsighted is what makes you interested in physics and chemistry. I shuffle warily back toward the screen and watch.

"Hi!" the woman says. "I'm Dr. Smith, and I'm the Deputy Director of Operations here at Sequest. Ansel, Elena, and Ingrid, I want to welcome you here. I hope you feel rested after the past few days of sleep."

I've been asleep for *days*? A flash of memory—the needle going in my arm. Instinctively, I cover the place with my hand.

So my friends are somewhere around here too. The thought comforts me, even as I shift inside my weirdly silky pajamas.

"This video is just a little orientation to help you find your bearings after what must have been a strange and difficult time."

After? It still is.

"No doubt you will have a lot of questions. I have answers for you. But first I'd like to draw your attention to the small device at the back of your neck."

My hand flies to the spot. There's a tiny *something* stuck to the skin, like a rectangular pimple.

"You may hear some things that upset you over the next few hours. However, it is important that you remain calm. Violence against any of our staff will not be tolerated. That device on your neck may be activated remotely at any time to render you unconscious. I have a controller for it, and so do some of my security staff." She pats the pocket of her lab coat to demonstrate how close to hand it is.

I do not like where this is going. At all.

My eye is drawn to my wardrobe, where I keep my X50. I fling open the doors. Let's see how far I can get.

But of course it's not in there. Just a load of weirdly pristine versions of my clothes, on *hangers* no less. That and the absence of screwed-up laundry under the bed are the essentials that show they really haven't nailed my room as well as they think. The fact gives me a bizarre flash of hope.

I move reluctantly back to the screen as Dr. Smith continues.

"Hopefully the use of this device won't be necessary. We expect to have a long and mutually acceptable partnership with all three of you, and once the basics have been explained to you, I feel certain you will come to the conclusion that cooperation is in your best interests. With that in mind . . . let's meet in person."

The screen goes blank and a swish behind me tells me the door has opened. Warily, I turn. Standing there is the same woman, this time for real. She looks identical to her video image, except there's a long red scratch across her cheek.

She smiles. "Good morning, Sel. I hope my video didn't scare you. It's just a precaution, to avoid misunderstandings."

"Scare me? No, you come across as totally normal and not like a psychopath at all."

If she registers my sarcasm, she doesn't show it. She steps back and beckons me out into a curved, gleaming white corridor. It's empty, other than the two of us, and has a few more doors along it. I wonder if Elena and Ingrid are behind any of them.

"Put your shoes on, Sel, and come with me. You may ask questions as we go."

She begins to walk off, clearly expecting me to follow. I can't think of a good alternative, so I shove my unworn sneakers onto my feet and go after her.

"What is this place?"

She tuts quietly, as though annoyed. "This was covered in the video. You're at Sequest HQ."

I tut right back at her. "Yeah, but what *is* Sequest? Like, really? Harold said it was a health research company. He was lying, though, wasn't he?"

Her hair swings slightly as we round a curve in the corridor, revealing more corridor ahead. Her shoes echo on the floor.

"We are a technical services company," she says.

"What does that even mean? What services?"

"Anything. Everything. We conduct research on whatever is useful to our clients."

"What clients?"

"Various governments around the world. Other, less official entities too, if they can afford us. We share our findings exclusively with our funding partners, and they use the information however they wish—for their defense or to improve the lives of their own citizens. We do not share our methods with them. And they do not ask."

It takes me a few seconds to figure out what she's talking about, and then it clicks. All that stuff Harold said about Sequest trying to make the world a better place . . . of course it was all lies. It's about the money. Finding a cure for the virus was never their priority. "Defense? You make weapons?"

She tuts again. "Please listen more attentively. We trade in *information*. Scientific findings. Our clients choose what to do with the data we sell them." She pauses. "But yes, many of them are looking to improve their defense capabilities, as I said. Making the world a better place takes many forms. Some of it needs to be healed. Some of it needs to be destroyed. There's no point being naïve about it."

"Funny how it's the ones with the most money who get to decide which is which."

She ignores that. "Up until now, you've been part of the most ambitious scientific endeavor ever undertaken, though most of the world doesn't know it exists, and believes Tremorglade is a wildlife reserve."

My mind is racing. "So . . . you made Rippers? *Corpus pilori* is yours?"

"We didn't make the virus. We found it, dormant, in a fossil and reactivated it in Tremorglade, after sealing off the community and fabricating the Disruption. As for Rippers being a weapon, obviously they have great potential. But currently *corpus pilori* is too infectious for us to use in the outside world. No point having a weapon that hurts us all indiscriminately. We're still looking for ways to harness the phenomenon without the infectivity. Also," here she sighs with what sounds like long-held frustration, "we need the Turned to be aggressive without having to douse them with infrasound the whole time. It's impractical."

I smirk behind her back. "So it's not going well. Shame. Bet your clients aren't happy they've been paying for a dud."

She stops and turns so suddenly I almost walk into her, her expression venomous. Wow, that really touched a nerve.

"Oh, it's going *fine*, Sel. Plenty of our other experiments in Tremorglade have yielded excellent results. Most particularly the psychological ones—an entire population of children caging their parents. And manipulating the hostility between you and Ingrid was a spectacular success. Easier than we imagined. Our clients will put that data to good use among their own populations. And of course, the operation to persuade you to escape without revealing your plans and disturbing the other subjects in Tremorglade . . . well, up until the small screwup right at the end where you ran from the library . . . you were *impeccably* manipulated. Don't you think? I'd call that a win."

My face grows hot, while a cold hatred creeps up my spine at the same time. She notices my humiliation, and a hard little smile appears. "You know, we could have picked you up the moment you washed up on the riverbank by the wall. It was my idea to let you keep going. I felt it was too good an opportunity to miss: tracking your reactions and responses, controlling your slow realization of the truth in the library, reeling you in. We never stop our research, Sel. We're very good at what we do." Her eyes search my face, though I can't tell what she's hoping to find.

My throat feels tight. My fists clench. I can feel it again—the part of me I never knew was there, the part that wants to hurt, to punish, to go far beyond justice, to be savage. But I have a feeling she'd activate that thing on my neck to drop me before I even got close.

She's still watching me intently, her pupils dilating in excitement. "That's it, Sel. I can see it in you. The aggression we need. It's there. I always knew it was. We can nurture it, help you access it when you Turn. You could be so much more. It's why we brought you here. Where we can do more bespoke research, with your help."

I growl through clenched teeth. "As if we'd help after what you've done. Dream on."

She merely continues around the next bend and stops at a door.

"Perhaps. You'll be happy to see your friends, I expect." Her fingers hover over a panel next to the door. "Just a little reminder: if any of you act inappropriately, you'll be unconscious before you can take your next breath."

The door swishes open to reveal a small, square room with another door on the other side. It's empty, except for my friends.

Ingrid is kneeling with her arm around Elena, slumped against the wall. Elena looks woozy and confused, but when she sees me, there's recognition in her eyes. I want to run over to them but am wary of making any sudden movements.

"What did you do to Elena?" I demand.

"Exactly what I said would happen if her behavior was not acceptable," Dr. Smith says, her finger going instinctively to the welt on her cheek. It's still bleeding a little. Elena's handiwork, I'm guessing. "She reacted inappropriately when I mentioned her brother. She'll be fine, unless she does anything like that again."

Ingrid glares over at Dr. Smith, then says to me, "She told Elena they'd used Pedro to help us figure things out, but that they were always going to kill him rather than let him leave."

Dr. Smith sighs. "Pedro was infectious. *Of course* he couldn't leave. Now, get up, Elena. I have more to show you all, so that we can work together as soon as possible."

Ingrid and I help Elena stand up, wobbling, while I process the obvious point: no one infectious has ever been allowed to leave. So Dr. Adebayo wasn't transferred three years ago. The drone that took her . . . I'm guessing it never made it over the wall. She was taken for some transgression we'll never know; another Sequest victim. I bet there are a lot more.

The far door opens onto a vast, hangar-like room. We enter and stand on a metal deck overlooking a huge area full of desks and banks of computers, a constant hum of conversation and electronics. There are people sitting and typing, others walking between the desks holding papers, and a few standing around apparently chatting. A couple of them look up to the deck and nudge each other, and gradually an uneasy silence falls as they all clock us.

Dr. Smith claps her hands, once. "Back to work, everyone." Slowly, warily, they begin to move again, though the murmur of voices is distinctly quieter than it was when we first walked in. She brings her attention back to us. "This is our center of operations for Tremorglade. Its beating heart, if you like." She begins to clack carefully down a set of winding metal stairs to the main floor, motioning us to follow.

"This room contains some of the technology we used to gradually isolate Tremorglade, over a period of years, until it was entirely enclosed without anyone realizing it. Your experience is controlled from here." She pauses, gesturing at the banks of computers.

"Our experience? What do you mean?" Despite the fact that it feels like cooperating with her, I can't help but ask. I need to understand.

She's happy to oblige. "Every time you buy something online, you're buying it from us. Every time your rather dim Sergeant Hale gets a message from . . . say, Forensics in Hastaville—it's us. Your school board—us. Your father's job interviews, Elena—us. When your mayor believes he's talking to government ministers—us." She glances around to make sure we're getting it. "Every Tremorglader's interaction with the outside world is in fact an interaction with Sequest HQ. The only resident who knows the truth is the man who volunteered to live there right from the start—our director, Harold Poulter."

"Harold is your *director*?" My jaw drops open. That snake...

She nods. "Sequest's founder. When his bloodwork showed that he was immune to the virus, he was determined to be our man on the ground rather than leave it to a subordinate."

"So Mayor Warren, Sergeant Hale, Dr. Travis ... *they* don't work for you?"

A pitying smile. "Everyone works for Sequest, Sel. They just don't know it."

"But Warren killed Pedro for you! How did you make him do that?"

Dr. Smith doesn't respond, just flicks a glance back over her shoulder at Elena, who mutters to me, "He didn't do it."

She stumbles slightly and Ingrid slips an arm through hers, presses it close, then explains for her. "*They* sent Pedro that text pretending to be from Warren, then made sure we found it," she says. "To keep us paranoid."

I'm overwhelmed with confusion. Then it hits me. There's only one person who could have injured Pedro and shoved him into that shed, right next to Shady Oaks. There's only one person in Tremorglade who *would* have.

I feel sick. I think of Harold's hands dealing cards for us, stroking Eddie. The same hands that brought a blunt object down on Pedro's head, that set up the trap over the river, that led us to Pedro's "lost" phone in the bushes. With a little help from his friends right here.

As we reach the bottom of the stairs, I deliberately push Harold from my mind, like throwing out something rotten. We might be trapped, but we're in the one place where we have a chance of disrupting these scumbags' plans, whatever they are.

Clearly Dr. Smith wants us to know this stuff, but I can't tell why, or where she's going with it.

And it's not just us I'm worried about. It's the people back home. Dr. Smith talked about getting us out without disturbing the other participants. That must mean they plan to keep them alive, right? But Harold said they were all going to be killed.

Harold lied about a million things.

That had better be one of them.

CHAPTER THIRTY-THREE

We reach the main floor and follow Dr. Smith as she walks briskly between the consoles. I notice people leave a space around us, like they don't want to get too close. As I pass one desk there's a logo on the screen I recognize: Righteous Rippers.

I look over to read what the woman sitting there is typing. She's just finished adding an advert for a brand of smoothie to a video of a Ripper being pelted with fruit. As I lean closer, my arm touches her shoulder and she flinches and screams, lurching away from her desk so abruptly her chair almost topples over.

Dr. Smith tuts. "Oh for goodness' sake, Arya. How many times do I have to tell you? You're in no danger. They've got at least a couple of months to go before they start being infectious. You've all seen their blood test results—clear as clear can be."

Arya nods apologetically, but she still leans away.

"The guy in the library talked about werewolves. Is that what we are?"

Dr. Smith makes a disgusted face. "We don't use that word here, and we made sure your parents didn't either. It's deeply inappropriate. We are not in the business of fairy tales."

We walk around a corner to find row upon row of cubicles. In each one, a person is tapping away at a keyboard—mostly they seem to be in their twenties. Some of them sip coffee, some of them are typing intently, others sit slumped in a pose my mom calls "noodling about." I recognize the FIN app on the screen. They're chatting.

"This is our FIN area. It's shift work. We have a lot of Tremorgladers who want to chat, so we try to always have plenty of colleagues available. We often put our new interns to work here first," she adds, resting a hand lightly on the closest man's shoulder. "Which is why occasionally mistakes are made. Such as failing to check the file for the correct name for a dog . . ." He doesn't look at us but his ears go bright red.

I can't get over how ordinary the team looks. Like normal office workers.

"You people are sick," I say, half to myself, then I repeat it louder. One or two of them half turn, but don't catch my eye.

"How can you be involved with this?" Ingrid shouts. She grasps a guy by his collar.

"We take care of you," he says, like he's repeating a catchphrase, eyes swiveling around in terror, hoping for rescue. One of the security guards moves toward them, and Ingrid lets go. The guy drops back into his seat, breathing heavily.

Elena grabs the nearest chair and tries to turn it toward her, but the woman in it scrambles up and backs off. "What's wrong with you all? We're not animals!"

Dr. Smith tips her head to one side. "Except . . . you sort of are, aren't you? You're not fully human beings, anyway. You are . . . something else. The dormant virus we found in that fossil was millions of years old. At some point, it seems the Earth may have been full of . . . well, creatures like you. But they were wiped out. Like the dinosaurs. You're relics from an ancient time. Utterly fascinating."

She turns to me and suddenly grasps my hands, her eyes blazing with intensity. "We still have so much to learn about you, and we want to do that here as well as in Tremorglade. Now that you understand our aims, you can cooperate with the experiments. We'll make faster progress."

I pull my hands from hers and shove her away from me; she takes a stumbling step back. At the corner of my vision, the security guard comes closer, drawing what I guess is a controller from his belt pouch. My eyes dart to

Dr. Smith's pocket, but she makes no move to take out her own, and motions him to hold off.

I swallow. "What are you going to do with us?"

"The three of you will be kept here at Sequest, in your *very* comfortable rooms. Even when you begin to Turn in a few months, it won't be a problem. Your rooms are hermetically sealed, and you can be fed remotely, via a hatch in the wardrobe. I do understand you might miss social contact. But once you're infectious, our workers will still come in from time to time in hazmat suits to satisfy your need for conversation, and our need for closer study. Your every requirement will be met, and you can play as much Happy Trappers as you like. We'll study you. All being well, you can even be allowed some contact with selected people back in Tremorglade. Scripted, of course."

"That's it?" Ingrid asks, incredulously. "That's your offer? To keep us in cells, experiment on us, involve us in torturing our families and friends, and in return we can play your stupid game?"

Elena spits. "Get stuffed."

Dr. Smith nods and looks at her feet for a moment, as if she was expecting this. "Then, without your cooperation, I'm afraid the entire Tremorglade experiment will need to be terminated."

"Good!" I say. And then it dawns on me what she means. "Oh. No."

"We'll bring Harold out first, of course. Then Tremorglade and its contents will be disposed of in a humane manner. One of our drones will drop a bioelectrodynamic bomb. On impact in central Tremorglade it will stop the heart of everyone within a ten-mile radius."

My body feels cold, limbs stuck to the floor. Faces rush through my mind. My mom, Elena's dad, Ms. Boateng, Mika, Amy, and Bernice. Even Dr. Travis doesn't deserve that.

"The cleared area will then be treated with antivirals before being opened up."

"I thought you said it was going well," I say weakly. "Why would you end it?"

Her lips purse a little before she replies, and I realize that for the first time, she's uncomfortable. There's something she doesn't want to admit. "Our clients are demanding a speedier return on their investment. If we don't make faster progress, they'll take their money out. With you here, cooperating, we can take some areas of study to the next level. Then Tremorglade will keep its funding."

So that's what this is about. Her job is under threat. Her and Harold's precious project.

"You're lying." Ingrid's voice is low. "It's what you do. Even if we decided to cooperate, you could kill them all anyway, and we'd never know."

Dr. Smith considers this. "We could. You'd have to trust us. That would be an interesting psychological experiment, wouldn't it?"

A flash in the corner of my eye. Ingrid's foot connects with Dr. Smith's jaw, sending her pirouetting into one of the terminals, which crashes to the floor.

Nobody moves for a few moments. Ingrid stands there panting, looking ready to take on the entire room like she's at the tae kwon do championships. Dr. Smith slowly clambers up, touching the back of her wrist to her mouth. There's blood. On the desk, a couple of what I think are her teeth. Her shaking hand delves into her lab-coat pocket, digging around for the controller to zap Ingrid.

"Looking for this?" Elena asks, holding it up. Her eyes are bright with fury, and I feel something ignite inside me. We can't win this. But we can go down fighting.

Dr. Smith clutches her jaw and regards us with loathing. "I'll let you have that childish outburst for free. And a chance to reconsider your attitude. But my patience is finite. Quinn, call first-floor security to take them to their rooms." She clicks her fingers at the guard hovering nearby.

Just then, a thin man in a lab coat sidles up from behind us and whispers in Dr. Smith's ear. His face is pale and sweating. Her eyes narrow and a frown cracks her brow. "I thought you said they had been dealt with."

The sweating man licks his lips. "Yes, but . . . it seems

there were others we missed." He glances at me. "His mother, for one. She didn't buy the idea that Dora ate the kids. And she found some of our reports under the boy's mattress. She's gone around causing trouble."

My ears prick up. "Mom? What about my mom?" It's been a while since I went missing. I don't even want to think about what she's been through.

The man ignores me and keeps talking to Dr. Smith. "The gossip they started went further than we anticipated. It seems to have precipitated some sort of crisis in Tremorglade. And . . . " He swallows. "We've picked up some chatter locally, about real-life werewolves being hidden behind the wall."

"*Locally*? People are talking here in Hastaville?"

He nods, scared.

"That's not possible. These three were monitored the entire time. They can't possibly have gotten word out here." Dr. Smith looks furious. She snaps back around to glare at the three of us, as though expecting us to be sorry about it. "I don't know how you did this. But if it's true, their blood will be on your hands. Not mine."

Judging by Ingrid's and Elena's faces, they have no more idea than I do about how we did it, either. There's a buzz and a hiss as the nearest door slides open and someone in a full hazmat suit, complete with helmet, bundles through clumsily, knocking into a desk and causing a pile of papers to scatter to the floor.

"Ah, here's your escort back to your rooms. Just as well. I need to sort this mess out." Then she does a double take, noticing what the guard is wearing, and I can practically see the last strand of her temper break. "How many times must I say this, people?" She raises her voice to address the entire room. "Look at me—I'm no more Immutable than any of you, but you don't see me shying away, do you?" Turning back to the new arrival, she puts her hands on her hips. "Take off that suit right now before you break something. Did *nobody* read my email? Hazmat suits are to be worn in isolation areas only. For the last time: these children are *not infectious.*"

The hapless guard bows in apology, unclips the helmet, and uses both hands to take it off.

Time stops. I feel my heart stutter and then soar out of my body.

"*They're* not. But what about me?"

Pedro runs his fingers through his sweaty bangs, grins, and drops the helmet. It rolls across the floor and comes to a halt just by Dr. Smith's shiny shoes.

I scream in delight and rush to hug him. Elena and Ingrid are close behind. He laughs as we all pile on.

There's another scream, louder than mine. It goes on and on.

From somewhere behind us comes another scream, and another, spreading like ripples through the room. The scrape of chairs being pulled back, feet running.

From Pedro's clunky embrace, somewhere in his armpit, I squeeze my face around to look back at Dr. Smith.

I'm not sure exactly how I'd describe the emotions that seem to be taking her over. But if she could study her own feelings right now, she'd probably call them "fascinating." Her mouth is open wide, lip bloody and already puffing up from Ingrid's kick, but I can't tell if any sound is coming out. It merges with the chaos.

CHAPTER THIRTY-FOUR

Dr. Smith can't seem to get a grip. It's the first time I've watched someone scream themselves not only hoarse but literally blue in the face. When Ingrid approaches her to try to calm her down, touching her arm, she starts hissing, cursing, and writhing, and backs off into the far corner of the room, where she sinks to the floor and continues to wail. We leave her to it for the time being.

"Get those things off their necks," Pedro demands of a couple of workers hanging around nearby. Oddly, they jump to it, looking like they're in total shock. I guess they're used to following orders, and they're certainly not getting any more from Dr. Smith.

As they apply various numbing chemicals and loosen the devices on our necks, we listen to Pedro's story.

He's been out for two months—an anonymous stranger found long after dawn, wandering naked and seriously injured, washed up on the riverbank, taken to the hospital to recover from his wounds. He couldn't get anyone to listen to his wild stories, at first. He thought they were messing with him when they said they'd never heard of Rippers. They thought he'd lost his mind.

Very quickly it became clear that to free Tremorglade, he had to find a way into the heart of Sequest. He made it his mission to get hired and, being the charmer that he is, soon enough he was taken on as security, wearing a fake mustache and beard to avoid detection. It's amazing how a bit of facial hair could trick a load of people who are supposedly experts in a virus that causes it to sprout all over the body. He barricaded himself inside an abandoned warehouse so that he could safely Turn without causing panic and risking capture or being shot. During the daytime, he's been observing the workings at Sequest HQ, looking for a chance to sabotage the system, and nights have been spent on the internet, posting anonymously on crank sites, sharing the truth about Tremorglade.

Of course, rumors aren't the only thing he's been spreading. That crafty virus will already have made its way silently across the entire city, probably much farther. Next full moon, a lot of people are going to get hairy for the first time.

It's not Pedro's fault. By the time he realized, it was already far too late. You don't need to *try* to spread *corpus pilori*.

Dr. Smith knew what it meant, the moment she recognized Pedro. I'm totally dazed—a few minutes ago we were doomed to spend eternity locked in a cell, and now everyone else is staring down their inevitable future as Rippers. Elena, Ingrid, and I can barely take our eyes off Pedro, for fear he might disappear again. But he looks more solid than he's ever been—strong and defiant.

A few of the staff are still hanging around, looking scared. A couple are sitting at their desks, sobbing quietly. One is positioning and repositioning a photo on Righteous Rippers, over and over again. Security guards tried to stop people leaving at first, to quarantine the room, but got trampled in the rush. It's an instinctive thing, I suppose. It will probably take a while for them to grasp that it's pointless. Leave, don't leave—it's all the same. *Corpus pilori* is already inside them.

Elena, Pedro, and Ingrid grill one of the more cooperative senior staff about how we can keep Tremorglade's essential functions going until we can get it opened up. With no one running Sequest's systems, there will be no deliveries in, and everything will shut down. If we don't get control shortly, they'll run out of medicine, food, crucial supplies. It's going to take a while to break our town open.

As they talk, my eye falls on something happening at the other side of the room. Dr. Smith is no longer wailing.

She's busy at a console. Something about the intent way she's typing makes me uneasy.

As I approach, she pushes back her chair.

"What's that?"

The smile is back, though it's a hard, spiteful one. "You've destroyed our world. It's only fair to repay the compliment. Harold will understand. The captain goes down with his ship."

The screen in front of Dr. Smith shows a bunch of code that I don't understand. But from her look of triumph, I already know what she's done.

Pedro shuts Dr. Smith in my fake bedroom, to stop her interfering any further. In the end, when she knew she'd lost, and she had the chance to finally do the right thing, she picked revenge instead. Maybe she spent so much time trying to observe the effects of hatred and find ways to weaponize it, it was too tempting to put it into practice.

Apparently, the launch is automatic now. The drone is small—only about the size of a football, with its fatal load hidden inside—and will take just over an hour to reach its target, at which point it will run out of fuel, and fall to the ground, detonating on impact. Everyone going about their business will just drop dead. The town silent.

Pedro is sweating as he thumps the console in frustration. "Without Dr. Smith's personal passcode, it can't be brought back. We're locked out of its controls."

Elena is crying. "There must be something we can do."

He's racking his brains, we all are, but it seems hopeless. Then Ingrid grabs one of the staffers nearby, the one who's still repositioning photos on Righteous Rippers.

"Hey, you have drones, right? Can we access those?"

The woman blinks at her. "Y-yes. Top floor. They take off from the roof."

Ingrid turns to Pedro. "Right. So we send their fastest one after it, intercept it."

But he shakes his head. "No. If we knock it out of the sky, it still goes off as soon as it hits the ground."

Then I remember Dr. Adebayo. "Hey," I ask the woman. "You have drones that can take a passenger, right?"

She nods. "Two-person reconnaissance copters. We normally use them for trips around the walls."

"And they're fast? Faster than that . . . bomb drone? We could catch it?"

"I . . . I don't know about that. It's not my area." She shrugs, turning back to Righteous Rippers as though she's got important videos to be faking, rather than saving thousands of lives. She's on autopilot, her brain taking a back seat.

"Pedro," I say, "you can control it from here, right? I'll be inside. What if you fly it right up next to the drone, and I'll grab it out of the sky?"

He makes a *What?* face but it fades as he gets thinking. "Actually . . . it might be possible."

"I'll go as well," Elena declares, and starts dragging me toward the lifts.

"No, sis," Pedro says. "I can't keep an eye on everything at the same time—the drone path and the copter controls. I need you here."

Ingrid is next to me like a shot. "I'll come."

For a moment I think Elena's going to argue. We don't have time. The drone's been gone ten minutes—we can all see its blob moving on the screen, heading slowly but steadily on its murderous course. But then she nods. "Do it."

Ingrid and I have to shout to be heard over the propellers. The sliding doors are open on both sides, and the wind rushes through, buffeting our hair, whipping the words from our mouths. There are no controls inside the copter—it's designed to be flown entirely remotely.

Through our earpieces, Pedro tells us the distance we still have to cover—the good news is, we're gaining on the drone. The bad news is it's going to be tight. Once we pull alongside, we'll only have a few seconds to grab it.

We're quite close before we see it—it's just as small as Pedro said, a silvery sphere glinting in the sunlight, slightly lower than we are under a blur of propellers.

Pedro deftly maneuvers us so it's directly to my left, a few feet away.

"Just a bit more," I say, unclipping my seatbelt and grabbing the door, ready to reach for it.

Pedro curses through the radio. "It won't let me! The copter's crash sensors won't allow me to get you any closer. Can't you reach it from there?"

I clamber carefully out of my seat to sit on the edge, my left foot on the metal skid underneath the copter. As my head leaves the safety of the interior, I immediately feel a tug upward, my hair getting sucked toward the rotors. I duck reflexively, grabbing tight to the top of the door, and feel the copter jerk slightly, tipping toward the trees. Ingrid squeals in warning, but it quickly rights itself. The drone flies parallel alongside. It's hard to tell with the noise of the copter and the wind, but I feel like the drone sounds quieter now. Like it's running out of juice.

Experimentally, I stretch out my arm. A hand's width short. If I try, I might just be able to touch it, but that could easily knock it out of the sky. I need to be closer, to get a hand right under it, to be sure.

Pedro's voice crackles through the radio, static cutting him off intermittently. "Guys . . . you . . . about twenty seconds . . . it's . . . or never."

I pull my other leg outside so both feet rest on the skid, and stand up slowly, grabbing the top of the door with one hand. Just need to not let go.

"Um, can you hold on to me?"

Ingrid sees what I'm doing and her eyes widen. She starts to clamber over to the seat I've vacated to reach for me, but as her weight comes to the same side, the copter lurches. My feet leave the rail as it tips, and for a moment all that prevents me taking flight is my sweaty white-knuckle grip on the edge of the door.

Ingrid throws herself back over the other side, there's another lurch, my legs thump hard against the body of the copter, and I scrabble wildly until I feel the rail under my feet again.

"It's too much with you hanging off outside, Sel. I've got to stay here or it's unbalanced." She leans out her side and holds tight. "Try now."

Below us, the treetops swaying like waves on a green ocean are suddenly gone, and there are houses instead. Familiar streets. Tiled roofs. Tiny figures moving, stopping as their faces lift up at the sound of the copter.

"Ten seconds!"

There's a sputtering from the bomb drone, and as I watch, the blur of its propellers resolves into solid shapes as they begin to slow.

Seconds stretch out. The fingernails of my right hand dig into the tight space where a strip of metal meets the door edge, my left hand reaches for the space under the drone, palm up. Every sinew in my body is pulling, my neck muscles straining. I bring my hand up underneath, gently. Inches away, I can feel its warmth, the electronics inside whirring. My skin makes contact, and then it's in my palm, fingertips curled round the smooth bottom edge, just as the propellers on top sputter and die. I'm bringing it in.

And then my wrist cramps, holding on to the top of the door.

Pain shoots down my arm and I cry out, cheeks bitten so hard I taste blood, in an effort not to let go. But my muscles betray me. My fingernails are sliding along the top edge of the door, losing grip. And then they're grasping at air, and I'm tipping outward. I start to lose the drone from my left hand, and instinctively bring the other one around so I'm gripping it in both. I don't know why—it doesn't matter. We're both on our way to the ground. Maybe if I wrap my body around it, it won't go off when I land.

I see it all in slow motion, as my head and chest swing downward. There's a crowd in the street below, faces upturned, mouths open. I'm right over the school, ironically. An image flashes into my brain—everyone standing around my squished corpse on the playground, Ms. Boateng saying, "Well, at least he finally made an impact."

And then there's a massive jolt as my foot catches on something; it feels like every bone in my body is yanked out of its socket, and the drone starts to leap out of my arms, but I reflexively squeeze hard with my elbows and somehow keep hold of it. The copter whines horribly in protest at being almost on its side. Hanging upside down, I look up: the loop of the seatbelt is hanging out of the door, hooked round my ankle.

Slowly, the copter rights itself again.

"What's going—" comes Pedro's panicked voice in my ear. "Did you—" Then he must get a glimpse from one of the onboard cameras because he swears very loudly. "I see you. Gonna bring—back. Just . . . hang on—"

I have no other plans.

There's an electronic buzz as the seatbelt starts to wind itself in, taking me with it, then a hand grabs my ankle, helps pull me up.

"Got him," says Ingrid, letting go of the seatbelt lever and dragging me the rest of the way in until I'm lying across the footwell. "Here, give me that," she says, trying to take the drone so I can get myself onto the seat. But I don't seem to be able to let go. My arms are locked around it, trembling with exhaustion and adrenaline.

"Mom," I say. "I want to see Mom."

EPILOGUE

I'm locking up again.

I stand on tiptoes to grab the metal shutter and pull it down, click the padlock, and give it a little rattle to check.

Mom's bakery closes an hour before dusk on Howl night—we don't call it Confinement anymore. Sequest knew all along that, when not being tortured by infrasound, when they're not afraid, Rippers don't have a lot of interest in attacking anyone. Which is just as well, because no one had time to prepare. So there are no cages. In that sense, the world outside Tremorglade is the same as it ever was. In other ways . . . not so much. I suppose you might call this time a Disruption.

The shop's only been open a couple of days, but it's doing really well—everyone loves Mom's cinnamon-and-raisin rolls, her whole-grain loaves, and her doughnuts, airy-light and sparkling with sugar. After everything changed, she decided she wanted to make some changes of her own. Now that the road's fully open, she gets customers from Hastaville, and even farther afield. Tourists. They step off the bus, blinking like moles emerging into sunlight, staring at everything. We stare right back.

I know things aren't easy out there. Sure, we've had to adjust here, too, but outside . . . well, there's been a lot more to get your heads around.

Part of me wonders if things would have been any different if you had known about Tremorglade before. Would you have kept us in there anyway, when the alternative was . . . well, this? Would you have shut your eyes and pretended not to see?

I try to give people the benefit of the doubt. And when that doesn't work, I just choose not to think about it.

Because the world needs our support. And I don't just mean the doughnuts.

Harold Poulter and his cronies might once have been the experts on our condition, but we're the ones who know it best. Sequest is being "cleaned up and repurposed" now—Dr. Smith is in prison awaiting trial, along with a load of other senior staff—and the fresh faces say they're trying to make things right. I don't know if I believe that, but we have no choice but to rely on them to help clear up the messes Sequest made. Because it looks like Tremorglade isn't the only secret project they were working on.

When we opened up the files, we found a few things that have been keeping me awake at night ever since. Whole projects are missing—there are folders named after towns and villages around the country, and farther afield, where Sequest has branches. Inside are empty files. Investigations have begun, but something tells me it's with an intent to cover up rather than expose.

There's only so much my friends and I can do. For now, we have to look after our own.

Like Eddie. He lives with me and Mom, now. He turned up on my doorstep, all thin and forlorn, and Mom let me keep him. He loves me just as much as he ever did, and there's no evidence that he misses his old owner at all. I know not to give him chocolate. And that's pretty much all I have to thank Harold for.

Dr. Harold Poulter was the beginning, but we've moved on, left him behind. He's our history, not our future. He's missing—has been since that last night. I half wonder if Ripper-Dora went back to take a chunk out of him. Of course, she can't remember, and that's probably for the best.

I can't feel sorry for Harold, after what he did to us. I wonder, sometimes—if he *is* still alive—whether he listens to us howling on full moon nights, alone, and feels left out, instead of special and superior.

Yeah, I said "us"—I headed for the litter box last month. It was a bit of a surprise. I reckon it must have been brought on by stress, because Ingrid got her fur coat too, the very first month after we came out. Elena's still waiting, though I don't think it'll be long.

I heard they've actually started making congratulations cards for it.

It's hard to believe, but there are still some folks out there who think the whole thing is a hoax. Fewer every day, of course. It's harder to deny it's real when it actually happens to you. Although there are some die-hards in dark corners of the internet who insist that they *don't* actually turn into Rippers—the sprouting hairs and entire-body swelling is only an allergic reaction, and if they just put enough calamine lotion on it, it'll go away.

I pity them, really. When authorities have lost your trust, the danger is you start to disbelieve *everything*—even the truth, when the evidence is all around you. You can cry "fake news" all you like, the virus doesn't care. Sorry, dweebs, it's "fur real."

And don't put calamine on. It makes your fur crusty as it dries.

Full moon nights are ... different now. I can't describe them for you—you'd have to talk to the kids about that. They're the ones who watch us Turn and gallop past them in the streets, play-fighting as we go. We still don't remember anything when we wake up the next morning.

But we're left with exhilaration, a sense of togetherness. Joy, if you want to get sentimental about it. There are no headaches for the kids anymore, no nausea. No gnawing sense of dread. It's party time—at least in Tremorglade. The rest of you just need a chance to catch up. You'll get there in the end, just like we did.

Elena was right, as she is about most things, about the raw meat. No one bothers with that. As long as your loved one eats a good hearty dinner before dusk, they're ready to rock and roll. By all means stick a bloody rump steak in front of your Turned parent if you really want, and they'll definitely eat it. But there's no need. We've got places to go, legs to stretch, howling to do. Apparently, we do chase the occasional squirrel, I'll admit, but we don't mean anything by it. If you're too young to Turn, and you wander the streets on Howl night, you can peek through windows and see scenes of domestic Ripper bliss: great furry bodies lying draped across the sofa while kids share popcorn and watch TV; play-fighting with the family dog; or in my case apparently, digging up the house plants that I'll have to repot the next morning.

It's hard to scare us or hurt us. I can't *guarantee* your safety if you do, and I'm not sure why you'd want to try. Best not, eh?

Elena says it's kind of eerie but beautiful, when she sits at her open bedroom window to listen to the midnight howling. It's calming, she reckons. Like we're singing her to sleep. She recorded us, the other night, and played it back for me. I couldn't make out my own howl, of course. Probably just as well, given my human singing voice. I bet hers will be something special.

I thought I'd discovered that my life in Tremorglade wasn't real, but I've come to see that's wrong. My community, my friendships, all the things that matter ... those things weren't fake. They just work differently now.

Pedro is selling T-shirts online, as a side gig, just for fun. He's printed a load that have a still from the Fen Zhao movie where she's in full Ripper mode, with headphones photoshopped onto her head. He's captioned it: IF YOU'RE CLOSE ENOUGH TO READ THIS, CONGRATULATIONS! YOU'RE ONE OF US!

To be honest, they're probably a bit tasteless at this point, but I told him they looked good. "Maybe Fen Zhao will finally sign one for you."

"You kidding? She'll probably want *me* to sign *hers*," he replied.

Fen Zhao almost certainly *is* one of us by now, and she'll have been better prepared than most. She had no idea when she was making those movies that they weren't entirely fantasy, but they'll have given her a good head start on the basics. Personally, I think it's probably still too raw to send her the T-shirt.

So here we are.

Life as you used to know it is over.

Your world wasn't as bad as we in Tremorglade had been led to believe. But ours won't be as bad as you expect either.

There's been a lot of misinformation floating around, about how it happened and what it means. That's why I've started making educational videos and putting them online, to tell the truth, give tips on how to handle Turning parents, and explain that it's not so bad. The videos are getting pretty popular—I suppose you could say I've gone viral. And they're nowhere NEAR as cheesy as *Your Changing Body*, despite what Ingrid keeps saying. People seem to find my advice helpful.

I tell them they're not monsters. They'll make mistakes as they get used to it, and that's okay—we're all human.

Most of the time.

ACKNOWLEDGMENTS

A lot of people were essential to the making of this book. I would like to thank:

My husband, Rob, and my sons, Fraser and Cameron, who each read multiple drafts and gave perceptive feedback, and whose enthusiasm kept me going. I am very, very lucky to have you all.

My agent, Kate Shaw, for her unwavering support and wisdom through ups and downs.

The whole team at Simon & Schuster UK, led by Rachel Denwood, for taking on the series and fueling it with so much creativity and imagination.

In particular, my extremely talented editors—Lucy Pearse and Katie Lawrence—for their many insights and suggestions to improve the text. Also Alexa Pastor at Simon & Schuster US, and Anna Bowles for her thoughtful copyediting.

Jose Real, for the coolest cover art imaginable.

I'm very grateful to all those who generously gave their time and expertise to help me, by reading extracts, or giving advice, or being supportive friends, including: Tiggy Lee, Dashe Roberts, A. M. Dassu, Louie Stowell, Alom Shaha, Fiona Barker, Eiman Munro, Nicola Baker, Sarah Medway, Priscilla Mante, and all the incredible Swaggers. Any errors are entirely someone else's fault. (Okay, yes, mine.)

Finally, thanks to you, reader, if you got this far. Stick around. It's not over yet.

ABOUT THE AUTHOR

S. J. Wills grew up in Chelmsford, Essex, where her parents let her choose any books she wanted from the library, no matter what. She has worked as a freelance copyeditor since 2003, alongside rediscovering her childhood love: writing her own stories. She lives in Kent with her writer husband, two sons, and a large, bouncing poodle.

WE WEREN'T ORPHANS AFTER ALL. THAT WAS THE FIRST SURPRISE. THE SECOND WAS THAT WE WERE GOING HOME.

In a new series by *New York Times* bestselling author Margaret Peterson Haddix, Rosi must decide what she's willing to risk to save her family — and maybe even all of humanity.

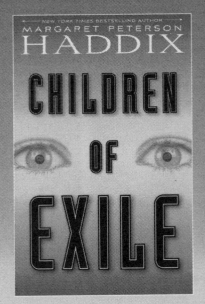

When Eden stumbles into Everdark, a parallel wo
death and the afterlife, she encounters a dreade
wants her as an eternal daughter. Is she stron
fight the witch's magic, or will she be stuck here forever?

"Stunning, moving, and marvelously strange. I loved every page."
KELLY BARNHILL, bestselling and Newbery Medal-winning author

Eden's EVERDARK

KAREN STRONG

"A haunting yet beautiful exploration of grief, love, and
—KWAME MBALIA, #1 *New York Times* bestselling au

"Stunning, moving, and marvelously strange. I loved every
—KELLY BARNHILL, bestselling and Newbery Medal-winni

"A can't-be-missed novel working in the beautiful folkloric
of Black American storytellers."
—DHONIELLE CLAYTON, *New York Times* bestselling a

DEBUT NOVEL WITH AN ACTION-PACKED
CLIMAX THAT WILL LEAVE READERS EAGER TO
SCOPE OUT THE WEIRDER SIDE OF NATURE."
—School Library Journal

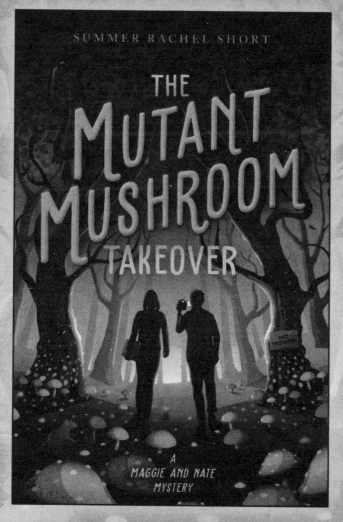